Obitus served in Germany, Cyprus, Singapore, Malaysia, Hong Kong, and Borneo. He was a Senior Police Officer and taught ethical police interviewing, neurolinguistics, body language, and the *Anatomy of a Lie*. He currently heads Checkmate, a publisher of informative materials that provide training aids for police officers.

To Jana

Obitus Hades

NOBLE CAUSE

AUSTIN MACAULEY PUBLISHERS™

LONDON • CAMBRIDGE • NEW YORK • SHARJAH

Copyright © Obitus Hades 2023

The right of Obitus Hades to be identified as author of this work has been asserted by the author in accordance with sections 77 and 78 of the Copyright, Designs and Patents Act 1988.

All rights reserved. No part of this publication may be reproduced, stored in a retrieval system, or transmitted in any form or by any means, electronic, mechanical, photocopying, recording, or otherwise, without the prior permission of the publishers.

Any person who commits any unauthorised act in relation to this publication may be liable to criminal prosecution and civil claims for damages.

This is a work of fiction. Names, characters, businesses, places, events, locales, and incidents are either the products of the author's imagination or used in a fictitious manner. Any resemblance to actual persons, living or dead, or actual events is purely coincidental.

A CIP catalogue record for this title is available from the British Library.

ISBN 9781398470637 (Paperback)
ISBN 9781398470644 (ePub e-book)

www.austinmacauley.com

First Published 2023
Austin Macauley Publishers Ltd®
1 Canada Square
Canary Wharf
London
E14 5AA

Chapter 1
Let us pretend a fiction, and suppose…this.

The Prime Minister has called a snap general election. The electorate will cast their votes on Thursday, just five weeks away. At last, the chance to establish an effective government, wiping away the present shambolic mess of intransigence, indecision, and incompetence brought about by the sheer lust for power. The game is, as they say, afoot.

In the provinces, MPs had a great deal to worry about, re-election, or disgrace. At Aqua Ponds in the county of Wessex, the local Member of Parliament, Khom Ting, congratulated himself on having the answer to his survival as an MP. He called the Home Secretary to confirm the timing of their meeting on Saturday.

	"Kelvin dear boy, Khom here, about Saturday's meeting…"
Kelvin interrupted	"Sorry, Khom, out of the question. I've just had an audience with the PM who has charged me with the duty of coming up with an election-winning idea touching on matters relating to police and prisons."
Khom said	"Exactly so. I have the answer to both which I intended to run past you on Saturday"
Kelvin said	"Good god, man, run them past me now, time is of the essence."
Khom whispered	"Bit of a secret, dear boy, not for the phone, walls have ears, do they not?"
He continued	"Besides, vis-a-vis our conversation during our last drinkies meeting, and at no expense, I have installed a pleasure room to meet all our requirements."
Kelvin said	"Yes, yes, go on."
Khom said	"Not now dear boy, that particular matter is top secret."

Kelvin said	"Well, can you say anything, give me a taster."
Khom said	"Tuppence, dear boy."
Kelvin enquired	"Tuppence, Tuppence, what is Tuppence?"
Khom smiled and said	"Her name."
Kelvin gushed	"Splendid, well done, what a perfectly delightful Victorian name."
He enquired	"How old?"
Khom corrected him	"No dear boy, not Tuppence in the sense of a delightful Victorian name, but Tuppence in the sense that she is not quite the full shilling, do you see?"
Kelvin said	"Yes, I believe I do, yes quite so. Not much going on upstairs then?"
Khom replied	"You might say, it's all going on downstairs."
Kelvin enquired	"Last word then, how old?"
Khom said	"15, 16 soon."
Kelvin said	"Yes, top secret, as you say. Don't be late for Saturday's meeting at Police Headquarters, I have to present a couple of medals to our brave boys in blue, a useful photoshoot, free lunch and drinkies in the Officers' Mess, I will disclose all then."

The medal ceremony, as ever, was attended by the usual suspects, described by the media as the Great and the Good. The Chief, Home Secretary, Lord Lieutenant, and a handful of local MPs, and other lesser rascals. The headquarters was a new building, awash with the latest wizardry, it gave new meaning to the word high tech, the taxpayers had indeed been kind to the Wessex Constabulary.

The vision of so many policemen in one place, somehow explained why they are rarely seen on the streets. What on earth are they all doing here, surely this is not the scene of a major disaster? Their ID badges gave the game away, their name, under which was the course they were attending. Public Order, Homicide investigators, Interview Techniques, First Aid, and so it went on, Negotiator, Firearms, Mortuary, not unlike a UN convention in many ways. And so it was clear, if you're to become a victim of a firearms incident, then you'd do well to live near the headquarters, where, in a moment, you'd be attended by a first aider, a murders squad detective and a mortician.

There was in excess of 200 in the Sports Hall, where medals were to be presented. In the front row was Sergeant Shear and his task force unit of six men. Shear's medal was for an act of gallantry, arising from an incident where he disarmed an armed man exiting a post office in the city centre. The citation read:

In recognition of an Act of Conspicuous Gallantry, when Sergeant Paul Shears, acting on his own, was, without warning, confronted by a drug-fuelled man, armed with a firearm attempting to escape from the scene of an armed robbery, single-handedly, disarmed the man, and saved passers-by from resulting danger.

Or so it read. The truth was that this was no altruistic undertaking. Shear had finished work earlier that day and had spent the last two hours in the pub. Lukins, a local reprobate aged 83 years, had been at the other end of the bar complaining bitterly that his government handout had not yet arrived at the post office next door, and that he was going to sort them out. When the landlord finally refused to serve him, he stormed out of the pub muttering, "I'll be back." In the event, he didn't come back because Shear, who was as drunk as Lukins, finished his drink and left a minute or so later, just in time to bump into Lukins who was leaving the post office when they both fell over one another. Lukins believing he was under attack began to fight but was overpowered by Shears. The post office door opened and the postmaster fell over the two miscreants, just as a passing police car pulled up. The postmaster called out that Lukins had just pulled a gun on him and demanded his money. This was taken to mean the postmaster's money and not the money Lukins was waiting for. The uniformed police officers pulled the sergeant to his feet, congratulating him on his arrest, handcuffed Lukins, and dusted down the dishevelled postmaster. The charge against Lukins was reduced to one of threatening behaviour when it was realised that, according to Lukins which the evidence tended to support, was demanding his own money, and when the postmaster made light of his demands, Lukins became outraged and produced a pistol to reinforce his demands. Seeing how old Lukins was, and guessing the gun much older, the vexed postmaster chased him out the door. The ballistic report on the gun stated that it was an antique, with slightly bent barrel, incapable of firing, and in the hands of a drunken old man, more a danger to himself than others, as was borne out by his arrest.

After the medal ceremony, the top brass gathered in the officers' mess for drinks. Kelvin was anxious to hear from Khom about the delights that awaited, but had to wait until pleasantries had been exchanged, favours acknowledged and the usual hollow promises made. Finally, Khom beckoned Shear to join him and Kelvin to an anti-chamber where, what was said would remain. All three sat around a small table.

Khom began	"Home Secretary, may I introduce Sergeant Shear, a task force commander. He has specific responsibility for reducing all crime related to drugs in the southern part of the county."
Kelvin said	"Good god man, since my appointment I've been trying to do precisely that for the whole of the country, and if the BBC can be believed we're failing on every front. Time was when religion was the opium of the people, now it seems that opium is the religion of the people. It seems to me that the great unwashed need a thorough cleansing, but legislation proposals are stopped at every turn by bleeding heart Liberals and the Labour Party who have some ludicrous idea in their heads about the freedom of people to choose. Well, I'll give them freedom to choose, they can spend one year in prison or five, their choice."
Khom said	"Sergeant Shear, your thoughts."
Shear began	"You are so right, sir. A total redefinition of tolerance levels is what is needed. I tell you privately that drug-related crime in the area I control has reduced by sixty percent plus…"
Kelvin interrupted	"Sixty percent, ye gods, that would get us re-elected at once and secure my position for the foreseeable future. How long have you known about this reduction and, more importantly, why do I not know about it?"
Shear continued	"My crew were each chosen by me for the fundamental understanding of the human condition, and who should have the power to shape how society works. To that end we have begun to reshape our area of responsibility by making it easier for drug dealers to conform to societies' norms than to deal in drugs."
Kelvin asked	"How?"

Shear continued	"Some secrets have to be guarded by lies. So the story we will put out is that we have introduced a number of new initiatives based on..."
Kelvin continued	"Yes, of course, based on...initiatives by me and your local MP, secretly trialled here in the provinces...yes, yes, I see it all now. Khom and I will at once announce that a strategic review of our drug laws has revealed a quote...new approach...unquote resulting in the most favourable outcome, and...let me think..."
Khom continued	"Legislation will now be drawn up to ensure that..."
Kelvin rejoiced	"Yes, the Prime Minister's brief will be met. With a 60% reduction in the use of drugs, there will be the same percentage decrease in the numbers appearing before the courts, a reduction of drug offenders in prison, and the same percentage reduction in crime."
Khom added	"Not overlooking the percentage increase of what high esteem the population will have on the Police, win, win."
Kelvin concluded	"So that my brief from the PM will at once have been realised. Police and prisons, both at a stroke."
Khom asked	"The truth you mentioned Sergeant, the one that has to be guarded by lies..."
Kelvin interrupted	"Khom, be a good chap, let us not cloud the issue with facts. The facts, or truth, will be, as is always the case, whatever we say it is. If it appears on the BBC as the news, then, de facto it is true. Now, Khom, you and I have important matters of State to address. So, Sergeant Shear, if there's nothing more?"
Shear got up.	"Well, if you have your full support, sir..."
Kelvin said	"You have, Shear, well done, continue to good work."

Shear left the room and switched his recorder off.

Kelvin and Khom, now alone in their cauldron, put their heads together and cobbled up a plan that could be sold to the masses as a brilliant new conservative strategy designed to bring about fundamental changes to the approach to crime and its causes. His boffins at the Home Office would find a form of words sufficient to hoodwink the all believing public. Yes, all this, and at a time of national debate on the party best suited to lead the nation into a new age of equality, growth and prosperity. A country where every hard-working person would flourish, and each and every person would be rewarded, blah, blah, blah. The usual stuff repackaged, buy one, get one free sort of thing. It was agreed that this would be aired on primetime slots and repeated until everyone knew it to be true.

Kelvin enquired "Time now for full disclosure, Khom, what delights have you laid on. I know that she's called Tuppence, aged about 15 or 16 you said..."

Khom interrupted "Before that, there is something else to discuss."

Kelvin said "Do tell."

Khom continued "Well, we've discussed how this matter is to be sold to the public, but..."

Kelvin sighed "Yes, yes, but what?"

Khom continued "A sixty percent decrease in drug related activity is an enormous achievement by any standard, perhaps we should find out precisely how this was brought about."

Kelvin said "My dear Khom, you really are an innocent abroad, it certainly hasn't come about by diligence and hard work, that only ever keeps things five or so percent above or below a silly sociology graph the loony left burn the midnight oil studying. No, such enormous results are achieved not by hard work, but by smart work. People who follow the rules achieve nothing, well maybe a pension, but only the smart cookies in this world achieve their goal, and in Shear we have one very smart cookie. Let's leave it to him, shall we?"

Khom lamented "Yes, I suppose if we knew the facts, we wouldn't really be able to give it the go ahead, now would we?"

Kelvin concluded "If we knew the facts, we would be co-conspirators, colluding in the dark depths inhabited by the Police."

"No, we don't want to know what they get up to. Should the wheel come off, the bubble burst or the balloon go up, you and I dear boy, like Caesar's wife, will be squeaky clean. So official line is, we know nothing. Our meeting with Shear was a two-minute affair where we thanked him for his outstanding bravery, nothing more. Now let us leave matters in the capable hands of the Boffins at the Home Office to shape the minds of the proletariat. You and I, Khom, need only bask in our own reflected glory, what say you to that?"

Khom sighed	"Well, you've got everything right...so far, so onwards, if not to heaven, then hand in hand to hell."
Kelvin concluded	"The matter is settled then, let me ring my close protection people and reward their stalwart efforts on my behalf with the remainder of the weekend off. That will cheer them up. You and I meanwhile will make our way to your place in the country where we can hammer out national strategy, which of course is codified language for frolics and fun with Tuppence. Let's get in your car where you can tell all, I can't wait to hear what's laid on."

Sergeant Shear collected his crew who made their way to their crew-bus which went under the name of Cerberus, a three headed dog from Greek mythology that guarded the gates of the underworld, his duty was to ensure that no one interfered with the contents of his environs. Shear and his crew made their way back to their patch to continue where they left off.

Shear asked	"Who's next?"
Boots replied	"Jonah's being bailed at about six, Sarge, he's disqualified from driving so he should be on his way out of town about twenty past."
Shear smiled	"We'll pull him just after the motorway bridge, nice and quiet, perfect location."
Shear said	"Tony, check low tides with Google, should be about eight I think."
Tony replied	"Yes, ten past, Sarge."
Shear smiled	"And dark at seven, perfect."

Shear's crew-bus pulled into a lay-by just outside Aqua Ponds. They played the tape of Jonah's interview. It was clear that Jonah had been in possession of half a kilo of cocaine when he left the city, and yet there was nothing found in his vehicle when searched by police on his return home. The question to be answered, was where is the coke now. This question could best be answered by Jonah who was about to be bailed by the police, and twenty minutes later he would be liberated from his freedom by Shear's crew who, unlike the regular police with their rules, codes of practice and other protocols, were free to get results. No rules, just results. They would soon have hold of Jonah then with the use of Einsatzgruppe techniques, the cocaine. If all went well, Jonah would then disappear sometime a little after eight.

The crew-bus radio broke silence. Foxtrot 13, foxtrot 13, receiving over. This was the official name of Cerberus. The call was taken alerting them to the fact that Jones had been bailed, he was a disqualified driver and that they should keep observations in the event he became mobile. As they waited, a local scallywag stopped to have a pee behind Cerberus. Boots left the vehicle and advised that if he didn't put that away, they would put him away. The kid had been drinking but still had the wit to grunt like a pig, but not the courage to actually say the word pig. His bashfulness did not save him. Like a frog he was wheeled into the open side door of the crew-bus where he was introduced to the members of Foxtrot 13.

	"This plank thinks we're pigs."
Shears said	"I see you are suffering from both a mobility and an identity crisis."
The kid said	"What!"
Shears continued	"You don't seem to know where the toilets are, and the only pig here is you, sunbeam…"

The kid interrupted "Yeah, but…"
Boots advised "Shut it, listen to the Sergeant."

The miscreant fell silent as he observed the focused menace on the faces of both Boots and Shear.

| Shear continued | "Now there are two types of pigs, you sunbeam are a member of the lowest order of pigs, the type who wallow in mud, who have no sense of shame and who labour under the erroneous belief that they can do as they please without consequence. Well know this, it stops here. The other type of pig, the elite, can be found in a book called *Animal Farm*. In the book, the animals get rid of all the humans and take charge of the farm. They soon realised that they needed someone to police their new society, the smartest animals on the farm. Now guess which animals on the farm were the smartest?" Shear grunted. |
| The kid said | "The…pigs." |

Shear enquired	"And what do you think the pigs eat when they're hungry?"
The kid said	"…Dunno."
Shear said	"Bacon sandwiches, they pull one of you little horrors out of the mud and chop you up for bacon, capiche?"
The kid said	"Yes, but what's capiche?"

The kid was dragged from the crew-bus by Boots. His face showed solemn remorse, he was scared and knew that somehow he had just had a narrow escape.

Boots advised	"Think yourself lucky son, we could have done you for urinating in a public place, indecent exposure, insulting behaviour and bestiality."
The kid enquired	"What's that?"
Boots said	"What's what?"
The kid said	"Bestiality."
Boots said	"Calling the police the wrong type of pig, now do one…"

The kid walked smartly away, broke into a trot and then did one.

Shear's crew sat quietly waiting for Jonah. Another ten minutes or so should do it. They checked their equipment and other non-issued kit. Two shovels, 20 or so Sainsburys' plastic bags, a tailored folded blanket and a battery driven hand drill. All crew-buses were customised to suit the requirements of the crew. Shear's bus was fitted with two seats installed behind the driver. The side of the bus could be accessed from a large sliding door on its nearside. To the rear of the bus there were two sets of seats, two to the left and one on the right with central access to the rear bench seat which sat four, not unlike a small-town bus. All told the bus seated 12 plus the driver. Saaz usually drove with Shear upfront, the rest of the crew sat where they pleased. Ken often took the seat at the back next to the supply of plastic bags. Saaz spotted Jonah in his rear-view mirror and alerted the crew, 200 yards and closing. Jonah was slow to spot the crew-bus due to failing light and abundance of trees. As he drew level, Shear caught Jonah's eye.

Shear said "Get in Jonah."

Jonah knew this wasn't a request. He was no stranger to the formal arrest thing, whereby his front door would be kicked in, warrants read out followed by search, then if unlucky off to the police station. He could handle that. He had a good working knowledge of the drug laws and police procedures. He also had access to very expensive lawyers resulting in him having no convictions for Class A, notwithstanding the fact that he sat at the top table in the Gang of dealers. This was something else, an invitation into a police van full of hardnosed no-nonsense cops. Everyone knew, you don't fuck with these guys, they don't fuck!

The van drove off, the light was fading and low tide was in about an hour. But before that, games. Jonah was sitting on the floor of the van handcuffed to a rail, a blanket draped over his head, no one spoke. Jonah self-interrogated, on each occasion coming up with worse possible scenarios. The journey continued in silence. Jonah's mobile kept ringing and ringing. Jonah was desperate for someone to speak, small talk, anything. He felt his bowel move, he felt quite sick suddenly vomiting over his legs and the floor of the crew-bus. No one moved, no one spoke. The journey continued to the sound of the mobile phone. Twenty minutes later the crew-bus drove down a long lane, just before driving into a large barn. The silence was broken.

Shear said	"Are you into BDSM Jonah?"
Jonah replied	"What's that?"
Shear said	"Bondage, discipline, submission and sadomasochism."
Jonah said	"What do you mean?"
Shear replied	"A bit of torture."
Jonah said	"No, I'm bloody not."
Shear said	"We are."

Jonah was sick again and again. The crew-bus finally stopped. The blanket was removed from Jonah's head. He could see that he was in a dimly lit barn. He was moved to the second seat from the rear, his hands cuffed behind him and cuffs on his ankles which in turn were cuffed to the legs of the seat. Ken sat in the rear seat, immediately behind Jonah.

Jonah said	"What's going on, you know you can't get away with this…"

Shear said	"Let me assure you, we can. What happens now Jonah is this. You will tell us where the half kilo of coke is, we know from one of our informants that you left Bristol with the gear and we know that when the police stopped you at Aqua Ponds it was gone. You now have a decision to make, you will tell us the truth or be subject to the most unspeakable pain."

Ken pulled a gag over his head reducing his protests to a muffled report. Tony handed Shear the hand drill. Shear brushed his finger past the trigger causing the drill to emit a low growl. Jonah knew he was in big trouble. He was on his own and he knew that there was going to be a bad outcome if he didn't strike a deal with Shear. Shear held the drill up to Jonah's face and again fingered the trigger…another growl.

Shear said	"The moment of truth now Jonah, the gag will be slackened and you will tell us where the coke is, if not you'll be kneecapped, got it?"

Jonah shook his head vigorously. Ken loosened the gag.

Jonah said	"You won't tell that I gave you information, will you?"
Shear said	"Wrong answer son."

Shear now put the drill on full power…

Jonah said	"OK, OK, I stopped at my brother's house, he's got it honest."
Shear said	"Your brother Steve?"
Jonah replied	"Yes, Steve, he's holding it for me."
Shear said	"You'll now ring Steve and tell him to put the coke just inside the front door, leave the door unlocked and it will be picked up later this evening."
Jonah said	"OK, Steve always does as I say, no problem, the coke will be there, I promise."

Ken called the number and held the mobile whilst Jonah told his brother what to do, his brother asked no questions.

Shear said	"Well done, Jonah, you've just saved yourself from a great deal of pain, that just leaves you to pass or fail part 2 of the test."
Jonah enquired	"What's that?"
Ken said	"It's a matter of mind over matter."
Jonah said	"I don't get it."
Ken said	"We don't mind and you don't matter."

Ken tightened the gag and pulled a Sainsbury's bag over Jonah's head and held it tight at the neck. In one minute, Jonah lost consciousness and in two he was dead. Boots and Saaz carried him in the blanket to the pull-in by the beach, got their bearings from the top of the concrete platform arrowing the way. Boots and Tony carried the shovels. They put Sainsbury's carrier bags on over their boots and walked in the dark the four hundred yards to the low water mark. It took only a few minutes to dig a three-foot grave in wet sand, not that it mattered, so long as he was covered then for three quarters of the day thirty feet of Bristol Channel salt water would keep him and his pals well pegged.

Shear said	"Lewis, when we get back to the factory, you and Rohan drive to Steve's place, Rohan can wear his Muslim kit to pick up the coke, then meet us back at the cottage."
Saaz asked	"Well, that was number four, two more and I reckon the infestation will be extinct. Funny how no one ever enquires where they are."
Boots said	"This lot are the worst of the worst. Evil bastards destroying kids with coke, heroin and every other evil that exists. They are rats, vermin, wild bloody animals. When the fumigators clear them out, no one asks where they are. The fact that they are not here is all that matters."
Ken added	"A good extra strong insecticide always does the trick, never fails."
Shear said	"The answer is always the same. We wait until they are facing serious charges and then strike. It's always assumed they jumped bail and are tucked up."

"In Spain trying to Habla Espanol. Besides, if you get rid of decent folk, they call it homicide. The vermin we deal with are different. They destroy the lives of good decent hardworking people, people who are just protecting their kids, that's not homicide, it's insecticide and no one's got a problem with that. Not unlike an anal crustacean, never spoken about and when it disappears, you're somehow very happy."

Kelvin and Khom pulled into Khom's weekend country house in the Hills a few miles from Aqua Ponds. Kelvin had been briefed as to the delights which awaited them both later that night. Kelvin spent time on the phone with the ministry boffins. They advised that they should air the new initiative in the third slot of the national news following the Prime Minister's address to the nation. Everything had been finalised. Both now settled down for a drink.

Kelvin asked	"What's the plan then, Khom, you're not bringing her here surely."
Khom said	"Good god, no, we'll make our way to the docks where we will engage in festivities."
Kelvin enquired	"The docks you say?"
Khom replied	"Yes, I've arranged her accommodation on a canal boat neatly anchored at the end of the dock, overlooked by no one. The dock is surrounded on three sides by high rise apartments so it's a busy place, so busy that two middle-aged gentlemen will go unnoticed. Her boat is at the end of the line so there is no passing traffic."
Kelvin mused	"Rumpy pumpy on a canal boat, this is a first for me, how splendid."
Khom continued	"In the event of difficulties, I can have the canal boat moved from the canal to any location up or down the canal. So you see, everything has been thought of."
Kelvin said	"How marvellous, a secure home with no address, so secure that its location is moveable. Unique I'd say."
Khom continued	"No one of course would hire a canal boat to a schoolgirl, so arrangements were put in place whereby the tenancy was signed for by her mother."
Kelvin said	"Excellent, it's not as though her mother's going to be there is it?"
Khom said	"Ae contraire mon ami, her mother will be there, but that's the good news. No one expects the girl to be on her own, that would draw unwelcome attention."

Kelvin interrupted	"For god's sake, man, how can her mother being there possibly be described as being good news?"
Khom said	"Perfectly simple, they are both coke heads and the mother is an alcoholic. Mother lives at one end of the boat and Tuppence has her own quarters. Canal boats are up to seventy feet long so they live independently unless they choose to get together. But there are other benefits…"
Kelvin said	"Go on, other benefits?"
Khom said	"Yes, her mother is no stranger to Brutus Erectus and I have enjoyed her pleasures on many occasions. She is about forty, well put together, independently sprung buttocks and a heavily laden chest, a body of pure joy, the downside is, she has the social skills of a warthog."
Kelvin exclaimed	"Not so much a ménage a trois, more a menage de project, or in the parlance of the day, a veritable gang bang, oh how well you've managed events Khom, well done. Now, when do we start?"
Khom said	"We need to tool up first."
Kelvin laughed	"My tools are in my underwear."

Khom disappeared upstairs returning a few minutes later with two transparent bags containing white powder. "In here, my friend we each have five grams of coke, enough to fill two teaspoons." Khom began to transfer the powder into two small plastic containers, each with a secure lid.

Kelvin said	"I know I'm unfashionable but I don't do drugs."
Khom replied	"No, nor do I, these are for the ladies by way of very special delivery. What happens is, and wholly unknown to them of course, is that we get them kneeling on the end of the bed, then we put on condoms, dip tools in coke, and then my friend penetration is given new meaning, elevated to a state of ennoblement. She'll think you're god."
Kelvin replied	"Yes, opium has indeed become the religion of the people, and we two its high priests. Tell me, where do you get your coke?"
Khom said	"You met my supplier earlier today. The gallant Sergeant Shear."

Both Kelvin and Khom made their way to the docks.

Kelvin asked	"Has the boat got a name?"
Khom replied	"Indeed it has, Narrow Escape, an appropriate name for a narrow boat, to which people escape."
Kelvin asked	"Talking of escape, what's the plan in the unlikely event of trouble arising?"
Khom said	"Never happens my friend, Shear deals with everything."

Shear does indeed deal with everything, down to the smallest detail. As the Right Honourable Home Secretary and the conservative MP for Aqua Ponds made their way on board the Narrow Escape, Shear and his crew relaxed in their comfortable seats at the cottage and watched events unfold on the Narrow Escape CCTV. All was well with the world, the human condition and its place in the universe dutifully recorded for prosperity. Truly a copper-bottomed insurance policy rivalling any futures market.

Chapter 2

Kelvin and Khom relaxed with drinks, congratulating themselves on their recent elevation to high priests. The BBC early evening news began as usual. Heavy duty mood music suggesting we all sit up straight and be prepared to call out 'we believe'. The newscaster, holding papers, but reading from the script on the screen, looked perfectly solemn. Her gender was evidence of equality and her colour, not quite white, further evidence of Auntie's colour-blindness. The BBC mission statement to inform, educate and entertain was about to be tested. The first item covered the breaking story of a mass shooting in Texas. Viewers were warned that they may be distressed by some of the images, a further alert followed concerning flashing cameras, finally viewers were shown the footage of the event. The shooter was clearly calling out to the police, but the editor had seen fit to bleep out his words. The newscaster rolled her eyes in a gesture of resignation reinforcing the "we don't want to see that sort of thing, do we?" Add to that a telephone number appeared on the screen for those viewers who had become overwhelmed and who were now in need of counselling. Clearly the edit button should be renamed remove the truth button, and this is the channel viewers actually pay to watch. A tax on half-truths.

The remainder of the news comprised blistering attacks by the Conservatives on the Labour Party, and equally vociferous counter attacks by Labour. The Liberals, noted for their ability to sit on the fence with both ears to the ground, came up with their usual platitudes seeking not to rock the boat, which had been boarded and bested by their opponents. They had learned nothing from losing power in the twenties and looked blissfully happy to remain the minor pressure group they had become.

Finally, news of the government's latest initiative. The newscaster introduced the crime correspondent.

"...and breaking news from Aqua Ponds here in Wessex. The Home Secretary, Mr Kelvin Bragg has unveiled plans to reduce drug related crime following a successful trial here in the west country, where it was shown that by introducing a number of new measures, based on zero tolerance, could bring about a reduction by, in some cases, fifty percent. This news has been greatly welcomed by the local community..."

And there it was, cameras showed historical film of Aqua Ponds in bright sunshine and uplifting music. Scenes of people leaving prison vans and being escorted into court. Children walking to school hand in hand with their parent on the now drug-free streets. Oh how well it was all done. As this was the last item of news, and introduced without warning, the opposition had been ambushed, no right of reply at the point of disclosure. Their probing questions holding the government to account would have to wait until tomorrow when they will have lost their bite. A perfect coup.

Khom said	"Bit of a disappointment, Kelvin, I rather thought I might have figured in the broadcast, but no a mention."
Kelvin assured him	"No, no my friend, my job is to outline broad policy to the nation, the strategic objective so to speak. Matters of detail, the tactics of implementation is your department. Good god man, this will result in your appearance on the local television on a daily basis. You'll become a household name. I expect you'll make the national news from time to time."
Khom replied	"Yes, that's my fear. I couldn't begin to guess what these new measures are. Unlike you I don't have the creativity your boffins provide, I have to come up with the actual facts."
Kelvin said	"Facts my friend are what we say they are. It has appeared on national news, therefore it is so, it's a fact. The populace will discuss the matter in a favourable light and so the fact will be reinforced.
	"How can it fail, everyone wants it to succeed. Those, Khom are the facts. Best get your head together with Shear, he deals with these matters on a daily basis, he'll put you straight, I'm sure."

Khom said	"Yes, I'll get on to it as a matter of urgency, I'll set up a meeting."
Kelvin said	"Now remember, the election is less than five weeks away, speak to the courts, probation, police, all stakeholders, we must all be singing from the same hymn sheet, now I'm leaving you to make this happen. Don't get it wrong, there's a good chap."
Khom replied	"Of course not, if I get this wrong, I'll be hung, drawn and quartered."
Kelvin said	"And of course, if all goes well, I'm sure the PM will look favourably upon your part in the matter."
Khom asked	"Do you really think so, Kelvin?"
Kelvin smiled	"Re-election and control of the country would satisfy most Khom, but for special people who have made the extra effort…"
Khom enquired	"Yes, what?"
Kelvin said	"I'll deny saying this of course, but with my full backing, there just might be a Knighthood in the offing for those of our supporters who go the extra mile as I know you will Khom. So twix now and our second term of office, onward."

The following afternoon Shear and his troops were on plain clothes patrol in an old battered undercover van. Their brief was to keep observations on a suspect farm on the Quantock Hills where it was heavily rumoured that a large consignment of drugs was to be dropped. This farm had been staked out before with negative results, but rumour control kept throwing up intelligence reports that known couriers were seen to be in the vicinity of the farm, but never anything strong enough to amount to evidence justifying a search warrant. Shear was armed with a standard Ordnance Survey map showing that there were two entrances to the farm. The map was the standard issue to officers engaged in observations and took no account of technology. Shear clicked on Google Earth which showed a third footpath leading to the farm from a nearby lane behind the farm. This area is where they would keep observations. Camouflage kit, binoculars and a dense wood hid them well enough. Only one known dealer was seen to enter the farm, he exited 15 minutes later.

Once darkness fell, they left the scene and made their way back to the nick. En route two vehicles were spotted heading toward the farm. Each contained known villains.

Shear said	"Soon be time to spring a trap, boys. So back to the factory now and report that we were in the woods opposite the farm entrances. Nothing was sighted and the day passed without incident. That will be in keeping with all the other reports, resulting in the obs being called off on the grounds of cost v reward, it's costing a fortune and no one is getting nicked. Now that won't do, will it?"
Boots said	"Yeah, the boss keeps calling us his secret weapon and if we can't get a result, who can?"
Shear said	"OK standard ambush then. Now the plan will be an outside hit or so it will appear. Saaz and Rohan will be dressed in their Muslim kit, the full works, black hijab and full kit head to foot so it appears that two Muslim ladies are walking along the lane…"
Saaz interrupted	"It's called a Niqab, Sarge."
Shear said	"Hijab, Niqab, Alibabajab, what does it matter, be completely covered, yes, room only for two peering eyes."
Rohan grinned	"Yes Sahib."
Shear continued	"The ladies are walking along the lane. We will be in front of the target vehicle in the battered van when you two stop us for directions. The target stops behind us then you two show them a sawn off. They won't be able to reverse because Ken and Tony will be in a vehicle behind them."
Lewis said	"Sounds good Sarge."
Boots asked	"When were you thinking Boss?"
Shear replied	"Soon, this week sometime when we've worked out who's worth the hit. The best way to get that information is to ask."
Lewis said	"Ask who?"

Shear explained "The people who know. We'll pull a courier and offer him a deal. The deal being that they get nicked and spend a year or two in jail, or, they can tell us about a bigger fish, that way they remain free, keep their drugs, make their delivery and go home with their ill-gotten gains. We'll make sure they are from out of town, that way they'll be more ready to give information as they will have no loyalties at this end."

Boots added "Well, we're here again tomorrow, might be best to do it then before they call the operation off."

Shear replied "Tomorrow it is then."

The next day Shear's crew were working four 'til midnight. They made their way to the lane and stopped half a mile from the rear entrance to the farm and waited. They pulled their van off the narrow lane into a track just inside the forest. They had ANPR on board so that when a number plate is recognised, the computer will come up with all intelligence held on the vehicle. Two hours later a yellow mini came into view as it left the bend three hundred yards away. Boots could see that the registered keeper was from Gloucester and that he had a number of convictions.

Boots said "Battle station boys, the yellow mini contains a juicy target."

Shear enquired "How juicy?"

Boots replied "He's got form for drugs, is disqualified, and guess what…?"

Shear asked "What?"

Boots said "He's wanted on warrant for non-appearance at Crown Court."

Shear said "Bingo, he'll do, let's give him a pull."

As the vehicle grew closer the van pulled out of the track and onto the lane where it stalled. Lewis and Tony walked out of the wood closing in on the rear of the mini which now faced an enforced stoppage. Tony was a few years behind the driver when the vehicle stopped. Tony opened the driver's door and took the key from the ignition and dragged the driver from the vehicle. The mini keys were thrown to Lewis. Shear strode forward.

Shear said "Hello, Mr Selby, welcome to our world."

Selby spluttered "What's going on, who the bloody hell are you?"

Selby was bundled into the van which was then pulled back into the wood. His mini was pushed off the track where it was searched by Lewis. Lewis remained with the mini suggesting to any passers-by that the vehicle was his. Selby had been cuffed and searched Tony. £3K was found in his jacket pocket. He was cuffed to the seating in front of Ken.

Shear said	"Who do you think we are?"
Selby said	"Bloody cops."
Shear said	"You had better hope so, 'cos if we're not you're in big trouble."
Selby said	"Well, I've done nowt wrong, why have you stopped me, and you haven't said I'm under arrest or anything."
Shear said	"We're off-grid cops and we've grabbed you because we don't like you."
Selby said	"Well, what have I done wrong, nothing."
Shear said	"Tell him Officer."
Boots said	"Your name's John Ian Selby and you live in Gloucester, right?"
Selby said	"So what?"
Boots said	"So, this, if our computer can be believed, you've got convictions for public order, theft, and drug possession."
Selby said	"Yeah, that was all a long time ago."
Boots said	"You were disqualified from driving three months ago, right?"
Selby said	"Yes but I've put an appeal in, haven't I?"
Boots said	"You are now driving whilst disqualified."
Shears interrupted	"You've been asked half a dozen questions and told us two truths and five lies."
Selby said	"How do you know?"
Shear said	"I saw your lips move."
Selby said	"I'm not saying any more, I don't have to speak to you."
Shear said	"You don't understand your position here. We ask questions and you answer them. If you lie or don't answer, this is what happens."

Ken pulled a plastic bag over Selby's head, tightened it at the neck and began to count. Selby struggled and tried unsuccessfully to speak…seventeen…thirty-two…forty-five…at this point the bag was removed. Selby pulled himself up, gasped for air whilst trying to speak. He eventually gained control and said:

	"OK, OK…what do you want to know? Just tell me what you want."
Shear said	"Like I said, welcome to our world. We don't inhabit the world that you think we inhabit, we inhabit your world when there are no rules. We are off-grid and we deal in the international currency of communication, you know what that is, don't you?"
Selby said	"No, what?"
Shear said	"Pain."
Selby said	"Yeah, OK, just tell me what you want, I'll tell you, honest."
Shear said	"Now here's the deal, we can nick you now for disqualified driving and being in possession of enough Class A to charge you with possession with intent to supply…"
Selby interrupted	"I haven't got any drugs, honest, you can search my car."
Shear continued	"If we search your car, we'll find enough Class A to get you banged up for the foreseeable, in fact…let me see…where's that coke?"
Ken said	"Under your seat, Sarge."
Shear continued	"Yes, this stuff, that's what we'll find. Are you with me so far, are you keeping up?"

Selby nodded.

Shear continued	"Now we are going to let you go. You will continue to the farm and buy your three grand worth of drugs. On your return, you'll tell us who's at the farm, numbers, names and what they're holding. You'll also take a few pictures of the layout and note anything worthwhile. Now who's got the mike?"
Ken said	"This mike is going in your inside pocket, we will hear every word spoken and if you put a foot wrong we will be

	straight into raid the place and we'll tell them that we followed you in."
Selby complained	"You'll get me killed."
Ken said	"That's right, we will."
Shear said	"So, young Selby, it's up to you. You can have a good result, go to the farm, do your business and drive safely home with enough coke to make you King of Gloucester for six months, or you can get nicked now and go to jail for six months. Up to you son, King of Gloucester or detained at Her Majesty's pleasure."
Selby said	"What if they find the mike on me, I'm dead."
Shear said	"It's a torch, the mike is behind the bulb, if they find it, then it's a torch, nothing else, understand?"
Selby said	"And then you'll let me go?"
Shear lied	"Yes, of course, that's what we've just agreed."
Selby said	"What guarantees have I got?"
Shear said	"I guarantee that if anything goes wrong, we'll make sure it's all down to you and that they will be looking to kill you, and remember, we'll be listening to every word that is said and if we spot a mistake, you're toast."

Selby drove along the lane and turned into the farmhouse. He knew that he only had to stay cool, buy his coke, try and take a picture or two and get out as quickly as safety permitted. He knew that he wouldn't be doing business with these people again as the police were about to take them out. If he was smart, he'd be back to Gloucester in a couple of hours as top dog.

Shear said "Do you think he believed the bit about the mike behind the bulb bit?"

Ken laughed "You convinced me, Sarge."

Shear's mobile phone rang, he could see that the Honourable Khom Ting, MP was calling. He answered and said he was on an active operation and asked Ting to text, he then cut Ting off. The text followed…Need to speak soon, can you do tonight? Shear replied…Working 'til 10, how about 10.30…? Ting said…"OK." Twenty minutes went by when the mini appeared from the farm track, a minute later it stopped by Shear. Selby carefully handed over the torch and said:

"There's only two of them, some big fat guy called Jay and some kid he called Fink. Jay went out the back and into a green barn, they keep a tractor in there, then he came out with my stuff, I paid him and that was it."

Ken said	"Pictures?"
Selby said	"Sorry mate, I didn't have the nerve, sorry."
Shear said	"We couldn't hear the chat between you and Jay very well, what was he saying?"
Selby said	"Just chit chat really, he mentioned that he was having a load of stuff delivered Friday, they've got an old post office van carrying it, no one ever stops it do they, it's post office."
Shear said	"Let me see your mobile phone."
Selby said	"That's not the one I use for business."
Shear said	"OK pal, that's it, consider yourself as having a narrow escape and if you ever come to light again, I'll tell Fat Jay you fingered him, and I'll give him your name and address."
Selby said	"What about my phone?"
Shear said	"What about it?"

Selby drove off wiping the sweat from his brow. He considered his lucky escape. He could be lying in police cells now charged with disqualified driving and Class A drug possession. It wouldn't take them long to discover he skipped Crown Court and that would keep him banged up for ages. In the event, he played a blinder and is off home with street value coke of about 25K, sweet.

Shear said "You can use Jonah's mobile to make that call now, Ken."

Shear's crew were finishing their written reports back at the nick when Chief Inspector Cole called him to his office. Shear had reason to believe that Cole couldn't be trusted with serious information. He spent too much time in the bar and he was too free with his tongue. Anyone looking for quality information didn't have to ask, they only had to listen. Shear told him that they had received intelligence that a large consignment of drugs was to be delivered to the farm on Friday. By way of bait, he told Cole that they were using a post office van to sneak the stuff in.

Cole had been drinking and didn't have the wit to interrogate Shear further. Shear was anxious to get away as it was nearing 10 pm so he told Cole that he had put a pint in for him behind the bar. Cole looked at his watch and agreed to meet Shear for the next briefing on the farm. Shear returned to the report writing room.

Ken said	"Have you heard the news, Boss?"
Shear enquired	"No, what news?"
Ken said	"Traffic nicked a guy on the M5 northbound loaded with cocaine. They thought he might have been sourced from somewhere on our ground."
Shear said	"What's his name?"
Ken said	"Selby."
Shear said	"We had better arrange for him to be interviewed before he's back on the street."
Ken said	"No problem, Boss, he'll be remanded in custody, he failed to appear at Crown Court for sentencing. It looks like he'll be banged-up for three or four years."
Shear smiled	"Oh dear, Mr Selby seems to be having a bad day."

Shear made his way to Khom Ting's place in the country. A walled estate tucked away at the foot of the hills. The approach was pleasing and appealed to Shear's sense of security. A half mile country lane leading to a clump of trees hiding antique wrought iron gates. Shear thought it sterile, uninviting. He liked it a lot. The gates opened and Shear drove in, he noticed the gates close behind him. A further 300 yards brought him to the Portico leading to the entrance to the building. The Portico was supported by two Ionic columns in the Greek style. Here was a man with real wealth, old money, with all the nuances of speech and behavioural patterns that attended his class. This was going to be fun he thought. Ting appeared at the door clutching a drink. Shear checked that his voice activated tape was on and well hidden. He left the car. Ting led him into the living room.

Khom said	"Thanks for coming out old chap, do come in and have a drink."
Shear enquired	"Who else is here?"
Khom said	"We are perfectly alone, I let the staff go earlier, this meeting is totally secure, no problems on that front, I've even turned the security cameras off. There will be no record of this meeting ever having occurred. Drink?"
Shear replied	"Black coffee, no sugar, thanks."

Shear looked around at the opulence of the room, lavish beyond belief. He guessed the place to be 300 years old, maybe more. Oak beams, high narrow leaded windows, Inglenook fireplace, the whole place dripped with antiques.

Shear enquired	"So this place is what, 300 years old?"
Ting replied	"Built 1601, last of the Tudor piles you know."
Shear said	"So why am I here?"
Ting replied	"I'm in a bit of a fix really. I am instructed by the Home Secretary to deal with the nitty gritty of this drug reduction thing, you know, the more important aspects of the matter, the practical details of how this reduction was brought about. The fine-grain detail so to speak."
Shear said	"I saw on the news that the Home Secretary had sorted the whole thing. It seems he ran a trial here on our patch, and by the use of a number of initiatives based on zero tolerance he has brought about this change, and all this just as a general election was called. A perfect strategy and perfect timing."
Ting said	"Well, we both know better than that. This whole thing is down to you alone, it was you who…"
Shear interrupted	"Let's just deal with what we've got now. What is the fix you say you're in, tell me about that?"
Ting explained	"Well since it broke on the news, I've been deluged by important people who want to know how this has been brought about. No one can get hold of the Home Secretary, his people are very protective and shield him from every enquiry. When asked by the opposition, he refers them to me with some nebulous nonsense about a paper being disclosed concerning the trial supposedly carried out here. Well for goodness sake, what am I to say. I need your help here old chap. Tell me what you can about this reduction?"
Shear asked	"Who are these important people?"
Ting replied	"Well, everyone really, the media, the Crime Commissioner, Magistrates' court chairman, leader of the local Council…"
Shear interrupted	"…any of these people life threatening?"
Ting replied	"Career threatening, yes. The Crime Commissioner and the council leader, a couple of bastards really, both ardent socialists."

Shear asked	"The council leader, isn't that Derrick Fold, didn't he stand against you at the last election?"
Ting replied	"He did, yes, I beat him by an overwhelming majority and he now spends his life questioning my every decision, I have to meet both next week for their monthly audience. Oh my god, it'll be a disaster, they will oppose whatever I have to say and make political gain at every point. So you see I need hard facts, lots of them, enough to silence them both."
Shear said	"I think Fold bats for the other side, he's got a strong reputation for it."
Ting said	"The man's a strutting sodomite I tell you. Spends half his life giving me a hard time and the other half seeing who'll entertain his hard on in the local toilets, the man should be exposed for what he is."
Shear enquired	"Do you know what pub he uses?"
Ting replied	"Yes, the Pelican, that gay bar by the park, they all meet there."
Shear asked	"Do you have a photograph of Fold I could borrow?"
Ting said	"Yes, I believe I have, upstairs somewhere, it'll take a while to find, do you need it now?"
Shear lied	"Yes, I'm not entirely sure what he looks like and I'll need to show his face to my people."
Ting said	"Well, I'll get it now, it'll take a couple of minutes, make yourself another coffee."
Shear said	"I need to ring the nick, can I borrow your mobile phone, mine needs recharging?"

Ting opened his mobile, entered his password and handed it to Shear then disappeared upstairs for what Shear hoped might be at least two minutes. Shear made his way to the kitchen, put the kettle on and then secreted himself in the toilet where he began to work on Ting's mobile. In less than a minute, Shear had installed an EyeSpy tap and track device in the phone. He returned to the kitchen just as the kettle boiled and was awaiting Ting when he returned with the newspaper photograph.

Ting said	"Here it is, local council meeting which I attended, Fold is the tall guy on the left."

Shear said	"I know the Crime Commissioner pretty well, like you say hard-core left wing, cloud cuckoo land material."
Ting said	"Yes, they both are. Now what I need from you is a synopsis that I can put to them next week, enough to keep them quiet until after the election. I cannot over emphasise how important this is to me."
Shear said	"OK, leave it with me. I'll let you have the facts and figures before the meeting. I suppose you'll want some more coke for your next visit to the Narrow Escape."
Ting nodded	"Yes, thanks, I'll take as much as you can provide, those girls just can't get enough."

Shear left the house and made his way to the cottage. He stopped in a lay-by and listened for a moment to his voice activated tape. He then tapped on his tap and track app and smiled when he saw Ting's house appear on his GPS app. A good night's work.

Shear received a text from Chief Inspector Cole requiring Foxtrot 13 crew to attend a briefing at Headquarters concerning ongoing action following observations on the farm. He guessed that the post office van was to be targeted as it made its way to the farm. A successful operation would be a good result for Cole, but Shear had his doubts.

Foxtrot 13 met in the canteen and took their usual place at the window.

Shear said	"A small problem has arisen that we need to sort sooner than later. The local council chairman is causing difficulties for one of our patrons and we need to remove the threat soon. Councillor Fold, does anyone know him?"
Lewis said	"Yes, he drinks down the Pelican, it's a gay pub, I can look at that Sarge, I know a few people in there."
Shear said	"OK, you and Tony get down there and get some black on Fold, shouldn't be too hard. Now that it's legal they think it's safe, well let's see if we can quote 'unseat him' unquote."
Lewis laughed	"His seat is about to be taken out, but not in the way he likes it."
Shear said	"No delay, we need a result soon."

Everyone made their way into the briefing room. Three task force units were present. Shear was a little surprised that Cole was making a big issue of something that might come to nothing. A low-profile operation would have been much better, then in the event of failure it would have passed without comment, but more than 20 cops on a simple drugs bust had better get a result otherwise the boss will be answering difficult questions from the Chief. The bust was to take place on Friday, they would first take out the post office van and then execute a warrant at the farm. Cole asked Shear to produce an operation order to be issued to officers involved, it was a classified operation so limited copies would be made and distributed 'For Operational Officers Only'. Shear resolved to incorporate his own security measures in the document on a just in case basis. Each copy of the document would be secretly marked. A typo would be made on each. So that addressee no 3 would have a typo on page 3, line 3. Simple enough, worked every time and fool-proof. After the briefing, Foxtrot 13 boarded Cerberus and made their way around town.

Shear enquired	"What do we have on the Commissioner?"
Boots said	"Nothing Boss, he's whiter than white, never makes a bad move and always says the right thing. Every time he appears on the television it's to extol his own virtues as the common man whose been elected by the community to guard the guards."
Saaz said	"Yes, and we're the guards and he's the guy they voted to guard us. I want to know who guards him."
Shear smiled	"We do, of course."
Boots asked	"How do you mean, Boss?"
Shear explained	"We all have flaws, we're just people. We make mistakes, we have our dirty little secrets, no problem, everyone is hiding something. It becomes a problem if you set yourself up as something special."
Saaz helped	"What like a Crime Commissioner?"
Shear said	"Yes, if not him, then someone or something connected to him. All we have to do is find it."
Ken said	"His kid was cautioned for possession of a minute amount of cannabis, nothing to speak of, he's been clean since."
Shear said	"Well done, Ken, get the file and see what you can find out, speak to the officer in the case and get from him what's not on the file. Get a photo of the kid, we'll need that. In fact, let's get back to the nick, you Ken can find that file and Saaz and Tony can get into plain clothes and go for a drink down the Pelican."

Shear and his remaining crew continued their mobile patrol of Aqua Ponds. It was nearing midnight and the end of their tour of duty. Just before midnight control directed them to the local free mason building. The caretaker's wife had called the police to report that she had been speaking to her husband on the phone when she heard him cry out, the line went dead and she thought he had a heart attack. Shear was looking forward to getting into the inner-sanctum of this international secret society, or as they describe themselves a society with secrets. He reflected on the occasions when certain senior officers had asked him to join. He always refused without giving reason. He also knew that being a mason was career enhancing and at senior officer level downright necessary. There was evidence of Masonic activity everywhere.

Shear said	"Boots, Google free-masons."
Saaz asked	"What do they get up to, Boss?"
Shear replied	"It's an international self-help group. People who are anxious to get on, ambitious, determined people. As a mason you can be your bosses' boss."
Saaz asked	"How does that work?"
Shear replied	"When you join the masons, at the end of the initiation ceremony your blindfold is removed. At that point, you are the new boy who is then exposed to the people above you in the pecking order. Now it may be that you join as an inspector then there is every chance that there will be half a dozen constables present who are now well above your newly hatched station."
Boots exclaimed	"Bloody hell, so back at work if you have to see the inspector who is below you in the masons then you're going to have a good result, yes?"
Shear said	"Yes, Boots, exactly correct, and imagine if you've applied for promotion with half a dozen other guys, who is favourite I wonder, you a mason or the non-masons?"
Boots said	"My god, and people think we live in a fair society…ah, got it, Google Wikipedia…Christ, half the kings of the world are masons. Four British Kings and…the Duke of Kent is the main man, he's the Worshipful Master…my god, if you're not a mason you don't stand a chance. It says here there are about a quarter of a million of them. They have lodges in every town."

Shear said	"Yes, nearly as many as Chinese takeaways."
Saaz	"I think I'll join."
Boots continued	"Listen to this, they've got ranks, apprentice, journeyman and master mason, oh my god where does it end."
Shear said	"Muslims are against the masons, Saaz, they think they are pro-Jew and you know what that means."
Saaz said	"I thought everyone was against the Jews."
Boots asked	"So do normal working people join, probably not."
Shear said	"They do, yes. Just imagine, if you move into town and open a butchers' shop near two other butchers, all the masons will tell their wives to shop at your place so that you have a captive audience, that's how it works, they look after their own people."
Boots said	"And I thought they only sold meat."

Cerberus pulled up outside the front door of the Masonic lodge. They found the magnificent front door locked, there was no lighting and the place was silent. He asked the control room to call the lodge, there was no answer. The only key holder was the caretaker, so they decided to banjo the door. Two minutes later the door lay open and they were in. The place was empty and the phone was on the receiver, no trace of the caretaker.

Boots said	"Is this the right place, Sarge, it looks a bit like a church, look there's a bible on the table and candles."
Shear said	"Oh, yes, this is the Masonic lodge, look at the pictures on the wall. These people Boots are the illuminate, with Lodges like this all over the world. It's no wonder that the conspiracy theorists believe that these guys effectively rule the world."
Boots said	"Why don't the government close them down?"
Shear said	"Because they are the government, anyone who's in a position of power is a mason, or a friend of a mason, they possess the power free from elections, and everything is a secret, but not from us, we've just captured this lot."
Boots asked	"Is there anybody who can't join?"
Shear said	"Anybody can join, the problem is most religions are against them, especially the Islamic lot. Even the labour party have got it in for them, the good thing is that nobody knows who 'they' are."

37

Boots asked	"What about blacks, can they join?"
Shear said	"Yes. Funny really, black men can join but women of any colour cannot."

They looked at the pictures, over a hundred or so. People dressed in their Masonic kit, sashes, pineys and gloves. The pictures showed the general activities of the lodge, ceremonies, meals and general festivities. Shear was transfixed by the number policemen in the pictures and the company they were in. He knew each of the policemen, most of the solicitors and some of the businessmen. This was a goldmine. They split up the wall between them and photographed all the pictures.

They called control on the air and reported that there was no trace of the caretaker. The response was that he had been picked up by an ambulance outside a public telephone box a few hundred yards from the Masonic lodge.

The crew met at the cottage the next morning, three hours before they started duty. It was time to sum up what intelligence they had and what to do with it. The election was less than five weeks away and things had to happen, and they had to happen now.

Shear began	"OK, let's look at what we've got. Ken, how did you get on with the Commissioner's son?"
Ken replied	"The kid was turned over outside the school by the local bobby who found a bit of cannabis on him, not much, about enough to roll two ciggies."
Shear asked	"Do we know who supplied him?"
Ken said	"He wouldn't say but that's Fink's ground, so a thousand to one it was him."
Shear asked	"Lewis, Tony, any hard information."
Lewis replied	"Well, the target didn't show but we got into conversation with a couple of his pals. It didn't take long to be invited to one of their meets. They get together most Saturday nights at Fold's caravan to party and bang each other. When they were drunk enough, they showed us pics on their mobile phones of a recent meet. The good news is that Fold is a dresser, black stockings, suspender belt and knickers…"
Shear interrupted	"Did you get the pics?"

Tony said   "Only after we promised to bring a few lines of coke to the meet. Have a look."

They all gathered around and ogled the pictures, three pictures in all. Each showed a number of naked men engaged in sexual activity. Two were dressed in lingerie and wigs. Fold was in his panties and stockings and despite being the subject of a pig roast was clearly identifiable.

Tony said "Lovely isn't it, when it was illegal nobody would have taken pics and now because it's legal, they think they can do what they want…"

Shear interrupted "Yes, the only rule they have is no holds barred so to speak."

They left the cottage and prepared for their hit on the post office van and farmhouse.

Chapter 3

Chief Inspector Cole took his place behind the lectern in the briefing room. He asked Shear to hand out the operation orders, ten in all. There were two task force units, two traffic cars, a scenes of crime officer and a dog handler. 23 officers to stop one vehicle and raid a farm. Shear knew this was overkill and that Cole was making something out of nothing. Of course, if it resulted in a major seizure then this would reflect well on Cole and perhaps change his fortunes. Cole began his briefing taking a sip from his Coke bottle. He made a big play of a simple job. The traffic cars would sit on the motorway and spot the post office van. As the vehicle was stopped the farm would be raided and the warrant executed. Shear allocated this job for his crew. What was the point of an operation order that didn't favour you?

Shear made the case for the farm side of the operation to be undercover, meaning his crew would be in the old battered van and in plain clothes. He also persuaded Cole that as operational commander he would be best placed to be at the scene of the post office van stop in the event of a major haul. Cole was happy with this and offered no resistance to whatever Shear suggested. After the briefing Cole went to speak to the traffic cops to ensure that he was in the car that stopped the post van. Shear took advantage of his absence and had a sip from his Coke bottle. Sure enough, brandy and Coke, a functioning alcoholic. At 6 pm, all units were deployed to their jump off points and waited.

Shear's crew pulled their vehicle into the woods a few hundred yards from the farm. Some minutes later a car pulled out of the farm driven by a well-nourished man. Shear knew it was fat Jay. Time now for a deception. Lewis then called the farm. The phone was on speaker and the crew listened in.

Lewis said   "Is Jay there?"
Fink answered "No, he is gone out. He won't be back for a while."
Lewis asked   "Is that Fink?"

Fink said	"Yeah, what are you after?"
Lewis said	"Jay's got a shipment coming in today but he hasn't called to say when I should come around."
Fink said	"It's been cancelled, it won't be here 'til Sunday morning."
Lewis asked	"What's the problem, I've got a lot of people waiting for their stuff?"
Fink replied	"We're expecting a visit from the cops, they won't find anything so you'll have to wait 'til Sunday."
Lewis said	"OK, see you Sunday."
Shear said	"That's interesting boys, we are no longer searching for drugs, we're searching for an informant."
Ken said	"You don't suspect Cole do you, Sarge?"
Shear said	"No, it's not him, he hasn't the wit for that sort of skulduggery. Let us see what we can get out of Fink, shall we? Rohan you and Ken can go in, get the camouflage gear out of the bag."

Just over an hour passed when the post office van was spotted leaving the motorway at Aqua Ponds. Cole announced on air that the van would be stopped in two minutes and that Foxtrot 13 should then make their entry. Two minutes later Shear stopped just outside the farmhouse. Two men got out. Rohan looked the part, dark skin, ample belly, short jet-black bear and turban. Ken lumbered from the vehicle. Big guy heavily muscled looking good in his pony tail wig and peel-on wash-off swallow tattoos, one on each side of his neck just below the ears. As they neared the front door Fink came out. He was clearly startled by these two heavies.

Ken asked	"You Jay?"
Fink replied	"He's not here, he's gone out, I don't know when he'll be back."
Ken said	"I'm Carter and this guy is Khan, we've just travelled over two hundred miles to get here, I've got twelve grand for my gear which I've arranged to collect today. Now get on the phone and get him back here now. Do it now!"
Fink fumbled	"He won't be back today…"
Ken interrupted	"It's like this, either you produce the goods, he produces the goods or you'll be providing two pints of blood."

Fink stuttered	"I would, I would honest, but the cops will be here soon, they're going to raid us…Jay's got what we had left, it's not much, he's taken it to town…"
Ken demanded	"How come you know the cops are going to raid you?"
Fink said	"We got a tip-off, that's why Jay moved the stash, that's why I'm leaving, they'll be here soon, we've got to go."
Ken continued	"Who tipped you off."
Fink said	"A cop, Jay knows him…"
Ken insisted	"What's the cop's name?"
Fink said	"I don't know, Jay deals with him, he's some high up in the cops that's all I know, honest, I'm telling you the truth."
Ken said	"Now tell me precisely where Jay is."
Fink said	"In town, I don't know where."
Ken said	"If you don't tell us where he is, they'll be calling you lefty."
Fink said	"…lefty?"
Ken said	"Yeah, Khan here will chop your right hand off and what's left is your left."
Fink agreed	"OK, he's in the apartment above the garage in West Street. If he finds out I told you, he'll kill me, honest he will."
Ken said	"When do you expect him back here?"
Fink said	"He told me to text him when the coast was clear."
Ken said	"Text him now, don't send it, just type it out like you do."
Fink said	"Why, what are you going to do?"
Ken said	"If he's not at the address, we'll send the text."
Fink said	"He's there, he really is."
Ken said	"Then you haven't got a problem. He will never know we've seen you. All you have to do is be here when he comes back, tell him some story about the raid, and be here Sunday when we come back for the stuff."
Fink asked	"What about my phone?"
Ken said	"What about it. Tell Jay you lost it."

Ken and Rohan returned to the van and waited. It didn't take long for the radio to report the outcome of the post office van stop. Cole was too ashamed to speak himself and it was reported by one of the traffic crew that the van had been stopped and found to be driven by an elderly lady and that nothing had been found. It was now their intention to drive to the farm and link up with Foxtrot 13. Shear called Cole on his phone and told him that there was no one at the farm. The farm was empty and vehicles previously seen parked in the driveway were gone. Shear suggested they return to the police station to de-brief.

Shear discovered that the other crews had been stood down by Cole and there was to be no de-brief. Cole was eventually found in the bar lamenting his bad luck. Shear consoled him and told him that the operation had much to commend it. Cole had seized command at the outset, organised personnel, prepared a plan to cover all eventualities and had led the operation from the front. A text book job. Shear assured him that everyone was impressed and that he would like to buy him a drink. Cole cheered up and thanked Shear for his support…and the drink.

Shear then spoke to a task force unit in the rear yard. He told them that he had just received information that a guy called Jay was about to leave the apartment in West Street with a substantial stash. He asked them to keep observations and turn him over if he showed. After ten minutes, Ken sent Fink's text to Jay. The trap was set.

Shear and his crew returned to work the next day, the incident report revealed that Jay had been arrested and found to be in possession of sixty-four grams of coke, half a cup of hash, two and a quarter ounces, enough to draw lengthy jail time. He had been interviewed by WDC Ward and was due to be released on bail later that day. Shear decided it was time to have a word with Jay, but before that a word with Ward.

Shear asked	"How did you get on with Jay?"
Ward replied	"A no reply interview, so he'll be charged with possession with intent to supply and with his previous convictions he'll be going down."
Shear asked	"Who's his brief?"
Ward said	"Simon Hanson from Bakers in Bristol, that'll cost him most of his ill-gotten gains."
Shear asked	"Did Pack produce photo ID?"
Ward said	"Yes, there's a photocopy on the file."
Shear enquired	"How much cash did he have when he got nicked?"
Ward said	"7K, we've seized that as part of the evidence. An asset recovery application will ensure that he has seen the last of that."

Shear spoke to the Custody Officer and got the nod for an off the record word with Jay. The Custody Officer said that Jay was in a foul mood and not amenable to a tea and biscuits chat. Shear opened the cell door to find Jay. The name fat Jay was fitting and he was in combative form.

Shear opened "Hi Jay, a quick word."
Jay replied "I'll tell you what I told that bitch Ward, I've nothing to say so fuck off."
Shear said "A mutual friend of ours has asked me to look in on you Jay, to see you're OK."

This drew a silence from Jay. Shear watched and said nothing. Jay stood up and eyed Shear who detected a meeting of minds, the atmosphere was tangible. Jay mellowed and looked a little coy.

Jay enquired "A mutual friend?"
Shear said "Yes, he said everything's fine, things will still go ahead tomorrow as planned, just stay calm and you'll be back on the street just as soon as…"
Jay replied "…I want to know who grassed me up?"
Shear said "No problem, a kid that Fink supplies."
Jay demanded "What's his name?"
Shear said "Don't know, Fink knows, it's the Police Commissioner's son."
Jay said "That stupid bugger, I knew I couldn't trust him."
Shear said "You can't trust anybody mate."
Jay said "I'll find out and when I do, he's dead."
Shear asked "Who?"
Jay thought "Both the bastards."
Shear advised "Be careful, our friend can only do so much to protect you."
Jay said "Yeah, but his boss can do a whole lot more."

Jay was bailed and Shear returned to the old battered van for undercover cops in another of Cole's no hope targets. They drove out of the police compound on its daily mission of protecting the good people of the Aqua Ponds. What lay ahead this day they wondered. They passed fat Jay on the street. He had a determined look on his face and was purposefully striding out as though he was on a mission. Lewis quipped that Jay was so fat that if he fell over, he'd probably roll downhill. The crew remonstrated with him enquiring how he could be so cruel, after all, charged, but importantly not yet convicted, did we not live in a just world where every man is innocent until a jury says otherwise. They all nodded in agreement. All was well with the world. They drove five miles out into the country to the salt marshes.

The van pulled up at the bottom of the drove in sight of the church. They were bedecked in camouflage jackets, beanie fishing hats and had two sets of binoculars between them. They knew the marshes attracted birdwatchers from the area and that they would go unnoticed. They could see their barn and with the aid of binoculars the small pull-in next to the beach by the concrete platform. What a perfect location, a protected salt marsh providing habitat for seabirds and young fish as well as flood protection, a place attracting twitchers, dog walkers and geeks, joyful serenity, tranquillity and peace. Time could now be spent looking at illuminati photographs blagged from the Masons' Lodge and try to piece together who was who and their relationship with each other. Shear reminded the boys that it was not about who you know, but all about what you know about who you know. The target Cole wanted them to keep obs on was not in the house that Cole had skilfully marked on the map, no, he was half a mile away under thirty feet of water. They had a couple of hours to kill.

Tony asked   "Are we looking for anything special, Boss?"

Shear advised   "Everything's special, just keep looking, try and ID as many as you can, and in particular where there's two or more in the picture, try and figure out any relationship they might have. The same goes if they are in different pictures, try to spot any commonality."

Two hours passed and they had gleaned what they could from the pictures. Cole was big friends with a number of senior officers, council members and the wealthy. This would be explored further at the International Police Association dance being held at Headquarters on Saturday next. Meanwhile Shear continued with his restructuring of the society he policed.

Shear said "OK boys time for action. When we get back to the nick Lewis and Tony can take a plain car out and see if you can clock the Post Office van. I'll report to Cole and bring him up to date with the non-events on the marsh and then we'll sit up and wait for events to unravel. Plan is the same, Saaz and Rohan will make the hit with us in front of postie and Lewis and Tony behind."

Shear made his way to Cole's office knowing that he was more likely to be in the bar, but fictions have to be pretended. Cole's phone rang and was answered by Shear. He then found Cole in the bar clutching his Coke bottle.

Shear said	"Not drinking Boss?"
Cole said	"No, I've got to keep a clear head, I've got a visit from the Deputy Chief and Chief Superintendent, complaints this afternoon."
Shear said	"I've just taken a call in your office about a double stabbing at Keenbourne, two kids stabbed and…"
Cole said	"Keenbourne, where's that?"
Shear said	"A small village about seven miles out…"
Cole said	"…Oh yes, I know it, how bad are they?"
Shear said	"Don't know, they've just been taken to hospital, probably best to get the major incident boys rolling."
Cole said	"It's not that bad surely?"
Shear said	"Well, we're looking at a couple of woundings and if anyone dies…"
Cole said	"I think I need a drink…and yes, get hold of the team, Christ this is all I need with the deputy here."
Shear said	"Might be good idea to get Oscar 11 airborne."
Cole said	"What's the point if they're in hospital, there's no one at the scene?"
Shear said	"You don't want a murder being reported on the local TV with pictures of an empty scene. Much better if you're there on camera with the Deputy Chief by your side and Oscar 11 flying overhead. I can see the opening broadside Local Police Chief Commander Cole heads hunt…"
Cole said	"Yes, well, let's get to it, thank you Sarge, you press on."

Shear and his crew made their way to the wood and reversed the van into the tracks just out of sight of the lane. Saaz and Rohan checked their niqabs and readied the sawn-off. They then listened to radio transmissions.

Boots asked   "What do you think Jay is doing now, Boss?"

Shear said	"He's angry, he'll be trying to work out how to contact his cop informant, trouble is, the cops have got his phone so he'll lie low to watch which way the wind's blowing. He won't go back to the apartment 'cos he got nicked there, so his only safe place is here at the farm just where we want him."
Ken asked	"I don't suppose his informant's number will show on his phone?"
Shear said	"No chance, too smart for that so we'll have to find who he is from Jay."

The radio called Cole and told him that one of the victims was DOA and they asked if Cole could deliver the message in person. They then gave the address. The Commissioner's address. Cole said he would contact control by landline for details.

Shear said "Dead on arrival. Shocking, I bet that was something to do with drugs. Another young life lost, where will it all end."

Tony texted Shear.

The Post Office van had just come off the motorway and would be with them in about twenty minutes. Two white males on board. They had just refuelled and looked at ease with the world, they suspect nothing. Saaz and Rohan got dressed. Tony again texted saying they had turned into the lane. Shear announced it was showtime, he pulled the van out into the lane. Saaz and Rohan got out and stayed at the driver's window.

Rohan warned "Here they come."

Saaz and Rohan began a conversation with the driver. The post van drew closer, Tony and Ken close behind them. As the van stopped, Saaz and Rohan made end of conversation noises and walked in their direction. They were boxed in. The two young female Muslims covered in head to toe in black peering out of their eye-slits were about to walk past them. The van driver opened his window.

Driver "OK darling, the mosque is at the end of the road?"

Saaz said "And your balls are at the end of the barrel?"

Rohan produced the sawn-off from under his Niqab, Saaz opened the driver's door and took the key. Rohan beckoned both youths from the vehicle. Tony and Lewis opened the back door and helped themselves to two heavy bags and reversed away. Saaz took their phones.

Rohan said	"You two can now kiss your ass goodbye."
Driver	"No, no, honest we can give you information, please we won't tell anyone, just let us go…please."
Rohan said	"Information?"
Driver	"Yeah, we know where all the consignments go, honest we can give you a list."
Rohan said	"You'll have to do better than that to stay alive."
Driver	"There's a guy in Bristol, he's the boss, he's a cop, top brass, he organises everything, honest it's the truth honest…"
Rohan said	"A name might keep you two little bastards alive."
Driver	"They call him Bubbles, I don't know his real name, just Bubbles. My boss deals with him on the phone nobody knows him, just Bubbles, that's all we know honest, just let us go we won't tell anybody anything honest."
Rohan said	"When I say go, you two start running back the way you came. Run for a mile then turn right and run through the woods, got it?"
Driver	"…Yes, OK thanks mate."
Rohan said	"Go."

When the youths were out of sight, their vehicle was rolled down the hill and into the woods. Saaz and Rohan joined the crew, got into mufti and drove off to meet Lewis and Tony. They returned to the cottage to discuss options. Boots took the two bags and disappeared out the back door as Shear received a text from Ting demanding an urgent meeting, it was agreed they'd meet later that night.

Shear announced	"The Right Honourable is having difficulties, I'll have to see him later and calm his fears."
Ken asked	"How come a twit like him can become an MP boss?"
Shear replied	"Because he went to a top public school, Oxbridge gave him a classics degree, he speaks frightfully well and he inherited old money."
Ken said	"Anyone with a bit of sense could do his job."
Shear said	"MPs represent just under a hundred thousand people. Ken, your two O levels and estuary English just won't cut it."
Saaz added	"And he's nice and white."

Shear said	"We've got what they would pay a fortune for and the higher up they are the more they would pay."
Saaz	"What's that, Boss?"
Shear smiled	"Anonymity my friend, anonymity, being anonymous is better than military grade camouflage. We can go anywhere and do anything without coming to attention. Everyone knows where the queen is and what she is doing, who'd want her job?"
Lewis said	"Prince Charles."

Boots returned to the cottage reporting that everything was set. With the crew together, Shear laid out the plan. It was time to pull Jay. Shear would enter the farm first and arrest Jay for murder, the crew would follow thirty seconds later. Jay would be cuffed and bundled into the van and the crew return to search the farm leaving Shear and Jay alone to speak.

Lewis said	"Do you think he suspects anything, Boss?"
Shear said	"Doubt it, there's not many witnesses in small villages and CCTV even rarer."
Tony said	"Have we got any actual evidence?"
Shear said	"Only the evidence of the chat we had in the cell this morning and the CCTV we'll say we recovered."
Lewis said	"The unofficial chat is inadmissible and the CCTV doesn't exist."
Shear said	"Only we know that."
Lewis said	"An interesting hour or so lies ahead."
Shear asked	"Low tide Tony, find out when it is?"
Boots said	"When do you plan to drop the stash, Boss?"
Shear said	"I had a text while you were out, could be tonight."
Tony said	"An hour and a half, Boss."
Shear said	"OK, remember, Jay thinks I am working alone, you guys know nothing so keep schtum."
Boots asked	"He's angry and probably on the bottle, Boss, are you sure you'll be OK on your own with him?"
Shear replied	"He's got more reason to be frightened of me, let's go."

The crew made their way to the farm. Jay's car was in the front yard in open view. No attempt had been made to hide it, he suspected nothing. Shear checked his Taser and made it more visible and made his way to the front door.

Shear shouted "Jay, open up."

As Jay opened the door Shear pushed him inside and into the kitchen.

Shear said "Half a dozen cops will be here in a minute, say nothing, you'll be going outside with me for a chat while they search the farm so keep it shut, don't speak, say nothing got it."

The crew entered the farm and found Jay in cuffs being escorted out to the van. They began their search.

Jay said	"What's the crack, what have they got?"
Shear said	"So, you managed to stick those two little bastards then?"
Jay said	"Yeah, they had it coming, nobody fucks with me and gets away with it."
Shear said	"Well, you might not get away with it. Fink is still alive and he's talking, where's the knife?"

Shear sat Jay on the floor of the van and secured him to the inside rail and covered him with the blanket. He briefed the crew and had Ken check the money was in the kennel. He told them to return to the vehicle in a couple of minutes and to take up battle stations. Ken was to sit in the rear seat behind Jay. Shear joined Jay.

Shear said	"A bit of luck, Jay, I told them there's not enough light to do the outside area so they're just finishing up. When you get back to the nick say nothing, do nothing, leave it all to me, we'll sort this little problem out. I've got the knife so I'll see to it that it's found in Fink's car, that'll get you out of the nick and Fink in."
Jay said	"Nice one mate. Tell Jock there's an extra ten in it for him."

The crew returned to the van and reported that nothing had been found, they gunned her up and made their way to the Marshes. Jay remained on the floor in silence. Such a big guy needed to be as close as possible to his crypt as he still needed to be carried. They stopped at the pull in and Lewis checked the directional arrow on the concrete pillar. Shear took a shovel and moved out onto the sand. The blanket was pulled from Jay who dutifully complied when asked to sit. His feet were cuffed and Shear gave Ken the nod. Less than two minutes saw Jay dispatched, the boys thought such a big lad may have lasted a little longer. Sainsbury bags were placed over feet and Jay was placed on the blanket and carried by all six of the crew. Shear had a large hole dug in the wet sand as the cortege arrived. And now back to the factory. Three minor jobs to complete, Cole, Ting and Hanson.

Cole, unusually was sitting at his desk with the life-saving Coke bottle nearby. Shear reported that his observations had come to nothing and suggested they be discontinued. Cole agreed that all observations were now off and that all energies would be focussed on the murder enquiry.

Cole said	"You know the boy who was killed today, Shear?"
Shear said	"No, Boss, just a kid on the edge of the scene, a bit of cannabis, nothing heavy."
Cole said	"No, Shear, not just a kid, he's the Police Commissioner's kid that makes it important. I've just spent an agonising two hours with the Commissioner who is devastated and quite inconsolable as you can imagine."
Shear said	"Yes, shocking news, sir, I'm sorry to hear of his loss, we're going to have to pull out all the stops on this one."
Cole said	"The Deputy Chief is taking a personal interest in this one, the Commissioner's a personal friend of his and he wants a result, he wants a result soon. The Chief has appointed DCI Farthing as senior investigating officer, the murder squad will be in residence in a couple of hours and then god help us. I can't stand Farthing, a flash bugger with questions always designed to undermine and mock us on the ground, and of course he's a member of the local mafia."
Shear Enquired	"…Mafia?"
Cole said	"Yes, those idiots in the Mason's Lodge, you know the secret society brigade."
Shear said	"Don't know anything about them, Boss, but I know if we can get a result before the murder boys get here…well it's going to show the Chief that you call the shots here, not Farthing."

Cole sighed	"If only."
Shear said	"I believe we've got one in custody."
Cole said	"Yes, a nobody called Blink or Fink, he's in hospital on the 'might pull through' list. God I wish it was him that copped it."
Shear said	"If it's Fink, I think we might have had dealings with him in the past, I'll see what I can turn up Boss."
Cole said	"Whatever…"

Shear spoke to the officer overseeing Fink. He said that they had operated and, apart from feeling sorry for himself, was perfectly well and would probably be discharged in a day or two. Shear looked through the window and saw Fink, a sorrowful little beast who was confused and in need of clarity. Shear entered his room.

Shear enquired	"You OK, mate?"
Fink asked	"Who are you?"
Shear said	"Jock sent me down, he heard there was some trouble down here between you and Jay, he wants to know if the consignment arrived. So what's been going on, did the gear get here or not?"
Fink said	"I dunno, Jay had some idea that I grassed him up to the kid I supply, he got me to get the kid to come out to Keenbourne and the next thing is he stuck the kid and then started on me, I don't get it, I don't understand, he's off his head."
Shear said	"Well, he's done a runner, he's got Jock's twenty grand and buggered off."
Fink said	"Well, at least he's gone, I don't fancy seeing him again, he's a serious bit of bad news."
Shear said	"What are you going to tell the cops when they see you?"
Fink said	"Dunno, I'll just say a couple of kids jumped us…"
Shear said	"…No, they've got CCTV from Keenbourne, they know it was Jay so stick to the story. Just tell them that Jay was well drunk and started lashing out at the kid, you tried to stop him and he stuck you too, that fits with the CCTV."
Fink said	"Oh nice one, thanks, mate. I think…"
Shear added	"…Tell them that Jay always said if things went wrong, he'll be on a boat for Porto and then to Spain."

Fink said	"What boat?"
Shear said	"Just a boat from Bristol, anything going to Porto, just tell them, they'll keep on 'til they think they've got all you know so that story should shut them up. Now I've got to see Jock and convince him that you haven't got his twenty grand and that Jay's snatched it."
Fink said	"Not me mate, Jay's had it away, he needs it to get out of the country."
Shear said	"OK, I'll square it with Jock, you make sure you tell the cops he's gone off with his girlfriend to Porto from Bristol docks, got it?"
Fink said	"He's not got a girlfriend, he's queer."
Shear asked	"Who's his boyfriend?"
Fink said	"Some guy on Fabguys, he speaks to him on that."
Shear said	"Fabguys, what's that?"
Fink said	"Yeah, it's on the net, Jay's called Chemagogo and his boyfriend is called Chocolate biscuit."
Shear said	"Chocolate biscuit?"
Fink said	"Yeah, when he bangs Jay, he gets a chocolate biscuit."
Shear said	"Too much information. Now what have you got to tell the cops?"
Fink said	"Yeah, Bristol and Porto got it."

When Shear arrived back at the nick, the murder squad detectives were beginning to arrive. They took over the conference and map rooms and most upstairs offices. They excluded everyone from the top floor including Cole who now spent most of his time between the control room and occasional visits to the bar. Farthing finally arrived, a tall slim man with the look of a sniper. His reputation suggested he'd been kicked out of the Gestapo for brutality, pugnacious, cantankerous, a proper street brawler, one lean mean bad ass. Cole tried to engage him in conversation but was brushed aside, for a moment Shear nearly felt sorry for Cole...nearly.

Shear said	"Boss, we need to speak alone."
Cole said	"Did you see that. Completely ignored, that bugger and his well-oiled machine will have this cleared up in a week making us look like the woodentops, I can't stand that bastard, I'd give anything…"

Shear said	"…Now that you've been chucked out of your office to the control room you have the advantage over sturmbannfuhrer Farthing, you are first to receive all calls on the murder…"
Cole enquired	"So…?"
Shear smiled	"You can decide who is told what and when."
Cole said	"For god's sake Sarge, I can't keep things from the murder squad."
Shear said	"Of course not, but you can let me know before they know and that might give us the edge."
Cole enquired	"What edge?"
Shear said	"It's just worth doing Boss, trust me?"
Cole said	"Yes, but do keep to the rules, we don't want to get discipline papers for breaching protocols now do we, you know what a ruthless bastard Farthing is."

Shear joined his crew in the rear yard. He explained that Cole had been nailed down to control room supervision and that Farthing and Cole were arch enemies. It was time for Shear to call on the right honourable Ting. He checked his Eyespy Tap and Track and sure enough Ting was at home. Shear asked Rohan and Ken to take a plain car and wait for Hanson at the farm, Rohan would meet him, and Ken's job was to remain outside and put a lump on his car when he arrived. Lewis would clock the murder squad arriving at the hospital and Shear and Boots would visit the estate of the right honourable. Saaz could remain on eyes and ears at the police station. The plot thickened nicely.

As Shear approached the estate, he rang Ting's landline so that he knew he was not walking about outdoors. He said that he would be there in a minute or so and that the gate could be opened. This allowed Shear to drive in and let Boots out into the estate without being seen. It was perfectly dark and approaching midnight.

Ting hailed Shear from the doorway.

Ting said	"My dear boy, welcome how very nice to see you again."
Shear said	"Are we alone?"
Ting replied	"Same as last time old chap, just you and I, now what news do you bring, I'm worried sick about this meeting with the Commissioner and that Fold fellow, I hope you have facts and figures sufficient to allow me a fair shot at them…"

Shear said   "I've prepared your statement, enough here to shut them both up I think…"

Ting read the handout. The handout to be distributed to all stakeholders and the media in two days' time…

"The Home Secretary and I have great pleasure in announcing the outcome of drug prevention measures trialled here in South Wessex during the past six months resulting in a fifty seven percent reduction in drug abuse and use in the trialled areas. This will be rolled out nationwide when parliament returns to its work in four weeks or so. We believe…"

Ting said "…Good god man, this is a bloody joke, do you really think I'll get away with this, they'll tear me apart, they'll make mincemeat of me, I'll be held up to public ridicule, no this won't do, this won't do at all."

Shear said "What you've read is what will be read in the papers, what you will dutifully trot out on the local TV news. The fine grain detail is not something that people want to hear, there's a general election in the offing, major issues are being debated throughout the country, local news headlines dwarf this rubbish. Now here's the stuff you have to bone up on, Google it, read it, understand it and rehearse, rehearse, rehearse to a point whereby it runs off the end of your tongue suggesting that you've spoken of nothing else for the last six months. Now look at this."

Proven interventions
Zero tolerance
Post arrest interventions
Post arrest contracts
Restorative agreements
Victims' accord

Ting said   "What the hell is post-arrest interventions and victims' accord, I don't get it, I just don't get it."

Shear explained   "Post arrest interventions is where they are dealt with without appearing in court and Victims' accord is where they have met the victim and after a heart to heart, been forgiven, so that…"

55

Ting said	"...So the crimes are not reduced, just the method of dealing with them, is that it?"
Shear said	"No. The position is that if none of the interventions had occurred, then there would have been an increase of fifty seven percent, so that the interventions stopped that increase in its tracks. I say well done to you and the Home Secretary, I say very well done indeed. A perfect example of the inverse futures market, economists would be greatly impressed with your methods."
Ting said	"The Commissioner will see through this, maybe even Fold, they're not complete fools Shear."
Shear said	"Just keep talking about restorative agreements, victims' accords and post interventional justice, nobody understands any of it, it's the usual high-brow nonsense they expect from politicians. So long as you keep repeating the fifty seven percent reduction then it becomes true, just say it often enough."
Ting said	"I wish I had your confidence Shear."

Shear left Ting with assurances that more important issues would be figuring in the local news, and that his master the Home Secretary would beat the drum on the national news and that all would be well. Shear picked Boots up as they exited the estate. Boots confirmed that the estate was sufficiently large to hide almost anything. It was particularly well suited to guard a stash of Class A. Everyone knew that MPs don't do drugs. Hanson was the last job of the night. Boots dropped Shear off at the farm and text Rohan. Rohan let Shear in.

Shear opened	"Hi, Simon, how are you?"
Hanson said	"Who are you?"
Shear said	"I'm Bubbles' representative on the ground."
Hanson said	"I don't know any Bubbles, who's he?"
Shear said	"But you do know Jock."
Hanson relaxed	"Yes, what's been going on here?"
Shear said	"Sad story really. Jay got off his head on crack last night on account of the facts that he'll soon be in jail for intent to supply Class A. He decided to nick what was here, including the contents of the briefcase, twenty K, I believe, Fink tried to stop him and got himself stabbed.

	One stabbing wasn't enough for Jay, he only went into town and killed a kid, and guess who the kid is?"
Hanson said	"Who?"
Shear said	"It's only the Commissioner's son, can you believe it?"
Hanson said	"We have a problem, do we know where Jay is now?"
Shear said	"Halfway to Spain, I think."
Hanson said	"No, he can't be, the police took his passport as a condition of bail, he won't be able to leave the country."
Shear said	"Wake up, Simon, money is a passport. Fink says Jay always said that in the event of escape, you go to Bristol docks, sign on as a deck hand or kitchen porter and you're sorted."
Hanson said	"Do we know what boat?"
Shear said	"Anything going to Porto, that'll take him to Portugal, Spain is only an hour away."
Hanson said	"OK, I'll speak to Jock and see if we can find him before he disappears."
Shear said	"Best thing Simon is to ring the local nick and mention the Bristol boat and Porto, the cops will then lead us to him and I can then arrange events to suit."
Hanson said	"You haven't said who you are."
Shear said	"I'm local, I deal with Fink and help him out from time to time, if you see me at the police station, we won't recognise one another will we. Oh, and tell your master that his twenty K will be here for collection next Sunday, same time."

Hanson made his way to Bristol. Shear, Rohan and Boots sat in the van. Boots checked the GPS and sure enough Hanson was moving north. The lump was active and so long as the magnet held, they would have Hanson spotted whenever mobile. A successful day.

Chapter 4

Shear's crew had the morning off and gathered to have a hard look at what lay ahead. It was agreed that the Home Secretary and the Right Honourable were their primary investments and protection. They had audio, CCTV and Eyespy Tap and Track cover so things seemed to be going well on that front. Only four weeks to the election so a couple more parties at the Narrow Escape might be useful. Boots outlined the result of his look at Ting's estate and it was agreed that most of the stash would be kept there. These things they controlled. Other matters needed debate.

Shear said	"OK, we know we have a spy, a tipster, what do we know?"
Boots said	"Top cop known as Jock, Scottish accent that's it."
Lewis added	"Twenty grand a month sounds like a retainer, this guy's in it for the long term."
Ken said	"Could be a woman."
Shear agreed	"Yes, could be. Sounds like his boss is some bugger called Bubbles. What else have we got?"
Ken said	"We know that the main distributions centre was the farm run by Jay and Fink…"
Shear interrupted	"…Fink is low life, just a runner, Jay was the main man."
Ken said	"Yeah…was…the main man."
Shear said	"Our link to the informant is Hanson, he collects the money and passes it on to Jock, so our link is the lump on Hanson's car which sooner or later, maybe later than sooner, but in any case will take us to Jock."
Rohan asked	"How good is the lump?"
Shear replied	"Best on the market, none of that police issue rubbish. Our magnets stick to the car."
Boots wondered	"How much are they doing a month do you think, Boss?"

Shear guessed	"We are one tenth part of the supply area, best guess is these boys are doing a hundred grand a month, maybe more."
Boots asked	"OK, so the lump takes us to Jock, but how do we get to Bubbles?"
Shear said	"Jock will either take us to Bubbles, or Bubbles will be attracted to Jock, our first job is to track Hanson and then Hanson to Jock."

Shear then outlined the activities at the police station. A murder being looked at by the squad led by DCI Farthing and the lamentable Chief Inspector Cole, a man promoted well beyond his capabilities by his membership of the Freemasons. Clearly Cole would need help if not to be eaten alive by Farthing. Shear invited Lewis to speak.

Lewis opened	"Farthing and a couple of his sergeants arrived very late at the hospital. They didn't stay long so they probably believed Fink on account of his injuries and information regarding the whereabouts of Jay. It was their first job this morning to give the West Street apartment a good going over by Forensics and then to take stock."
Shear said	"So far so good. I've fed Cole a story about how best to deal with incoming information, so he'll come to me on account that no one else seems to want to speak to him and he has no reason to distrust me and every reason to want to get at Farthing. So we'll use Cole to dismantle Farthing. Should prove interesting."
Boots asked	"Is the Right Honourable OK with his meeting with the Council Chairman and the Commissioner?"
Shear replied	"Good question Boots. We can play this either way. We can assume that the Commissioner will not show on account of his grieving for his son and Fold will not show because we can blow him out of the water. Our choice."
Lewis asked	"What choices, what have you in mind, Boss?"
Shear said	"We have pictures of Fold being pig roasted at a sex party, so we can load onto YouTube Dark Web for the world to view at their leisure, that will cause an immediate fall from grace resulting in his regrettable resignation, or…"
Lewis repeated	"…or…?"

Shear continued "…or we can use Fold to access more information, pictures and general intelligence on his associates and their activities. I think we'll continue to use him."

Shear checked his phone, he had missed a number of calls from Cole who seemed spooked by the speed the murder squad were moving. They had interviewed Fink and had searched the West Street flat and were now trawling for information on Jay. Time to get back to the nick.

The police station was awash with detectives. Cole was waiting for Shear in the rear yard and immediately engaged him in conversation. Shear intimated that they should find somewhere out of sight and hearing. They made their way to the bar which they found empty.

Cole said "Farthing's people have interviewed Fink and searched the West Street flat."

Shear asked "What did Fink tell them?"

Cole replied "Fink said that Jay was off his head on coke and booze and knifed some kid out of Keenbourne, Fink tried to stop him and got knifed too."

Shear asked "Is that the same guy that WDC Walsh dealt with yesterday, bailed him for possession of Class A with intent to supply?"

Cole said "Yes, that's him. The CID are all over it, it won't take long for Farthing to have him locked up, they're up in Bristol now looking for him."

Shear said "The Creeping Insect Department may take a little longer than you think…What did they find at West Street?"

Cole said "Nothing, just the usual stuff, nothing incriminating."

Shear asked "So why are they making enquiries in Bristol?"

Cole said "We've had three calls from the public that Jay is on his way to Porto…"

Shear asked "…Porto, where's that?"

Cole said "Portugal, Jay's going by ship from Bristol, jump ship at Porto and make his way to Spain."

Shear said "OK, Boss, I'll see what I can find out. I'll keep you informed."

Foxtrot 13 pulled out of the police station, Cerberus had been washed and another day lay ahead. The crew pulled up by the river to contemplate the day.

Shear said	"Hanson's call to the police station corroborated Fink's information and our two calls to crime stoppers have worked well. Farthing's lot are in Bristol looking for the ship Jay's managed to board. I would like to see Farthing's face when he finds out that the only ship going to Porto is the Marco Polo a luxury cruise ship carrying two thousand and more."
Boots said	"You know Farthing Boss, nothing stops him, He'll turn that ship upside down."
Shear smiled	"Yes, let's hope so."
Shear said	"When things are quiet, Saaz and Rohan can go to West Street and plant Jay's knife in the flat. Have a look at the scenes of crime photographs first then lay the knife somewhere not covered in the pictures. Meanwhile, let us think how best the knife can be found, and of course, by whom?"
Lewis said	"Might be time for Chief Inspector Cole to have a little luck, Sarge?"
Shear smiled	"Indeed it might, Lewis, indeed it might."

Foxtrot one three was directed to the mortuary in response to an alarm activation. It was known to activate on Sunday mornings and was always a false alarm. The alarm flashed at the control room but not the mortuary on account that it only activated for about five seconds before righting itself. Insufficient time to set off the main alarm. This strongly suggested that someone had gained entry and turned the alarm off before it sounded so that it was no doubt some medical staff, after all, what was there to steal in a mortuary? Cerberus drove along the perimeter of the hospital to the last signage on the road, a blue arrow and Mortuary. They drove around the rear and found a door open and a deck chair immediately outside the door. A man appeared at the door and began to sweep the outside area.

Saaz said	"Hi, do you know your alarm's gone off?"
The man said	"Oh, sorry about that, don't know what's wrong with it."
Saaz said	"Yes, no problem."

As they pulled away, Shear told Ken to get a picture of the man as they turned and went past him again. Cerberus turned about and waves were exchanged as the crew bus pulled away. Ken confirmed they got the shot. Shear said that the guy was up to no good he'd never seen so many deceit signals and why wasn't he wearing a name badge, all hospital staff wore name badges, enquiries would be made at the hospital the next day. Lewis confirmed that a friend of his worked in hospital records and would be only too happy to help. The matter was left to Lewis.

The crew were to report to the Briefing Room early evening to be brought up to date by the murder squad and to be given tasks of a door-to-door nature. Routine stuff, but a good chance to find out from slip of the tongue conversations especially later in the bar. As expected, they were tasked with enquiries from all known users and dealers to establish Jay's associates and possible location. This they already knew but would keep to themselves until needed. Lots to do but not tonight. Shear sent his crew to the bar whilst he sought out Chief Inspector Cole who was in the control room overseeing communications.

Shear asked	"Hi Boss, what news?"
Cole replied	"Farthing's in Bristol tracking down Jay, he seems very optimistic about making an early arrest and bringing him back here. Well just for once I'd give anything to see that flash bastard take a fall. He's so bloody cock sure of himself, trouble is he always gets results and people fall over themselves to congratulate him, I so hate him."
Shear said	"He won't be bringing Jay back here tonight, Boss."
Cole asked	"Why do you say that?"
Shear asked	"Have they got the murder weapon?"
Cole said	"No, all they've got is the kid in Hospital, Fink they call him, he says that Jay stuck the kid then stuck Fink who was trying to protect the kid…"
Shear repeated	"Have they got the murder weapon?"
Cole replied	"No, not yet."
Shear asked	"Everyone's in the bar Boss, can I get you a drink?"
Cole replied	"No, I have to keep my eye on what's going on here. If Farthing makes a mistake, I want to be on top of it."

Cole reached for his Coke bottle and took a long slow drink and asked Shear.

	"What do you know that I don't know, Sarge?"
Shear replied	"Farthing needs a body and a confession, the knife would be really useful too. Now just imagine…"
Cole said	"Imagine what?"
Shear said	"Imagine that Jay manages to escape and imagine that the murder weapon was found by one of your wooden tops, seems to me that would be one hard slap in the face for Farthing. His job is to find the killer and the weapon, he fails to find the killer and you find the weapon…"

Cole sighed "…if only."

Shear said "Let's see what happens."

The next day brought all officers back to the conference room. The Deputy Chief Constable was to address the troops and bring focus to the enquiry. The media were pressing hard for results and the Deputy needed something, anything to tell them, any result was a good result. On the stage was the Deputy and the head of the force drug squad who was introduced as Superintendent Alister McCoy. The whole of the murder squad was present, three task force units and sundry others co-opted onto the enquiry. The whole team waited.

Finally Detective Chief Inspector Farthing mounted the stage. The Deputy Chief outlined what had happened, what was now happening and what he proposed should happen, no surprises there. Farthing got to his feet and said that they had got the whole story from Fink and that Jay was almost in the bag. They had received a number of tip-offs from various sources all of whom pointed to Jay's planned exit to Spain on a Bristol based ship. The SS Marco Polo was favourite as it was the only ship bound for the Med stopping at Porto. They couldn't detain the ship as it was an up-market cruise ship with passengers in excess of 2,000, so four of the murder squad detectives sailed with the ship. An arrest was anticipated before docking at Porto.

Someone asked "Any sign of the murder weapon, sir?"

Farthing said "No chance of that coming to light, it'll be somewhere at the bottom of the sea, somewhere between Bristol and Porto by now so forget about that and focus on enquiries with local informants."

Shear mused that there was much evidence at the bottom of the sea but the murder weapon was not part of it. Soon be time for Cole to take a hand in finding the murder weapon he thought. Superintendent McCoy then spoke,

"The Deputy Chief has invited me here as a hands-off observer. You will know that the boy murdered was the Commissioner's son, a perfectly innocent schoolboy going about his lawful business. The media are calling for police action as is the local MP Mr Kham Ting. I will be speaking to both later today. Meanwhile I will be taking a close look at the question of drug supply in the local area and see how it relates to this most dreadful murder. To that end I wish to see all task force commanders in my office in an hour."

During the course of the hour, Shear and his crew looked at the scenes of crime photograph album of the murder scene. Most areas had been covered from most angles, portrait, landscape, black and white, colour, everything imaginable, but…no murder weapon. It was agreed that the knife, a standard eight-inch kitchen knife could be secreted behind a radiator in a standing position, an easy thing to miss. Saaz and Rohan would drop the knife at the apartment later than night.

Shear and two other task force commanders stood in front of McCoy. McCoy was a little over six feet, slim and trim, quite a handful by the looks of him. Two-inch scar below his left eye spoke of his Glaswegian antecedence, and, if asked, would have been described as a duelling scar. No one asked. On the table in front of McCoy was a dozen or so operational orders. McCoy said he wanted each operation looked at again to see what had been missed, or what could be deduced from the totality of each. They were each given a number of the orders and instructed to revisit each with a blade of grass mentality, every witness to be re-interviewed, each location to be revisited. He expected results in two days, not reports, results.

Afterwards, Shear gathered all the Operation Orders together saying he'd photocopy each. In the copy room, he redistributed the orders so that he had personal control of all operations in which he was involved. The other two commanders were each given three copies of each order, Shear keeping the farm orders for himself.

Cerberus pulled out of the police station yard with Shear and the crew who made their way to the farm to revisit one of their operations. The farm was perfect cover, Jay was dead, Fink still in hospital and all activities adjourned until further notice. Shear searched through the operation orders and found the original in which Cole stopped the Post Office van. He searched the pages and found that page two line two there was a typo. This was the copy that had been issued to

Cole. How come McCoy now possessed an operation order which was of no interest to anyone other than the officers involved? Everyone was asked to look again at all the photographs taken at the Masonic Lodge, Cole was known to be there, but McCoy…there had to be a link.

Saaz and Rohan sorted out their Pakistani clothing, shalwar kameez, fez cap and khussa footwear should do it. They put the murder weapon into a Sainsbury's bag and made their way into town on foot. Dropping the knife off at the flat in West Street should be easy enough. They would spend time mingling with Pakistani friends in the Chaaye Khana coffee house opposite the flat and drop the knife when the time was right. Shear rang the local council house and was put through to the leader's secretary.

Shear said "Hello, I need to speak to Councillor Fold."

A female voice said "Sorry that's not possible. Mr Fold is…"

Shear interrupted "…tell him it's a personal matter concerning activities at the Pelican pub which are about to be made public."

Fold enquired "Hello, who is this?"

Shear said	"Police here Mr Fold. We need to speak privately about…well I think you know what about?"
Fold replied	"Yes, yes, I have a caravan in town, if I send the postcode we could meet there?"
Shear said	"OK, I'll see you there in an hour, no later."

Shear and Boots turned up in plain clothes half an hour later and watched Fold enter the caravan. Twenty minutes later they knocked on his door and found a sheepish Fold looking through the door curtain. Shear pushed the door open. They recognised the interior from the pics they had of the pig roast. Fold looked quite different, no wig, no suspender belt, no panties, no alcohol and no coke, quite the gentleman with his expensive suit and tie, quite the Liberal leader of the Council.

They looked at Fold and said nothing.

Fold began	"…You said we needed to speak privately about…"
Shear said	"Yes, about…"
Fold searched	"You mentioned the Pelican pub?"
Shear said	"I did, yes, tell me about it?"

Fold said	"Me and friends drink there, it's never been a problem."
Shear said	"Here's your problem, Mr Fold. The Pelican is a gay pub…"
Fold interrupted	"…Gay is legal, there's nothing illegal about being gay, anyone who is anti-gay is in big trouble if they interfere with gay rights, that's right, gay people have rights…"
Shear said	"So you think that being gay is OK and that everyone should be left alone to do what they want so long as no one is harmed, is that it?"
Fold said	"Yes exactly, what's wrong with that?"
Shear said	"You ask me what's wrong with that, well you listen and I'll tell you exactly what is wrong with that. In the fifteen hundreds, Henry the Eighth had people hanged for it, the last hanging was in the eighteen hundreds and the last person to do time was ten years ago when a guy got three and a half years for buggery."
Fold said	"Being gay is OK, the Sexual Offences Act made it OK, it's not an offence any more. If anyone gives us a hard time about being gay, I'll sue them, especially the police, you should know better…"
Shear interrupted	"…Time for you to be quiet, if you stop being quiet, I will leave you here to sort out your own mess…"

Fold shouted "You can't tell me to be quiet, I'm the leader of the Council, I've been elected by the people to represent…"

Shear and Boots stood up and began to make their way to the door. Fold was flustered, his certainty become uncertain, maybe he was making a mistake, maybe he should listen, these were hard-nosed cops and at least he should let them tell him what they knew…

Fold said "OK, OK, let's just sit down a moment and talk about this, let's just sit down and talk."

Shear said "Mr elected leader of the council whose been elected to represent the people, know this, we are not in council chambers where there are rules and protocols and orders of speeches and who can say what to whom and how. This here is where you survive or you perish, your choice. Now here's all your worse dreams come true, are you now listening…"

Fold fell silent and sat down. He had finally been overtaken by the realisation that Shear meant what he said, survive…perish, worse dreams come true, he held his head in his hand.

Fold said	"I'm listening."
Shear said	"We nicked some pond life this morning who was setting people up for a bit of blackmail. He'd sent them a picture of an indiscretion together with an and or…"
Fold enquires	"…and or?"
Shear explained	"…and now you pay, or we publish this."
Fold asked	"How do you mean publish?"
Shear said	"We can send these pictures to your wife, or maybe your lover's wife or somebody who will do something to take you out."
Fold asked	"They can't get away with that, it's like you said it's blackmail, they'll get arrested, that's bloody outrageous."
Shear continued	"That's right, it's blackmail, they can't get away with it; and yes, it's outrageous, but guess what?"
Fold asked	"What?"
Shear replied	"To them it's not blackmail, it's a source of making money; and they think they can get away with it and the more outrageous the better, the more outrageous the more street cred they chalk up. Bit like robbing a bank really, nothing personal just hand over the money, latter-day stand and deliver merchants. The question is, do you hand over the money, or…?"
Fold asked	"I thought you said you'd arrested someone."
Shear corrected	"An arrest yes, but not someone as in a person, pond life as in a rat and you know what happens to rats…right?"
Fold said	"But if you've got him, that's it isn't it, you've got him, right?"

Shear said	"We're in talks with him. If he goes to the police station then the matter becomes official, there's a prosecution and all becomes common knowledge. Don't think that the person being blackmailed is somehow protected by the courts, this sextortion is in the hands of the CPS who have a prosecutors' pledge to keep the victim's identity secret, but that's down to the judge who will be swayed by compelling arguments from the defence. So you see, there is no protection for a person being blackmailed, even if the judge gives anonymity to the victim, jungle drums will soon have it out in public, it's an unjust world is it not?"
Fold sighed	"I don't know what to do."
Shear said	"A good starting place is to know what you're facing. Now put that TV on and I'll show you what was recently posted on the YouTube Dark Web."

Fold put the TV on and Boots streamed a YouTube Dark Web upload onto the screen. It was a standard video of a sex party, half a dozen guys a couple of transvestites, lots of booze with a few lines of coke in the background. Shear explained that the Dark Web was awash with anything you care to name and could be viewed by anyone anywhere. Even if the Dark Web took it down, you could rest assured that it would have been copied and shared throughout the known world.

Fold enquired	"So what else has this guy got?"
Shear said	"We nicked him on the strength of a whisper but since then we've found lots of other stuff including a book in which your name figures, so it looks like you were next to pay up or be exposed."
Fold stated	"So you've got anything he has on me then?"
Shear said	"Not quite, his bargaining tool is that if we don't charge him, he won't publish what he's got, trouble is we know he's got it but there's no proof until its published which is exactly what we don't want."
Fold asked	"What do we do not then?"
Shear said	"The first rule of doing, is don't. Do nothing and see what happens. If you do something and get it wrong, then you breach the first rule of holes, when in one stop digging, so here's the plan, you carry on as normal…"

Fold interrupted	"…yes, but…"
Shear said	"Having the powers of a prophet, I will tell our venomous little captive that in the event of any disclosure by him of any activities you may be involved in will be career ending as far as he is concerned. Now I believe that you have an audience with the local MP, what's his name…?"
Fold replied	"Khom Ting?"
Shear continued	"Yes, him and as we are on the verge of an election that audience will be televised here in Wessex, right?"
Fold replied	"Right."
Shear said	"So here's what you don't know and will save your ass when you do. Our little rat's brother died as a result of a heroin overdose a few months ago. So it's not gay people he's targeting, it's dealers and users. So, when you appear on TV with Khom Ting, you are going to approve of everything he says, you're going to support his new initiatives and nod approvingly at his every word against users and especially dealers. Whilst this is happening, we will be sitting listening with the rat who will see that you're not the kind of man he should take down, you're the sort of guy who should be respected and helped where possible…"
Fold asked	"…How can he help me?"
Shear sighed	"By not publishing the naughties, he possesses on you my friend, a kind of quid pro quo, a mutual back scratching so to speak. So that's it then, you support the new initiative by the local MP and your activities can continue as before."
Fold asked	"What are you going to do with him, you know pond life?"
Shear said	"Not for you to know Mr Fold, you are the Leader of the Council are you not."

Shear and Boots left a confused Fold in the caravan.

Boots said	"Looks like he had all of that Boss, what shall we do with the pond life?"
Shear smiled	"If he ever existed, back in the pond I suppose, could be we might need him again."

Shear and Boots picked up Saaz and Rohan on their way back to the police station. The murder weapon had been placed behind a shadowed radiator near the last vent. It was in a standing position and could readily be overlooked. The scenes of crime photographs showed the radiator but not the knife. Question now was, who was to find the knife, if not by the murder squad, then this would play hell with Farthing who already was on a wild goose chase. Time for reflection. Shear checked his Eyespy Tap and Track and found Mr Khom Ting was, as expected, at home. He checked on the lump on Hanson's car and was seen to be at an address in Bristol. At the police station, the crew met up. Ken, Lewis and Tony joined the others and they adjourned to the bar to pick up on the latest rumour intelligence. Chief Inspector Cole was sitting on his own…

Shear said	"Hi, Boss, can I get you a drink?"
Cole sighed	"Might as well I suppose, things can't get much worse."

Shear went to the bar and bought a large brandy, asked if he wanted Coke he said no, Mr Cole's got a can of Coke on the table. A murder squad detective at the bar intimated to Shear that the enquiry was going nowhere, Farthing was in Bristol organising the force helicopter in the event of an arrest on the Marco Polo and there was no sign of any independent witnesses or of the murder weapon. Like he said, going nowhere.

Shear said	"I see that Detective Chief Inspector Farthing will be on TV tomorrow night taking off from the good ship SS Marco Polo with his prisoner for murder safely tucked up. I expect the headlines will hone into the similarities with the arrest of Doctor Crippen…"
Cole complained	"Shut the fuck up, will you? Farthing, Farthing, Farthing, that's all I hear, anybody would think he's some sort of superman, if only…"
Shear continued	"I think we'll just have to accept Boss that he is a bit of a hero. After all the media have got him as the Force's Ace detective and cameras follow him about everywhere. So his every stroke will be recorded for posterity unless of course…"
Cole bit	"Unless of course what?"
Shear teased	"Kryptonite…"

Cole enquired	"…Kryptonite, what's that?"
Shear continued	"…the prevailing theory in geekdom is that Kryptonite is the stuff that can destroy super heroes, yes even Superman."
Cole disdained	"Kryptonite can only be found in comics Sarge, but if you ever find any I'll have as much as it takes to destroy that blaggard Farthing."
Shear demurred	"Yes, a pity it doesn't exist I could do with some myself. Tell me, Boss, is it true that they didn't use a dog when they searched the flat in West Street?"
Cole said	"They didn't, no, that bastard Farthing said his detectives would find anything worth finding but they only got fingerprints, no murder weapon."
Shear said	"Well, it's never too late for a dog, if it finds nothing then no one need ever know it was there. Just seems the sensible thing to do really."
Cole asked	"Do you really think so?"
Shear said	"I understand that you are appearing on the local show tomorrow night with Mr Ting, the Commissioner and the leader of the local Council on the latest way forward in dealing with drugs?"
Cole sighed	"Don't remind me, the Home Secretary and his sidekick Ting have created the latest elixir, the holy grail of drug reduction, now you see it, now you don't. I've read the bumf they've put out on it and I don't understand a word. It's all smoke and mirrors. I'm just there to represent local plod really. A sort of wooden tops anonymous."
Shear said	"If you appeared on the show with a bit of kryptonite, that would be a show stopper, would it not?"
Cole asked	"What do you mean?"
Shear said	"If you turn over enough stones, you're bound to find something surely; just keep looking, it's there to be found."

Shear and his crew pulled out of the police station in Cerberus for a last look around the town before going off duty. Shear received a text from Ting demanding a meeting before close of play. Tony and Ken were to stay at the police station and report when Cole returned to the control room. Saaz and Rohan were tasked with tipping off Crime Stoppers that there had been suspicious activity at the flat in West Street. His information would arrive in the control room just as Cole resumed his duties which would be spotted by Tony who would inform Saaz who would make the call. Lewis would remain in the bar and monitor rumour control. Shear and Boots returned to the cottage and picked up two bags of coke, they then made their way to Ting's estate.

Shear made his usual call to Ting's landline to ensure he was indoors. Ting opened the gates allowing Shear to enter with Boots who made his way into the undergrowth and disappeared. Shear found Ting at the front door.

Ting hailed	"Ah, there you are Sergeant, come in, come in, I'm not the slightest bit happy about tomorrow's meeting with the Commissioner and that fool Fold, it very much looks as if it's to be televised and…"
Shear interrupted	"…Here's what's going to happen…"
Ting said	"…No, you don't understand, this whole thing will crash about my head and…"

Shear put his forefinger over his closed lips and emitted "shhhhhh…"

He repeated	"I say again, here's what's going to happen. The Commissioner won't show on account of his son being murdered, you will understand he's devastated and not up to any public appearances…"
Ting smiled	"…Of course, yes, I see, I do understand, poor chap."
Shear continued	"And I have it on good authority that the Leader of the Council has been persuaded to support what you have to say on the matter of drugs…"
Ting, voice raised	"…Fold, support me rubbish. That fool will do anything within his power to harm the Tory programme of reform…"

Shear's forefinger again found his lips…Ting fell silent.

Shear continued	"Fold's power has been removed, you might say he's been caught with his knickers down, so it'll be you and a supportive Fold who will announce the fine grain details to the public, so remember. Zero tolerance, proven interventions, restorative agreements and, go on…and…"
Ting smiled	"…Post arrest contracts and victims accord."

Shear said	"See, how hard was that, you've even convinced me that you have the answer. It may be that your slot on TV may be cut short…"
Ting asked	"…Good god man, why would they cut it short, if there's support from the opposition…"
Shear explained	"…If the opposition supports it, then it's uncontroversial. Viewers don't want to listen to people in agreement, they want arguments, conflict, a bloody good fight. They don't want to hear that the day passed without incident that's not news, blood and snot is what's news, that's what they want."
Ting said	"Yes, thank you Sergeant, I believe I see it now. The issue made public without scrutiny, how bloody marvellous."
Shear added	"Besides, there will be much more on the news, Chief Inspector Cole may make an important announcement on the murder of the Commissioner's son."
Ting said	"Oh, I thought that Farthing was in charge of the murder enquiry?"
Shear smiled	"Yes, so did Farthing."

Shear received a text from Boots, a smiley face iconomotion.

Ting enquired	"The Home Secretary will be here at the weekend, Sarge. I need to know that we can use the Narrow Escape for a few friends we have coming down from London?"
Shear asked	"A few?"
Ting said	"Yes, the Home Secretary and I, and maybe three or four others, Brigadier and a General or two, shouldn't be a problem, should it?"
Shear said	"Problems only exist in the minds of the simple minded, no problem, you'll need a few extra lines of coke then?"
Ting smiled	"Yes, I believe we will."

Shear left Ting at the front door. Ting was so much happier, a TV interview on prime-time news with support from known enemies, no scrutiny, the prospect of a wonderful weekend on the Narrow Escape, two receptive females and coke sufficient to satisfy the Papacy ad the illuminate. His Knighthood was looking good, and already he could hear the words of the Home Secretary, "May I introduce Sir Khom Ting…Sir Khom, how well it sounded."

Shear picked Boots up at the gate and they made their way back to the factory. Boots explained that the coke was well hidden and fingerprint free. At the police station, it was clear that information had been received at the control room that the flat in West Street needed looking at again. In the absence of Farthing, Cole had a task force unit make the enquiry and ensured that they were accompanied by a dog handler. The crew of Foxtrot 13 went off duty and made their way to the cottage where they settled into the armchairs.

Shear asked	"OK, all the coke is well out of site on the Right Honourable's estate. Fold has been defused and will support Ting on TV. The Commissioner won't be seen for some time on account of his mourning, what else?"
Tony said	"Cole received two calls about the West Street flat and is having it looked at as we speak."
Saaz said	"Would love to see Cole's face when the knife is found."
Shear said	"No, it's Farthing's face that wants looking at."
Lewis said	"The guy we saw at the mortuary on Sunday is one Fred Forsyth Boss. No previous, lives in a bedsit in Belvedere Road. Been working there for about three months."
Shear said	"No one works at the mortuary at weekends, in particular Sundays, we need to get a camera into the mortuary for a look see, he's up to no good."
Lewis asked	"What do you reckon, Boss?"
Shear said	"A bit of necrophilia I expect, we'll soon find out."
Ken exclaimed	"Oh my god, he's not giving dead women a length surely?"
Shear said	"Why do you say women? Let's get some video of it and then we'll know what we know."
Tony said	"Superintendent McCoy is in the same lodge as Cole Boss. We have pictures of both at ceremonies and dinners but not together, but the point is that they are both Freemasons."
Shear said	"No surprise there then. Nor was it a surprise that he knew of the Post Office van stop. He is after all the head of the drug department, the surprise was that McCoy had a copy of Cole's operation order. Now that tells us a lot."

Boots asked "What's the plan for tomorrow, Boss?"

Shear said "Strategic objective remains the same, find the information."

Chapter 5

Foxtrot 13 appeared early for briefing. Shear and his crew made themselves aware of overnight activities from the incident report and knew that it was silent on the question of the murder weapon. A 'wait and see' policy was adopted. The briefing room quickly filled but there was no sign of Chief Inspector Cole, what could have delayed Cole they wondered. A dishevelled Cole eventually appeared clutching a stack of papers with one hand, his other hand on his Coke bottle. He looked flustered, he began.

	"You may be aware of overnight developments on the murder enquiry, as a result of…"
A DS interrupted	"We're the murder squad, Boss, we know nothing about overnight developments."
Cole continued	"…as a result of information received, I had the murder scene revisited last night and during the course of a search the murder weapon was found…"

With that, uproar broke out as though an ants' nest had been disturbed, detectives leapt to their feet and began shouting questions. One of their number began to leave the room but was called back by Cole who told him to remain seated. Cole was unusually commanding and finally had to call for order.

The DS continued "Boss, I spoke to DCI Farthing about an hour ago and I can tell you that he knows nothing new and nor do any of the murder squad officers here at the scene. Can you tell us what's going on, we should be the first to be told of any and all developments. Just tell us."

A political savvy Shear took advantage of the disruption and obvious difficulties that Cole found himself in, he was situationally disadvantaged and needed support, a subtle and wise turn of the scalpel was required here.

Shear called out "Oh, well done, Boss, murder weapon, marvellous. I thought the scene had been picked clean by the murder squad who found no weapon. You'd have thought the dog would have sniffed it out, they usually do."

Cole was given the lead he failed to see himself, but he was on it.

Cole said	"I don't think a dog was used by the squad…"
The DS called out	"There wasn't a dog available at the time, they were up the hills trying to sniff out some lost kids…"
Shear said	"…So a dog wasn't used then, a murder scene and you didn't use a dog, unbelievable."

Shear had done his work, mischief making complete, time now to let Cole take over from a position of authority and hammer home that a major flaw had been exposed and it was all down to the Creeping Insect Department who of course was run by the infamous DCI Farthing. Cole needed sufficient wit to let the mishandled enquiry be the subject of questions, and not how he had somehow been able to find the weapon, but find it without the knowledge of the murder squad. Shear knew that Cole's wit was insufficient to defend his position and that this would prove to be a useful tool in heightening tensions between uniform and the squad, thus distracting everyone from the main issue, where was Jonah?

Cole announced "I'm adjourning this meeting until Forensics have had a look at the knife and reported their findings."

The room quickly cleared. A cabal of detective sergeants could be seen engaged in whispered conclave at the end of the corridor from which one of their numbers emerged and made a call. No need to ask who he was calling.

Cole beckoned Shear and both left by the back door and entered the rear yard. Cole climbed into Cerberus followed by Shear.

Cole said	"Thank you again Sarge for your support, I know that the murder squad would explode when they heard the news about the knife, your intervention took the venom out of their attack…"
Shear replied	"Always here to help and support, sir, we work together for the common good. Don't be side-lined by a couple of DSs from the squad, they've got bigger things to worry about."
Cole asked	"Have they, what things?"

Shear explained	"They'll be working out who Farthing is going to blame for the absence of a dog, and as there was only CID there then it looks like one of them will have to be sacrificed. So you see, you're not the problem, Farthing is."
Cole said	"Yes, but DCI Farthing will know that I acted at the murder scene without telling him what was going on."
Shear said	"That's the least of his worries, he'll only be thinking of a way to explain his lack of forensic acumen, it seems to me that the hero here is you, at least that's how the Chief will see it."
Cole said	"Do you really think so?"
Shear lied	"Well, yes, I'm only repeating what others are saying, he who finds the murder weapon is the main man, so well done you."
Cole smiled	"Yes, I mean it was late when we got the information and there were no murder squad detectives about, so what could I do. I mean I took a punt, it's not as though I knew the weapon was there, it was found by the dog."
Shear said	"Yes, the dog that DCI Farthing failed to use, silly man. Don't worry Boss, you'll come out of this very well, whereas Farthing has some explaining to do."
Cole smiled	"Well, I hope you're right Sarge, I often rely on your judgement in these operational matters."

Time now for Shear to load the coup d'état, Cole looked good for it, he took a chance with the dog which came up trumps, all he could do now was go forward with anything he had, it was time for the scalpel to cut deeper.

Shear said	"Not only have you found the murder weapon Boss, but you're appearing on TV after lunch with the launch of the Home Secretary's new drug initiatives which are being outlined by Mr Ting, I believe that the Liberal leader of the local Council will be joining the debate…"
Cole interrupted	"…Oh yes, that bloody fool, he'll do what he can to undermine anything good proposed because…"
Shear said	"My understanding is that Mr Fold will be supporting Mr Ting on account of this initiative is really one brought about by the Home Secretary which means that it will make the national news, now I accept that he is against Ting, but taking on the Home Secretary would be like pressing the

	nuclear option, even Fold wouldn't do that so close to an election."
Cole said	"Yes, I see where you're coming from but…"
Shear said	"Boss, time for the kryptonite, time to dismantle Farthing on the national stage."
Cole enquired	"Oh, how?"

Shear set the scene. Khom Ting outlines the initiatives which are supported by the Liberal leader and the Chief Inspector. During the course of the debate, it will be mentioned that the Crime Commissioner's son was the subject of a shocking murder following a misunderstanding over drugs and that the Commissioner couldn't join the debate during this sad time. It would be at this point that the Chief Inspector would briefly update the viewers by stating that the murder weapon had been found only a few hours ago and was being forensically examined now.

Cole said	"My god, that would completely destroy Farthing, or at least cause him lasting damage. Problem is, he'll be here shortly and I'll have to explain everything to him and…"
Shear said	"He won't be here 'til lunchtime, lay low and have the TV debate concluded before he catches on to what's happening. That way he won't be asking you questions, he'll be answering questions from everyone who matters about his failures. No, you'll be the local hero and he'll be in disgrace. This is your one opportunity Boss. It's really up to you, I mean it you don't fancy…"
Cole snapped	"I'll do it, yes, after all it was me who found the weapon and Farthing was so bent on an early arrest that he made schoolboy errors. Yes, it's time to stand my ground…"

The radio in Cerberus squawked asking the location of Chief Inspector Cole. The TV crew had arrived and asked that he attend a pre-broadcast briefing. Shear and Cole watched as Ting drove into the rear yard, closely followed by Fold. They were met by the editor and taken to the briefing room which was being set up for the shoot. Wessex Constabulary signage was everywhere, heavy duty lighting and two cameras attended by a crew of three. The scene was set. Detective Inspector Knight walked toward the briefing room and was challenged by Shear.

Shear asked "Who are you looking for, sir?"

Knight said	"What's going on, Shear, who are all these people and why all the cameras?"
Shear explained	"They're filming some stuff for the local news, they intend…"
Knight said	"If it's got anything to do with the murder, then they'll have to wait until my boss gets here, he won't be long, he left Bristol half an hour ago."
Shear said	"Nothing to do with the murder, just some stuff about a new drugs initiative trialled by the local MP Mr Ting who will be challenged by the leader of the Council, a Mr Fold. Should be fun, these two hate each other."
Knight asked	"Does Mr McCoy know about this?"
Shear replied	"No idea, why should he?"
Knight said	"McCoy is the drug supremo for Wessex, if it's to do with drugs then he needs to know."
Shear said	"I think it's just a general debate, you know a political thing brought about by the election, no big shakes."
Knight said	"If it's any more than that, heads will roll."
Shear said	"Don't think so, anyway they're about to start."
Knight asked	"What's the new initiative, I know nothing about it?"
Shear sighed	"Nor me, some nonsense on how to reduce the drug problem, I think."
Knight said	"That's no problem, just hang the little bastards."
Shear smiled	"You should join the debate and tell the viewers what your thoughts are on the matter."
Knight said	"When Farthing gets here there's going to be hell to pay, your man Cole is going to be toast."
Shear replied	"He's not my man, the quicker he's toasted the better, nothing but a bloody problem if you ask me, besides I believe the murder squad has its own problems."
Knight asked	"What do you mean?"
Shear said	"When they searched the flat in West Street, they found nothing, fair enough if they'd used a dog but they didn't, big mistake…"
Knight said	"The boss had left the flat early, he told DC Book not to leave the search scene until the dog had attended but the dog never actually got to the scene so…"

Shear said   "Yes, I understand, trouble is the Chief won't understand, looks like your boss is in the frame."

Knight made his way upstairs to join the murder squad and wait for the arrival of his boss. Shear went to the bar and joined his crew who were having a coffee break. He brought the crew up to date with events and said that it looked like a DC Book was to be sacrificed on account of the dog that wasn't used. Shear asked Boots to keep an eye on the briefing room door and to report when the shoot finished. Lewis was tasked to keep an eye on the rear yard and report the arrive of DCI Farthing or D Superintendent McCoy, it was going to be a close run thing. The only question that now remained was to see if Cole had the balls to expose Farthing's incompetence to the world at large.

Thirty or more minutes passed when Boots returned to report that the TV crew were leaving the briefing room. Shear met Ting, Cole and Fold at the door and asked if they could quickly move their cars from the rear yard as space was needed for the scientific bus that was due to arrive. He hurried them outside to their vehicles. Fold left without saying a word.

Ting said "I'd like a word when you have a minute Sergeant, perhaps you'd be good enough to call on me this afternoon."

Shear said "What shall we say, about three?" They waved goodbye.

Cole asked "What's the Forensic bus coming here for Sarge?"

Shear said "It's not Boss, I needed to get rid of those two before Farthing and McCoy show. They're both due here any minute."

Cole said "Oh my god just what I need. They'll want to know what I said on TV and…"

Shear said "No Boss, you need to disappear until after the early evening news when it will be too late for Farthing or McCoy to make a difference. Now did you get a chance to mention the murder weapon?"

Cole said "Yes, but…"

Lewis came to the back door and intimated that both Farthing and McCoy would be in the rear yard in the next ten minutes. Shear told Cole to get into Cerberus and keep his head down. He then summoned his crew who mounted up and drove out of the station yard. They turned left in the knowledge that they would pass Farthing and McCoy on their way to the station. Sure enough, two very solemn figures passed Cerberus. It took only a few minutes for the radio to ask:

"Chief Inspector Cole, Chief Inspector Cole, your location over?"

Shear replied	"Foxtrot 13, we've just dropped Mr Cole off at Mr Ting's estate, I believe they're engaged in coordinating events for the Royal visit."
Control	"Estimated time of departure?"
Shear replied	"We are tasked with picking him up early evening, over."

The radio fell silent. It didn't take much to convince Cole that he should spend the next couple of hours with Ting where he would be free from enquiry. Besides, they needed to know how the broadcast was going to be delivered. They made their way to Ting's estate. Shear called Ting and said he'd be there by three, and so it was agreed, safety for a couple of hours when they would then know how things were playing out.

Shear had Ting open the gate allowing Shear and Cole entry. Lewis was tasked to return to the nick and communicate any intelligence he could source from the murder squad, control rook or just rumour control, anything that might prove useful. The rest of the crew would remain at the police station cleaning Cerberus and generally making themselves useful.

Shear and Cole appeared at the Manor's front door, Ting, who always greeted Shear was absent. Shear found the bell pull and gave it a solid tug. A bell could be heard ringing some distance away, still no Ting. Cole asked if he was sure that they were expected when Ting opened the door, he was clearly excited.

Ting said "Gentlemen, come in, come in. Exciting times, I've just spoken to the Home Secretary who says we have much to rejoice about. Come in, come in."

Shear and Cole followed Ting into the drawing room, Ting ordered tea and coffee and invited all to sit. This was Cole's first visit to the estate. He was truly amazed by how grand it was and the sumptuous eighteen carat fittings bedecking every nook and cranny, he was quite dumbstruck. Ting offered cigars from a Havana box, Shear declined and Cole was about to reach for the box when he was reminded by Shear that he didn't smoke. A portly lady delivered a tray of tea, coffee and cake to the table. Ting thanked her for her efforts and said he'd see her again at breakfast, the lady smiled and left. At last, they were alone.

Shear said	"I can see you're dying to tell us…"
Ting said	"Indeed, I am…"

Shear enquired	"Are we alone?"
Ting said	"Security always comes first with you Sergeant, yes, we are entirely alone I can assure you."
Cole asked	"How did you feel we performed for the cameras earlier Mr Ting?"
Ting replied	"I prefer to tell you how the editor felt about our performance, but then you know he was pleased with events, more importantly it's what the Home Secretary has to say that matters. He and I have just finished a long telephone conversation. He was able to preview the WTV tape of the interview…"
Cole interrupted	"…I didn't know Wessex TV allowed outsiders to preview…"
Ting said	"For goodness sake man, he's the Home Secretary, he has godlike powers, when he asks to see something it's not a request, it's a demand which in every case is obeyed."
Shear said	"Let's just hear what Mr Ting has to say shall we?"
Ting continued	"Quite so, now the thing is, what happens in the provinces is a microcosm of what can happen nationally. The Home Secretary is so pleased with what he saw that he intends to bump the interview from local to national news, which in turn will have an exponential effect on shaping the minds of the voting public, all this and just four more weeks to the election, a masterful stroke don't you think?"
Shear said	"Wonderful news, sir, I take it then that the Liberal leader didn't put up too much of a fight when you spelled out the fine grain detail of your initiative?"
Ting said	"All a bit of a mystery really, Fold is a known loose cannon who opposes all sensible Conservative initiatives, however we witnessed a complete reversal of his former rebellious self, he was almost compliant, docile, submissive even, it's as though he had read the Conservative Manifesto for the first time and, at last, had seen the light."
Shear said	"Amazing is it not."
Ting said	"I won't be a bit surprised if there's not a promotion in this for you Chief Inspector, I can see you being elevated to the drug squad supremo for the whole of the Wessex Constabulary I really can."

Cole was flushed with the news, he smiled broadly and said nothing. Shear could see that his eyes had glazed over and thought that if his mother was present, she'd give him a cuddle. Time to leave.

Shear said "I'm feeling a bit hot, Mr Ting, think I'll have a walk in the grounds if I may, I'm sure you and the Chief Inspector have much to talk about."

Shear took himself outside and text Boots asking the whereabouts of the stash. A couple of hours before the national news, the question was, would it be better to be here to watch the news with Ting and Cole, or back at the factory where he could gloat at the reaction of Farthing and McCoy to the news. Boots replied in codified text. Shear quickly found the stash and admired the creativity Boots had employed in the hide, Military grade camouflage, perfect.

Shear text the crew bus and asked that it pick him up in an hour. He then returned to the Manor House where he found Ting and Cole shrouded in cigar smoke reducing their limited mental capacity by guzzling large quantities of brandy and coke. When the wine is in, the wit is out. Now perhaps was the time for a few unguarded personal disclosures.

Ting called out	"Come on Sergeant, join us for a drink, after all, you've been instrumental in helping us with this achievement have you not?"
Shear said	"Well just one then, can't stop very much longer, unlike you I have the great unwashed to police. Let me fill your glasses."

Shear poured two large glasses of brandy and Coke and a large Coke for himself.

He sat next to Cole.

He said	"Courvoisier, a very good brandy indeed, drank by Napoleon, Churchill and the Right Honourable Mr Khom Ting, MP, I say a toast to us."
Both replied	"To us."
Ting said	"Following upon our election success if might well be…Sir Khom Ting, but I didn't say that did I?"
Shear replied	"Richly deserved and well overdue, but I distinctly did not hear you say it."
Cole said	"You're always too sharp with your replies Sarge, a bit unsettling you know."

Shear said	"The thing is Chief Inspector, it is shared with friends and aimed at our enemies."
Ting said	"You are so wise Sergeant, 'tis as well you're on our side."
Shear said	"You have my total loyalty gentlemen, working with you, working for you always, you have my total commitment at all times."

Shear asked "I wonder if I might ask your opinion on a personal matter?"

Ting and Cole were by now free of inhibitions, they were becoming louder and increasingly demonstrative in the way that drunks do. It would be back slapping and spilling drinks soon so Shear put the questions.

He asked	"What are your thoughts on the Freemasons, I ask because a friend of mine thinks that I could make a contribution to the charities they support and that…"
Cole interrupted	"Capital idea, Shear, capital. I can tell you that we have the top people in my lodge at Aqua Ponds and there are lodges in every town so you're never without a friend."
Ting added	"Yes, top people, I don't know where I'd be without them. I'm in the Home Secretary's lodge and the benefits are really quite unbelievable. Did you know that we have royalty on the square?"
Shear said	"You don't mean Prince Charles surely?"
Ting said	"No, not Charlie, but pretty close."
Shear continued	"My pal says he met some of the very top people including government ministers, top military brass, Bubbles and some…"
Cole said	"Best thing to do my boy is apply and if you're successful you'll meet all those people and more, find yourself a sponsor and apply."

Shear looked to see if he could see any noticeable change in speech, behaviour or atmosphere when he mentioned Bubbles, nothing was detected, these two know nothing of Bubbles, he was sure. Time to leave.

Shear said "Well I must up sticks and away gentlemen, I have a car picking me up presently, I'll leave you both to your celebrations, and again well done on a successful day's work I am honoured to be of some help to you both. If you care to open the gate, I'll see myself out."

Shear made his way to the stash and collected one of the bags. He then met Boots at the Gate. They made their way to the cottage where the bag was secured and then back to the station where Shear was told that DCI Farthing wanted to see him. He made his way to Farthing's office and found the door closed and much shouting coming from within. Farthing's voice was the only one heard and whoever was at the end of it was very much cowed offering no resistance.

A full two minutes pass, Shear could hear end of conversation noises when the door opened and two detective sergeants and DC Book snuck out of the office in silence and disappeared from view. Shear could see Farthing and Superintendent McCoy, both grim faced. They had the air of superiority seen in the faces of hyenas circling a lone lion with a kill. Time to play the innocent sergeant just doing his best in difficult circumstances.

Farthing spoke "Shear, isn't it?"

Shear said "Yes, sir, I believe you want to see me."

Farthing barked "Where is Chief Inspector Brown?"

Shear said "When last seen, he was being dropped off at Mr Ting's estate, Mr Ting, the local MP."

Farthing said "Yes, yes, we know who he is, now sit down, Shear, and tell me exactly what's going on."

Shear said "I believe the Chief Inspector is helping Mr Ting with his new drug initiative…"

McCoy spoke "New drug initiative, what do you know about that?"

Shear said "Nothing really, just that there is some new initiative and Mr Brown is helping out."

Farthing said "Now listen, Shear, I'm here to conduct a murder enquiry, I am the Senior Investigating Officer and I'm finding sinister activities afoot, what do you know about a knife being found in West Street last night?"

Shear said "Oh the murder weapon…"

Farthing shouted "No, no one knows if it's the murder weapon, it's a kitchen knife, that's all a kitchen knife…"

Time to take charge of this conversation. Shear would lay it out as he knew it to be without suggesting insider information. He would say what outcomes were expected and give Farthing a means of escape. McCoy should be encouraged to associate his name with this new drug initiative, after all he was the force drug supremo, would look very bad if politicians were seen to be acting on their own initiative. So,

Shear replied:	"Sir, a report was received suggesting something was going on at the flat, the Chief Inspector was in the control room and had a unit respond to what might have been burglars sizing the place up. In the event, a dog handler attended and it was the dog that sniffed out the knife. I believe that you told DC Book to ensure that a dog attend at the time of the first search…"
Farthing said	"Yes, but that didn't happen as you know."
Shear continued	"Yes, I'm sorry you were let down, but in fairness to Book the dog was being used to track some missing kids who…"
Farthing said	"Yes, but he should have stayed at the scene until the dog showed, no matter how long it took."
Shear said	"Yes, how wonderful hindsight is, but we have to face the fact that the blood on the knife will show it is the murder weapon and I suppose the best we can do now is hope that this advances your enquiry as SIO and that Book is wiser for the experience."
Farthing said	"Book is off the enquiry, he'll be in uniform tomorrow helping plod in Bristol."
Shear said	"Well, it's all looking good then, you have the murder weapon, Mr Brown is carrying out the superintendent's instructions on the joint initiative on drugs, a matter that the Home Secretary closely supports…"
McCoy asked	"…How do you know that?"
Shear said	"Well, I don't actually know it, but…well I suppose I can tell you, when I dropped the Chief Inspector off at Mr Ting's estate, Ting mentioned that the Home Secretary was delighted with the work trialled here in Wessex which of course Mr McCoy would have first-hand knowledge about as drugs supremo."

Things fell silent as all parties worked out their respective positions with this new found knowledge. Farthing could see that he had the murder weapon and that his enquiries were therefore progressing. McCoy could see that it was not too late to be seen to be the main player in whatever it was that the Right Honourable Khom Ting and the Home Secretary was up to.

Farthing asked	"What else do you know?"
Shear said	"That's it, sir, if I hear anything, I will of course let you know."
Farthing said	"OK Shear, what happens in this office stays in this office."
Shear said	"Fully understood, sir."

Shear opened the door and as an afterthought…

He said "Oh Mr Ting said something about being on the evening news, there's a TV in the bar, don't know if it's on the national or local, but it starts in half an hour."

Shear briefed his crew and I tasked Ken and Lewis to be in the bar when the evening news was broadcast and to try and video Farthing and McCoy's reactions if they could. Shear took the remainder of the crew to the Cottage for refreshments in comfortable seats where they could watch the news undisturbed. They didn't have long to wait.

It did make the national news but was the penultimate item, rather a low key, self-congratulatory affair twixt the Home Secretary, the Right Honourable Khom Ting, MP, the Liberal leader of the local authority and the local police chief. Each was gushing in their enthusiasm for this new initiative, in itself hardly mentioned, save for a few buzz words that somehow sounded reassuring. It was reminiscent of Maggie Thatcher coming back from Europe after protracted negotiations, having secured a staggering refund that everyone believed impossible. Cole was heard to link the initiative with information received resulting in the finding of a murder weapon and the anticipation of an early arrest concerning a major international drug dealer. Uplifting music and library pictures took the item off air and into the weather forecast. Utter perfection, it was as though the whole thing had been stage-managed and the participants were reading from prepared scripts. Excellent.

Shear rang Ting's home number, finally answered by what was by now a jubilant Ting. Shear congratulated him on his performance on the national stage, Ting was more incoherent than boastful and became more so when Ting reminded him that he had just appeared in front of twenty million viewers, each with a vote to cast in only four weeks. He then spoke to Brown saying much the same but alerting him to the fact that DCI Farthing and Superintendent McCoy were greatly impressed by their performance and that now was the time for them to get together to cobble together a joint strategy in relation to the murder and the drug initiative. Shear said that a conference had been arranged for the morning when they could all get together to prepare their joint approach. A minor lie which Cole would be too drunk to remember too much about save to say, he had a conference in the morning with his arch enemy who now sees him as a force majeure, a man to be reckoned with. Shear asked Brown if he needed a lift home as he was without a vehicle, Brown at once agreed.

Time for another lie. Shear rang Lewis and asked to speak to Farthing or McCoy Farthing answered,

"Yes Shear, what have you got?"

Shear explained "I don't know if you've seen the news…"

Farthing said	"Just tell me what you've got."
Shear said	"Well, I said I'd keep you up to date…well…the thing is…"
Farthing said	"For goodness sake man, what is it?"
Shear continued	"Well Chief Inspector Cole just called me about some local police issues and…"
Farthing sighed	"Yes, and…"
Shear disclosed	"He asked me to arrange a meeting between yourself and the Superintendent to hammer out a common strategy on the Home Secretary's new initiative…"
Farthing interrupted	"We saw that on the news and still don't know what it's about."
Shear continued	"Well, he'll make you privy to everything tomorrow and hopes you'll welcome the initiative."
Farthing said	"Of course we will, we're all on the same side are we not, once we have the confidence of the Home Secretary we can take the initiative on from its base here in Wessex, of course we will."

Shear picked Brown up from Ting's estate and began to journey home. Brown was awash with alcohol, eyes glazed, speech slurred, and very, very happy.

Brown said	"What wonderful news, do you know that millions of people saw me on television tonight Sarge?"

Shear answered	"I do Boss, about twenty million I believe, even DCI Farthing and Superintendent McCoy were watching, you gave a brilliant account of events, so proud to have watched it so pleased to be able to say to people, that's my boss."
Brown asked	"What about Farthing and McCoy?"
Shear lied	"Extolling your virtues Boss, proud as punch they both were."
Brown said	"Did you know that Mr Ting will get a Knighthood out of this, and we poor buggers at the bottom get bugger all, where's the justice."
Shear said	"If he gets a knighthood Boss, then you're definitely on for a QPM, no doubt about it."
Brown smiled	"Do you really think so?"
Shear said	"This is a major national initiative, how can the MP get a Knighthood and the local police chief, a national hero get nothing, no there's a QPM in this for you, sir, there must be."
Brown said	"Chief Inspector Brown, Queen's Police Medal…"
Shear said	"Superintendent Brown, Queen's Police Medal."

Brown was dropped off at home, dazed but very happy. Shear returned to the factory where he saw Fink in the front office signing for some gear.

Shear said "Hello, so you're out of hospital, I thought they'd have kept you in for a while longer."

Fink said "No, not nearly as bad as it looked thank god."

Fink collected his bits and pieces and made his way out the front door followed by Shear, who said "Get back to the farm, I've got the stash, speak to no one and I'll see you tomorrow."

Shear's crew had an early start, they gathered at the police station before seven, read the incident report and made themselves aware of activities planned for the day. Shear told everyone that they needed to get into the mortuary during silent hours and that in the event of a fatal accident or sudden death they should make it their responsibility to help out by way of evidence continuity. Shouldn't be too hard, there's usually two or three coroner's cases a week, sometimes more. Good timing was all that was required to secure covert entry.

As expected, Shear received a text from the Chief Inspector asking to be picked up. Shear replied that his meeting wasn't until 10 am and that he would pick him up at 8.30. Brown said OK, he didn't ask the question 'what meeting' that Shear knew he would be asked when he picked him up, a fun day lay ahead. The station was filling up, CID officers were dutifully preparing their house-to-house enquiry forms and checking maps for areas of the West end of town not yet canvassed.

DCI Farthing and Superintendent McCoy came in together. Farthing nodded to Shear and beckoned him upstairs. Shear follows them into Brown's office.

Farthing said	"Shut the door."
Shear said	"I've only got a minute, sir, I've got to pick up Chief Inspector Brown."
Farthing said	"You seem to be big pals with Brown, Shear so tell me, is he a competent hardworking guy, or is he as daft as I think he is?"
Shear said	"Just hard-working, sir, don't underestimate him, he's got friends in high places who sometimes take advantage but there's no hidden agenda, there isn't, honest."
Farthing asks	"So, you think there's something in this new drug initiative they're all talking about then?"

Shear looked a little confused. He actively withdrew from the Farthing Shear conversation and directed himself head-on at Superintendent McCoy.

Shear said "Superintendent, you are the head of department and have all information concerning drug activity. From the bits and pieces I pick up from Chief Inspector Brown and Mr Ting, it's pretty clear that the drugs trial over the last six months has been directed by you, so to suggest that you have somehow just become aware of events is a bit rich. No one's going to believe that even if it was true which patently it is not, after all, whilst Mr Brown is not the sharpest tool in the box, it's very clear that he couldn't have done this himself. No, Brown only has a head for tactics not strategy. This has the touch of a general. The trial has been held in secret, but last night's evening news has exposed the results so now is the time for complete openness on the matter and we can all work together."

Shear kept a straight face and looks as sincere as he could. Not one deceit signal escaped him. Question was, would they bite? McCoy smiled but stayed silent.

Farthing said	"What happens in this room stays in this room, Shear."

Shear responded	"Of course, sir. Mr Brown will be here soon and he will tell you everything, especially what the Home Secretary's views on the matter are. Best to treat him as a friend, he can be very useful and his masters unbelievably useful."

Shear left the room just knowing that Farthing and McCoy would bleed every bit of information from Brown as soon as they saw him. They had a lot of catching up to do and they had to find a way to immerse themselves into the initiative ab initio so to speak. Shear was quite certain that McCoy's modus operandi was to remain steely eyed and give nothing away. He rarely spoke and allowed his menace to strip away anything that might challenge his self-appointed position as alpha male. This worked well enough…mostly.

At 8.30, a bleary-eyed Brown climbed into Shear's vehicle, he was well hung over and looked a bit of a mess. Brown knew that he had reason to feel good about events but wasn't entirely sure why.

Brown said	"You said I had a meeting this morning."
Shear replied	"Yes, you asked me to arrange a meeting for 10 am."
Brown said	"Remind me what that was all about."
Shear said	"You're to brief DCI Farthing and Superintendent McCoy on the new drug initiative. Farthing's happy they've got the murder weapon but Mr McCoy needs everything you can give him in order to take the initiative forward."
Brown said	"Did you say the DCI is happy?"
Shear said	"Well, yes, his enquiry's progressing well, they have the weapon and he'll soon have the suspect behind bars."
Brown said	"So he's OK about me finding the murder weapon?"
Shear said	"Yes, no problem. It seems that one of his DCs failed to get a dog to the scene after being specifically tasked by Mr Farthing to do so, A DC Book, poor bugger, cost him his job."
Brown said	"Looks like I saved the day then by finding the knife."

Shear continued	"You did, Boss, Mr Farthing is not the problem. The thing is our drug supremo knows little about the initiative and it's important that you now bring him up to date with everything so that he can speak to the Chief from a position of authority, it rather looks as though he's got to have been in this from the outset, part of the main driving force, you do see that don't you?"
Brown said	"Yes, that was exactly my plan, best to keep your friends close and your enemies closer."

As they pulled into the rear yard, Brown left the vehicle and strode into the police station with a renewed vigour. He had suddenly become aware that it was he who called the shots and that others were waiting to hear what he had to say. Only he knew what was on the mind of the Home Secretary and his close aid Mr Ting, the local MP. He made his way to the briefing intending to be more prescriptive if not commanding.

Shear had Foxtrot 13 pick him up from the police station and they made their way out to the countryside on what was laughingly known as rural patrol. Shear noticed that the Sainsbury's bags had been replaced with white Lidl bags.

Shear asked	"Ken, the Sainsbury's bags have gone, whey have we got Lidl bags in the bus?"
Ken said	"Just fancied a change Boss, no reason really."
Shear said	"They won't do at all, ye gods what would our clients think of us if they knew we were dispatching them in inferior bags?"
Ken said	"Good strong bags, Boss, a bit colourful I know, but really strong."
Shear said	"Time for a vote then."

The question was put. Do we continue with our perfectly serviceable tried and tested bags from Sainsbury's or do we behave as though we live at the lower end of the socio-economic stratum. Hands up for Sainsbury's or ten press ups for Lidl's. All hands, including Ken's was raised.

Saaz said	"Steady on, Boss, I shop there."
Rohan added	"So do I."

| Shear said | "All things are said without prejudice gentlemen, you may shop where you wish but we have to have regard to our public image and maintain highest standards at all times. We can drop the Lidl bags off at the soup kitchen for use by the poor and needy." |

Only four weeks to the election. Shear had to see the Right Honourable Ting before the weekend to sort out his requirements for the weekend Narrow Escape adventure. He also had to see Fink at the farm and give him a supply of coke sufficient to keep his clients happy and to increase the team's wealth.

Shear said	"Don't forget, we're still looking for a reason to visit the mortuary, it has to be a weekend or night time job when the place is empty. So any sudden deaths or fatals that we can easily pick up is what we want."
Tony said	"When I was in my probation, I was taken to the mortuary at about 3 am. The sergeant told me to pull out number 3 which was recorded as empty and as I pulled it out there was a body covered in a white sheet. The bloody body was a PC who sat up and said, 'Fuck off, I'm in here.' Christ I nearly fainted, if we get a chance, Sarge, we'll try that one again, bloody brilliant."
Shear said	"We will, yes, bloody brilliant."

Chapter 6

Chief Inspector Brown arrived at the top of the stairs to see that his office, now occupied by Farthing and McCoy, had a number of detectives seated outside, each awaiting an audience. The door was closed. Now was the time for Brown to establish a new pecking order, no longer the long-suffering minor official to hand with offerings of menial help and support to his betters. The time for freeze and flight was over, time now for a fight. He pushed the door open and said to a seated detective,

"Sorry my friend, important matters of state, leave us will you, close the door on your way out."

Farthing and McCoy shifted nervously, quite taken aback by this new found confidence exerted by Brown whom both had previously shown short shrift, even contempt to the point of dismissal. Brown sensed his ambush tactics had gained him an advantage and decided to arm himself with weapons he didn't possess.

He said	"The Home Secretary has asked me to brief you on the new drugs initiative announced on TV last evening…"
Farthing interrupted	"You can't just walk in here…"
Brown asserted	"This briefing doesn't include you Farthing, this is a matter for Mr McCoy's ears only, if he chooses to share his thoughts with you then that's a matter for him."

Brown felt a swell of power, he had crashed into his office and without so much as a by your leave disrupted a meeting and was now attempting to divide the joint forces of the Creeping Insect Department, it was time to force McCoy to a decision, best done by falling silent. McCoy somehow sensed that it was his turn to speak but was beaten to it by Farthing who guessed he was about to be asked to leave.

Farthing said "I'll carry the interviews on downstairs, sir, I'll bring you up to date when you're ready."

Farthing had spoken slowly and quietly as though he was using the words as a cover for action he intended to take. However, action was now in the gift of McCoy who now had to make a decision, throw Farthing out and let Brown have his round, or…

McCoy said "OK, we'll pick this up later and I'll give you a full update on events here…"

Farthing left the room with a smile suggesting that leaving was somehow his idea. Brown closed the door and turned to McCoy who began to speak. Brown raised his hand silencing McCoy whilst he took a sea. Brown was now feeling quite pleased with himself, it was true that McCoy outranked him but it was McCoy who now needed Brown.

Brown spent a full fifteen minutes outlining the drug reduction strategy, McCoy listened intently to his every word. Victims' accord, post interventions, the list went on and on Brown added a refinement here, a caveat there, nice finishing touches rounding the whole package into an extremely creative game plan, a stratagem matching that of blitzkrieg itself.

McCoy asked	"When was all this thought up?"
Brown said	"Six months ago, sir."
McCoy said	"Yes, it was six months ago I was appointed drug supremo for the force you will recall. You will also recall that we had this very conversation at that time. We did a nook and cranny search of all avenues of drug intervention and I tasked you with the duty of preparing a new initiative which I now learn you have sold out to your local MP Ping, Ding, what's his name…?"
Brown said	"Ting, Khom Ting."
McCoy rasped	"What kind of name's that?"
Brown said	"He's of Asian extraction, but he was born here."
McCoy continued	"And your Ting has sold us out to the bloody Home Secretary, what were you thinking of?"

Brown and McCoy were engaged in surreal combat, McCoy to establish himself as a major player in this initiative and Brown as a necessary link twixt the police and his political masters, only four more weeks and his position would be improved greatly if only he could hold it all together. McCoy was equally determined. As drug supremo it was his duty to be the moving factor in all matters relating to drugs. By implication, they both knew that they faced a standoff, a confrontation where no strategy exists allowing either party to achieve a clear victory, it was clear that if either initiated aggression they might trigger their own demise. McCoy nor Brown could extricate themselves without suffering a loss. And so it was agreed, the initiative was a joint one given birth months ago at Aqua Ponds, and with the helter skelter of the murder, the drug initiative and the election, its birthplace and parentage would go unnoticed or so they believed.

McCoy said "Well you've got a problem Mr Brown, a problem so big that it you don't come up with a solution then your sixty percent reduction in drugs will be an increase that you'll need a calculator to work out."

Brown hesitated "So what you're saying is…"

McCoy leaned forward as though to speak. He produced a paper from a pocket and put on his half-moon specs. The silence was uninviting, McCoy read the paper and at the same time eyed Brown who was clearly cowed and uncertain. Brown decided to break this air of moral superiority.

He said "I think…"

McCoy raised a hand causing Brown to falter.

McCoy said "See you, Brown, you're just a wee man. You haven't got the balls or the savvy to deal with the main players. You and your well-educated Sloane Rangers can cobble together enough fancy words, terms of art and Latin to convince most of the people that you know what you're talking about, but you don't fool me son. You're just a silly wee man in a wee pond and sooner or later you'll be fished out of the pond and into the frying pan, so listen to this and listen well."

McCoy read some parts of the paper to Brown. It touched on a proposed new route for drugs to enter the UK. The south-east coast was becoming too expensive to the drug barons in terms of arrests and seizures. A new strategy had been identified by intelligence sources in Amsterdam, Dusseldorf and Bristol dealing with shipments in the tonnage, that meant boats, big ones, The only names McCoy had for the Bristol end of the operation was a guy called Charlie known to frequent Quanton and Aqua Ponds, nothing else was known of him, or maybe it was a her, no one knew.

McCoy said	"So wee man, if Charlie starts dropping tons of stuff on your ground that'll upset your figures a bit, won't it?"
Brown asked	"Do we know when this is about to start?"
McCoy said	"My people are looking at that now, what you've got to do is have your people rattle a few cages and do what it takes to get intelligence on the who's and where's."
Brown said	"Difficult to know where to start."
McCoy said	"Start at the beginning, speak to known dealers and offer them a…tell us what you know or we'll fit you up with a lengthy period at Her Majesty's pleasure. It's not hard son just do it."
Brown said	"I'll see what I can do."
McCoy said	"Wrong answer wee man, get out there, break a few arms do what it takes, but come back and tell me you got a result, don't tell me you'll see what you can do, just do it."

Brown made his way downstairs to the bar where most of the day crew gathered for refreshments and intelligence chat. He knew the bar shutters would still be down so he sat by the window clutching his Coke bottle. Lewis text Shear with a heads up on Brown's location, he added that Brown was clearly in need of a friendly ear. Brown caught Shear's eye as he entered the bar. Shear spoke briefly to Lewis then joined Brown at the window.

Shear said	"Tough day, I could do with a drink."
Brown sighed	"I'd kill for a drink."
Shear said	"A guy I know drops a ten-millilitre shot of brandy in his Coke can."
Brown lied	"I hope you don't think there's brandy in my Coke bottle Sarge, nothing but Coke in here."

Brown hastily guzzled what coke was left in the bottle transferring the evidence from the bottle to his belly finishing with a sigh of quiet content.

Shear said	"No, Boss, nobody's daft enough to put brandy in a bottle, it needs to be in a can, nobody can see it then. Even Mr McCoy keeps his in a can."
Brown asked	"Do you actually know that for a fact?"

Shear said	"I couldn't possibly comment on any minor flaws that afflict a senior officer, ye gods no, that would be like my saying I found you drinking on duty, that would never happen we're all in it together Boss, all for one and one for all."
Brown said	"I've just had a long conversation with Superintendent McCoy on the new drug initiative…"
Shear interrupted	"Was that a conversation or a monologue, he usually does all the talking."
Brown said	"I put him straight on a few things, but he changes everything to suit him. He's now saying that this new initiative was hatched here and it was mostly his idea."
Shear said	"Well, he would wouldn't he. He's the drug supremo and it's a bit obvious that all new initiatives would come from him, he is the main man after all."
Brown said	"What do you think, Sarge?"
Shear said	"Ideas should always belong to other people sir, 'cos when they go wrong everyone knows who to blame."
Brown said	"Yes, I'll think about that, I suppose lots could go wrong in four weeks in which case it would be the fault of the wee man."
Shear asked	"Oh, he gave you the wee man talk, did he?"
Brown said	"Yes, I don't get it, he sounded like a bloody gangster."
Shear said	"That's Bar L talk."
Brown said	"Bar L, what's that?"
Shear said	"All the bad bastards in Glasgow are held in Barlinnie prison, or as they call it the Big Hoose or the Bar L and if they want to assume power or influence over somebody, they just call them a wee man and if you accept the description, then that's what you are."
Brown enquiries	"What?"
Shear said	"A wee man."
Brown said	"Of course I don't accept it."
Shear said	"Next time just say I'm no glaikit."
Brown said	"Glaikit, what's that?"
Shear said	"He'll know, every Scotsman is brought to a standstill if you say you're no glaikit, try it."
Brown said	"It's a different bloody language they all sound like gangsters."

Shear said	"They are gangsters, Boss, they can even manage to bastardise the idea of café culture by calling al fresco a sit ooterie. God save us."

Brown told Shear that Superintendent McCoy would be calling all task force commanders together for an intelligence briefing on new inroads to the UK for main-line European drug cartel imports and that they had a name. Charlie, not much but it was what they had. Seems that this Charlie frequents Quanton and Aqua Ponds, so he's local.

Shear and Lewis made their way to the control room to see if anything was buzzing that might interest them. Unusually quiet. They met the rest of the crew in the yard and were about to mount up when the radio called them to a briefing by Superintendent McCoy. All three task forces eventually arrived in the briefing room. McCoy's bagman arrived and passed out a paper containing locations in Wessex where drugs might be landed in the force area. Shear noted that his favoured beach was not among them, so much for intelligence.

Shear asked	"Who's McCoy's bagman? I've never seen him before."
Tony said	"That's DCI Bradley Boss, joined up at the same time as me, a dour Scot, bit of an academic, but an OK guy."
Shear enquired	"A friend of yours then."
Tony said	"Yeah, we get on well enough, I haven't seen him for a couple of years but hell he's good for information if we need it."
Shear said	"We'll need it."

McCoy came to the briefing room and took Bradley aside for a tete-a-tete, then the briefing began. Nothing new, just the usual…we have information from intelligence sources that drug barons are seeking new import locations in the UK. Sources suggest that the Wessex coast will be targeted in the immediate future. The name Charlie recurs…

Shear said	"Tony, find out what you can from Bradley. We need all we can get on McCoy."
Tony said	"No problem, Boss, I'll speak to him when I get a chance."

Post briefing coastal maps and source information handouts were distributed. Informal chats vis-a-vis task force units ensued. McCoy asked task force commanders to the back of the room for a fine grain detailed list of his expectations. This informal briefing was white knuckled. Only McCoy spoke. He made it very clear that the units had carte blanche powers, total freedom to act as they wished and that he would personally deal with any complaints. They were to get results at any cost and the task force commander who brought him the head of Charlie could expect a promotion. McCoy nodded and they returned to their units, McCoy held Shear back.

McCoy said	"Are those wee Pakies yours Sarge?"
Shear said	"Pakies?"
McCoy said	"Aye, the wee black men you've got in your crew."
Shear said	"Saaz and Rohan are Muslims, not entirely sure where they're from but they were born here and they're British, is there a problem?"
McCoy said	"Where I come from there is only Catholics and Protestants and if somebody says they're Muslim, you should ask them if they're Catholic or Protestant Muslims, know what I mean?"
Shear said	"Both are good men, sir, I would trust them with my life."
McCoy said	"Protestant Muslims then."

Shear took his crew out into the yard and boarded Cerberus. Time to drive out to the countryside to reflect and take stock. They drive to the salt marsh and parked up.

Boots said	"So what have we got Boss?"
Shear said	"We've got Superintendent McCoy heading this hunt for something that might happen, looking for a Charlie who might exist and who might be floating between Quanton and Aqua Ponds. Believe me when I say that McCoy is a carnivore, he won't hesitate to eat anyone alive who gets in his way, he's one of those mad Scotsmen who hates everyone and everything so be alert."
Lewis said	"Yeah, they don't even like themselves, do they?"

Shear said	"We'll call in on Fink later and see what he knows, we're in plain clothes this evening, so there's lots to do with Fink and I've got to arrange things at the Narrow Escape for the Right Honourable and his friends, so busy, busy."
Ken said	"I see we're down for the royal visit on Saturday and a bloody football match the following Saturday."
Boots asked	"Who's playing?"
Ken said	"Plymouth and Liverpool."
Shear said	"Excellent, the money Fink makes for us next week we'll double come the match, trouble is we need a volunteer to go to Liverpool."

Boots said "Fink will give us a name, an away day at Liverpool, £100 cash and a few lines of coke will do the trick."

The crew listened in to radio transmissions from the other two task force units. Seems they're about to stop a suspect, trouble is they're using call signs we're not privy to, something's up. It didn't take long for them to announce two in custody please inform Delta 11.

Boots asked "Who's Delta 11?"

Lewis said "Superintendent McCoy."

Shear said "Back to Aqua Ponds boys, we need to get into the cell block and find out who's been pulled."

As they drove back to town, they were looking for a street arrest to justify a routing visit to the cells. Sure enough a known local was seen to pull out of the Kings Head, a pub known to harbour pond life. Automatic number plate recognition told them that the vehicle was owned by a disqualified driver named Wilson, trouble was, he was being driven by an unknown kid, a minor difficulty. Saaz stopped the vehicle. Tony and Ken got out to speak to the driver.

Ken said	"What's your name sunbeam?"
The kid said	"Dave, why?"
Ken said	"Not you son, your mate there, we've just seen you two swap places, don't you know you get jail time for conspiracy to pervert the course of justice?"

Tony pulled open the passenger door and dragged Wilson from his seat. Wilson made the mistake of resisting Tony and found himself face down on the ground in handcuffs and being arrested for disqualified driving.

| Wilson said | "I wasn't driving, honest." |
| Tony said | "Don't cloud the issue with facts. There's half a dozen policemen here who'll say you were, now we can add assault on police and resisting arrest if you want." |

Ken made a motion to the driver who started the car and drove off at speed.

Tony said "So much for your witness to not driving, seems he's got more sense than you."

Cerberus arrived back at the nick and Wilson was marched into the custody suite by Tony and Ken. The Custody Officer was in the cell block with a task force unit lodging their prisoners. Ken looked at the custody records for both arrests and took pictures of each. One of their number was a Charlie. He saw that the Custody Officer had noted on the record that a computer check showed Charlie to have two convictions for cannabis possession both resulting in fines, hardly enough to attract the attention of a task force.

After processing their prisoner, Ken and Tony met the crew in the briefing room for an update. They then went to the bar for coffee where they found the other task force unit who arrested Charlie.

Shear said	"Well done boys, I hear you nicked Charlie, that didn't take long."
Their boss said	"He's a nobody really, when you were speaking to Superintendent McCoy his bagman told us to get out there and nick any scally's called Charlie with previous for drugs."
Shear asked	"Has he got much form?"
He answered	"Minor possession only, a couple of fines, his only crime really is that he's called Charlie."
Shear said	"Oh, a really short interview then."
He said	"No interview, McCoy and his bagman are in the cells putting the fear of god into them, they'll then be released with an assurance that if they don't come up with some good information their lives won't be worth living."

Shear's crew sat at the window with their drinks where it was decided that the other task force unit had been separately briefed and that there was no covert move to exclude Foxtrot 13 from events. It was clear that McCoy was a desperate man who was intent on a blade of grass search for whoever Charlie was and that he and his bagman were taking a personal interest in anything and everything that might produce Charlie, and from Charlie they would extract the next point of entry of wholesale drug entry into the UK. A hard way to go about things, there were easier ways.

Shear said	"Well, we now know how desperate McCoy is to find Charlie, so desperate the he's going to personally have a chat to all prisoners himself. Time consuming and labour intensive I say. Happily we know a quicker way."
Rohan asked	"So what do you reckon Boss?"
Shear said	"We'll see Fink later and put a reward on the head of Charlie, two grand ought to do it."
Shear said	"Tony, your pal Bradley needs speaking to soon, find out how close he is to McCoy, if it turns out they're big pals then we'll need to monitor his movements, we're going to have to know where he is at all times."
Boots said	"We could put a lump on McCoy's car Boss."
Shear said	"McCoy is too smart for that Boots, he'd find it before too long and be aware that someone was showing an interest, much better if we tap his bagman, where the bagman is McCoy is not far away, but see what you can find out first."

McCoy and Bradley came into the bar. As usual they were focused and had their heads together. They sat in a corner and began poring over papers Bradley produced from a bag. Chief Inspector Brown then came in and began an about turn when he was spotted by McCoy who called him over. As Shear's crew got up to leave McCoy beckoned to him.

McCoy said "You haven't time to waste in here Sarge, get your troops out on the ground and start rattling cages and keep rattling until you've got something to tell me, have you got that?"

Shear looked at Chief Inspector Brown who was seated and clutching a can of Coke and said in a thinly disguised Glaswegian drawl.

"I'm no glaikit, sir, you've just interrupted our hunt for Charlie."

McCoy rolled his eyes in a gesture of resignation, formed his lips in a whistle-less pout and fell silent. Brown tried to hide a smile and Bradley had the vapours of a minor coup in his nostrils. Shear and his crew left the bar and mounted up in the rear yard. Shear instructed Tony to remain at the police station and report when Charlie and his mate were released and to engage McCoy's bagman in conversation if he could. Foxtrot 13 pulled out of the yard and began their mobile patrol of Aqua Ponds.

The radio in Cerberus squawked asking Foxtrot 13 to attend the town bridge where a young male was threatening to throw himself into the river. They arrived two minutes later and sure enough the young man was stood on the parapet of the bridge. He had attracted a small crowd who had happened upon the spectacle. They could see at once that it was Vince, an inhabitant of the local authority hostel for the homeless, who again was seeking attention from anyone who would listen. Ken left the vehicle and approached Vince.

Vince shouted	"Don't come near me I'll jump."
Ken said	"There's no future in that Vince, besides you're facing the wrong way and the tides out."

The crowd were quite drawn by the spectacle and could see that Vince had chosen the wrong location and the wrong time to stage a suicide by drowning. Feeling his frustration, they began to offer good natured and well-meaning advice on how best to top himself.

Vince said	"Why is everyone laughing at me?"
Ken said	"Well, it's not your youthful good looks or animal magic."

Only Vince was taking the matter seriously. He was something of a master of attempted suicides, he had tied himself to the wrong track at the railway station and had placed a rope around his neck and jumped from a window at the library, a distance of six feet with an eight-foot rope. Things were not going well for Vince and he was becoming a tad upset by the ridicule being offered by the crowd. He raised both his hands to his mouth as though to shout when he slipped and fell backwards a distance of some ten feet into two feet of mud below. Ken called for Fire rescue who plucked a disgraced Vince from the mud.

Shear quipped	"If Vince ever manages to top himself English Heritage could put up a number of blue plaques entitled Vince attempted suicide here."
Boots said	"Yes, a bit like the stations of the cross."

Lewis said	"It would attract so many lunatics to the area that Aqua Ponds could become a global supplier of village idiots."

They continued their patrol. A text was received from Tony that Charlie and his friend would be leaving the police station shortly without charge. They were returning home to Lowbridge a couple of miles north of Aqua Ponds. A quick chat with these two would prove useful, they could tell something of McCoy's interrogation techniques. They were found twenty minutes later walking out of town. Saaz pulled up alongside the pair.

Shear said "Hi Boys, they let you go then?"

Charlie said	"I should think so. I don't know why they arrested us, we've done nowt, I'm sick to death of police harassment. All we got was roughed up and then they refused to take us back home, we've now got a seven-mile walk."
Shear said	"Well, that's terrible, we always take people back to the place of arrest, it's only right."
Charlie said	"Well, you can give us a lift then."
Shear said	"It's the least we could do, jump in my friend."

Both youths clambered on board and sat on the floor of the vehicle.

Shear enquired	"How come they let you go so quickly?"
Charlie said	"They had nothing on us, we smoke a bit of dope if we've got money but that's it, we don't deal in it we just smoke it."
Shear said	"Who interviewed you?"
Charlie said	"Don't know, there were two of them, one kept telling us if we didn't come up with information things would get real bad for us."
Shear said	"So this wasn't a taped interview then?"
Charlie said	"No, we were both in the same cell and these two came in and threatened us. One did all the talking and his mate wrote stuff down."
Shear said	"Well, you weren't there long so they must have believed you."

Charlie said	"No, he didn't, he said the only way we'd keep out of prison was if we came up with names and addresses of deals going down."
His friend said	"And he said we'd become his snout and he'd pay us good money."
Charlie said	"We're not snouts, we don't grass our mates up, the one that was doing the writing gave us a number to text when we got information."
Shear said	"Well, that's bang out of order, they can't ask you to rat your mates out for cash, that's agent provocateur."
Charlie said	"What's that?"
Shear said	"It means it illegal."
Charlie said	"I thought so."
Shear said	"Don't worry boys, if he gives you a hard time let us know and we'll sort it for you. What's the number he gave you?"

Shear wrote a note and asked Charlie to text it to the number he'd been given, it read 'do we come to the station or text'. The reply was immediate. "Always text." He replied, "OK m8." Charlie and his pal were dropped at Lowbridge making encouraging noises to their new found friends.

Boots said	"Interesting Sarge, they've put the frighteners on those two and made promises of money hoping for a result."
Shear said	"Yes, standard stuff really, I somehow expected more from McCoy. At least we've got his interrogation technique sussed, all we need to do now is find out if the number belongs to McCoy or Bradley. Tony can do that."

Shear's crew returned to the police station to change into plain clothes and check out their battered van. Shear found Tony who had not yet made an opportunity to speak to DCI Bradley. Just as well, Shear gave him the number they got from Charlie and asked him to use one of their seized mobiles to see who answered.

Superintendent McCoy and Chief Inspector Brown came into the back yard and were in the midst of a row by the look of things. Shear told Tony to ring the number now to see if McCoy answered, he didn't. Bradley did. Shear asked Tony to find Bradley and renew his old acquaintance and see what could be found out, especially how close his relationship was with McCoy. If it was close, then they could use Bradley as their unsuspecting vehicle to keep tabs on McCoy.

Saaz fired up the old banger and they drove to the cottage to collect a bag destined for Fink. Enough stuff for Fink to bring in thirty grand or there about. The van was parked up a few hundred yards from the farm. Shear text Fink and established that he was alone, he then made his way there on foot where he met a sorrowful Fink.

Shear said	"What's wrong Fink you look a mess?"
Fink said	"No wonder, I've no money, nothing to sell and I'm on my own. People keep ringing for stuff and I've got nothing for them."
Shear said	"There's enough stuff here to keep you going for a week and plenty more when that's all sold, now how many buyers are waiting?"
Fink said	"About a dozen."
Shear said	"OK here's how it works. I've spoken to Jock who wants you to run things here. So you're the boss with total control, what you say goes…"
Fink interrupted	"What me, the boss. Bloody hell I wish my dad was here he always said I would amount to nothing, and now I'm a boss."
Shear said	"There are new rules so listen up. I supply you and you only sell to people you've dealt with in the past, that way you won't get robbed by a gang of outsiders."
Fink said	"Good idea, when Jonah was here people turned up from all over the place, he always sent me out to deal with them so I always had to carry a knife."
Shear said	"The knife you carry is the knife that stabs you, so no knives, just deal with people you know that way you stay alive."
Fink said	"I'll need a runner."
Shear said	"No runners, a runner is a person who starts by helping you, trouble is it doesn't take too long before they start helping themselves. If you need help you speak to me, got it?"
Fink said	"Yeah good."
Shear said	"Now your promotion is going to earn you good money, very good money, so you'll have to up your game son."

Fink said	"How do you mean?"
Shear said	"I want you to keep a list of all the people you deal with. Names and addresses if you can get them, but street names at least, so listen to what they say and listen to what their mates call them, but in every case it's your job to identify them."
Fink said	"But what if I can't get a name?"
Shear said	"A clever boy like you, newly promoted to a boss…"
Fink said	"Yeah, I'll get them."
Shear said	"A man will appear here tomorrow and set up a CCTV system."
Fink said	"What for?"
Shear said	"That's a dangerous question. Knowing stuff is dangerous but, as you're now a boss I'll let you know but this is privileged information."
Fink asked	"What does that mean?"
Shear said	"It means if you tell anyone I'll have to kill you."
Fink smiled	"Oh yeah, right."

Shear then explained the money laundering system favoured by the Scousers.

When Liverpool are playing an away game, say Plymouth, the locals in the know go and see the main man. They hand over say one hundred notes and in return they get two hundred back. They then spend the money in the pubs and clubs in Plymouth and everyone's happy.

Fink said	"I don't understand."
Shear said	"I'm only telling you this 'cos you're now a boss so this you keep in your head and never tell a soul."
Fink nodded	"Yeah, yeah."
Shear continued	"The locals in the know hand over one hundred good notes, in return they get two hundred back in counterfeit. That way the man launders his money and the bent notes are pushed over the bars in Plymouth."
Fink asked	"Don't they know they're bent?"

Shear said	"They get handed over in busy pubs and clubs nobody gives a toss. One in thirty notes are counterfeit and they only come to notice if someone says this is bent, if they don't then it's a good note. Do you ever look at a note you're about to hand over?"
Fink said	"No."
Shear said	"So the moral of the story is, it's only bent if someone says it's bent. If you know you had a bent note, what would you do with it?"
Fink said	"Hand it on."
Shear said	"Exactly, besides the notes Liz prints at the treasury are just as bent, they only work 'cos everyone passes them on, if you walked into a bank and said this note promises to pay the bearer ten pounds, what do you think you'd get?"
Fink said	"Nothing."
Shear said	"And if you take a counterfeit note into the bank, what do you think they thank you with?"
Fink said	"Nothing."
Shear said	"So now you know how money works and why they're forever changing the notes. Did you know that a firm in Debden in Essex prints hundreds of millions of banknotes each year for Liz, and the second biggest printer are the counterfeiters who print them for themselves."
Fink asked	"So why don't the bank give you the proper value of the bent note, that would soon get rid of them off the streets."

Shear said "No, if they gave you a tenner for every bent one you handed in, everyone would be looking at their notes and it would soon be realised that there are a number of printers in the country forging 500,000 fake twenties a year, resulting in the economy collapsing. So real or bent pass it on, no questions asked."

Shear left a smiling but somewhat bewildered Fink to reflect on his promotion and new found knowledge as to how the world works, everyone was at it, yes, even the Queen was at it. Shear rejoined his crew and made their way back to the factory. The radio squawked.

Control "Any crew near Lowbridge dual carriageway, report of a fatal call sign over."

Rohan said "There's our chance to get into the mortuary Sarge." Shear said "No Rohan, too early, we need to be there after hours but well spotted."

Foxtrot 13 arrived at the scene of the fatal accident in time to assist a local unit and help sweep the road. They then returned to the nick where Tony was waiting in the back yard. He climbed on board.

Shear asked	"What news, Tony, did you manage to speak to Bradley?"
Tony said	"Couldn't be better, Boss, James and I talked about the good old days and we're having a drink after work."
Shear asked	"Did he mention McCoy?"
Tony said	"No, best done when he's had a few beers."
Shear said	"Yes, when the wine is in, the wit is out, don't forget to record it will you."
Tony said	"Standard stuff."
Shear said	"If it turns out that he and McCoy are big pals we'll need to get a lump on his car."
Boots said	"What do you think they're up to Boss?"
Shear said	"Don't know, but we've got a lump on Hanson's car and we know he's the brief sent to look after the interests of all the dealers who are paying their tipster. The more lumps we have on cars the better, sooner or later they will come together and when they do, we'll have the name of who's got their nose in the trough."
Tony said	"I doubt if it's Bradley, he's straight up and down, I don't think he's got it in him to pull a stroke."
Shear said	"That's probably why McCoy uses him, he couldn't smell a parcel of flatulence in a spacesuit. An innocent abroad."
Boots asked	"What's next Boss?"
Shear said	"Nothing's changed. We're looking for the two top people, we know they're called Jock and Bubbles, we just keep looking, keep scratching and they'll make a mistake. They always make the same mistakes, their arrogance breeds complacency and they always underestimate their foes. It's only a matter of time."

Chapter 7

Shear and his crew had been called in early and gathered in the briefing room just as it got light. Chief Inspector Brown was seated and clearly was part of the audience. A second task force unit and dog handler arrived followed by an armed response team, a sergeant, six officers and a negotiator, the team was armed with Glock pistols and Heckler and Koch carbines. Maps were handed out and photographs fixed to the white board. Sergeant Bex took the briefing.

Bex began "Information is that a Marco D'Costa was seen entering his girlfriend's flat in Trull, an upmarket area of Quanton. He was seen to be in possession of a shotgun. He had spent the night drinking and he was off his head on coke. The informant states that it's his intention to sort his girlfriend out. The intention is to secure the area, establish communications with D'Costa and bring the incident to…"

The control room supervisor came into the briefing with updates that D'Costa had left the flat with a reluctant girlfriend in tow. It was confirmed that he was in possession of a shotgun. Oscar control had scrambled the force helicopter which would be overhead in fifteen minutes. The last known movement of D'Costa was that he was heading for the Quantock Hills in a white Nissan Qashqai. Last minute instructions were issued, designed to locate D'Costa, bring him to a halt and secure the area. All units had talk through with the chopper.

Control room instructed units not involved in the firearm incident to remain silent. Sergeant Beck was Silver commander and was responsible for all activities involving the armed response and supporting officers. He alone would dictate events. D'Costa's profile was transmitted to all units; previous convictions included drugs, public disorder, assaults and a wounding, he was on parole from Long Lartin prison having served eight years of a ten year sentence, this man was a serious player and seriously dangerous.

Sergeant Beck arranged his troops for best tactical advantage, they were laid up at strategic locations on the Quantocks overseeing all movement and waited. Shear knew he was in the hands of a professional. They only had to wait.

Lewis said	"What do you think Sarge?"
Shear replied	"D'Costa's back to prison or in the mortuary."
Boots asked	"Do you think it'll come to that?"
Shear said	"Well, he's a bad bastard who's just done eight years. He's full of psychoactive crap, liquor, coke and whatever else he injects himself with, and angry with his girlfriend so I'm guessing his negotiating skills are a tad rusty. Best guess is he'll go out with a bang, we'll bang him and he'll go out, suicide by police they call it."
Lewis opined	"And psychiatrists will tell you it's all because his mum didn't love him."
Shear replied	"Well, that's probably true, childhood is where it all starts and here's where it all ends. Life's like that."

The force helicopter was on scene asking Beck to confirm team locations. It confirmed that a white Qashqai was driving through Bishop St Mary northbound toward Aqua Ponds. Beck deployed his teams and asked Foxtrot 13 to come in behind D'Costa and block the road. The stage was all but set. Shears crew blocked the road and made their way north through the country lane, an area of outstanding natural beauty about to be sullied by the good guys taking out the bad. The other task force unit had blocked the lane ahead of D'Costa who was now in a tightening trap. The firearms team deployed themselves to tactical advantage and waited. The trap was now complete.

D'Costa stopped about sixty yards short of the road block. Shear's crew stopped a safe distance behind D'Costa who knew he'd been ambushed, his vehicle remained stationary, engine running, D'Costa remained inside.

An unarmed policeman stepped into the road holding both arms up and both hands facing forward. In response, D'Costa lowered his window and pushed the barrel of the shotgun out of the window, the barrel faced the nearside of the vehicle and was not an immediate threat. So long as D'Costa stayed in the vehicle he could not readily bring the gun to bear. It was all now down to the negotiator who remained still with his hands in the air.

Boots whispered "Who's he Sarge?"

Shear said "Trevor, the negotiator, every kid's favourite uncle…"

Trevor was a short man, aged about 45, an avuncular type who would easily have passed as a pipe smoking bee keeper. His voice was prescriptive and yet inviting, a gentle man who now held all the power. He called out,

"Marco, armed police, we only want to talk, we're here to help. Throw the gun from the car, You won't be hurt, we only want to talk."

It could be seen that D'Costa's girlfriend was giving him a hard time, she couldn't be heard but it needed no gift of imagination to see that she was pleading surrender. She tried to open the driver's door but was pulled back by D'Costa.

Negotiator "Marco, we only want to talk, throw the gun out, you will not be harmed, we only want to talk, we're here to help, we only want to talk."

Competition response was taking its toll. D'Costa's befuddled mind was trying to cope with a girlfriend intent on surrender, armed police making demands and his need for another fix, he knew his position was critical and prison was something that wasn't going to happen…

Negotiator "Marco, throw the gun out, you won't be harmed, we only want to talk."

D'Costa opened the passenger door and stood up bringing the shotgun to bear.

Negotiator "For fuck sake, somebody shoot him."

He was shot dead two rounds centre of mass. His girlfriend ran from the vehicle and the negotiator sat himself on the ground. Game, set and match. The scene was made secure. The radio was alive with requests for scenes of crime officers, police surgeon, ambulance and more. Somehow the press were on the scene looking for a winning picture. Shear's crew were stood down to return to the police station for debriefing by the post incident manager and the senior officer from professional standards. Time for a late breakfast. Foxtrot 13 pulled away from the scene.

Ken said "Like you said Sarge, suicide by cops."

On arrival at the police station, Chief Inspector Farthing was in discussions with a camera crew, two cameras, a sound engineer and lighting, must be big. Shear had never seen lighting used for a standard front of police station interview, he wondered what was up. Farthing made a beeline for Shear and told him aside.

Shear said	"What's on, sir?"
Farthing said	"You've just come back from the firearm incident."
Shear said	"Yes."
Farthing said	"You need to brief me, they're about to be interviewed for tonight's news, it might be shown nationally. So tell me what happened."
Shear said	"Well, the little bastard got himself shot, he needed shooting, long overdue…"
Farthing interrupted	"For Christ's sake, I can't appear on TV and say the little bastard got himself shot, now tell me what happened."
Shear said	"Well, the negotiator ended up shouting for fuck's sake somebody shoot him."
Farthing said	"You can't say that."
Shear said	"I didn't, the negotiator did."
Farthing said	"No, Sarge, that won't do and if you mention any of that to professional standards, you'll find that you're the one who'll get shot."
Shear said	"I speak from a position of authority, unlike you I was at the scene. They need to be speaking to Beck who commanded the firearms team, he was silver commander."
Farthing said	"Christ, that'll get us all shot."
Shear said	"Sounds like you want a sanitised version of events."
Farthing said	"Of course, and that's why I'm a chief inspector and you're not, the public don't want to hear the truth, they want to hear what goes down well with their tea and biscuits."
Shear said	"I'll get you a copy of the log from the control room and you can read it all for yourself."
Farthing said	"I'll get it myself."

As Farthing stormed off Chief Inspector Cole was dropped off. He immediately spoke to Shear.

Cole said	"What are all the cameras doing here Sarge?"
Shear said	"Well, sir, this is a bit embarrassing really, Chief Inspector Farthing is about to give a TV interview and he was asking me about the job and…"
Cole interrupted	"What job?"
Shear said	"The firearms incident."
Cole said	"What's it got to do with him, he's got a murder to sort out, besides he wasn't there, I was."
Shear said	"Exactly what I told him, sir."
Cole said	"He's murder squad, I deal with operational matters on district."
Shear said	"The cameras are ready to roll, you're the boss, you were at the scene so it's only right that you do the interview, besides the viewers are getting to know you now and they like you. Never know, it might make the BBC national news, two appearances on TV in one week, wow."

Shear's radio directed him to see Chief Inspector Farthing in the control room.

He said	"I'll leave you to get on with the interview then sir."
Cole said	"Thank you, Sarge, I'll deal with this, you'd better get on and see what the murder squad are up to."

Cole engaged with the camera crew and Shear made his way to the control room to find Farthing berating the civilian radio operator for taking too long to print out the details of the firearms incident.

Shear said "Chief Inspector Cole sends his compliments, sir, he's doing the interview himself as he attended the scene and it happened on his ground, nothing personal."

Farthing stared at Shear in silence, his eyes in obvious breach of the sixth commandment.

Shear's crew met in the canteen for a richly deserved breakfast. Professional standards took two at a time for debriefing. They all agreed that they were too far behind D'Costa's car to hear any conversation and expressed their disappointment at the tragic outcome to the day's events. They were each pencilled in to attend a post-traumatic stress disorder clinic and offered down time to be with family and friends should the need arise. It didn't.

Shear collected the operation order for the royal visit and noted that his crew were detailed to be in support of royal protection officers at the airport early on Saturday. The briefing was scheduled to take place at 32 squadron's office, the RAF VIP lounge. The operation order was marked secret but it was an open secret that a royal was a guest at a wedding in Quanton, no big shakes.

The crew finally became mobile and made their way to a quiet spot by the river which had recently become popular with users and dealers. The uniformed presence was supposed to act as a deterrent and to make local residents feel safe, or so went the theory.

Shear said	"How did you get on with DCI Bradley last night over drinkies Lewis?"
Lewis said	"Yes, interesting Boss, he's not a drinker but I managed to secrete a large brandy into his beer so he became quite unguarded very quickly. It's hard to see how someone like McCoy would choose him as a bagman."
Shear said	"McCoy is street savvy and chooses his people not for what they know but more for his ability to control them."
Lewis said	"Well, he's got a couple of degrees, philosophy and one in ancient something or other, but he's well short on common sense."
Shear replied	"Yes, such people can talk forever about compound adjectives and the pros and cons of adversarial jurisprudence, what they can't do is smell a rat."
Lewis said	"Exactly."
Shear said	"That's why McCoy chose him, he does as he's told, he does it well, but that's all he does."
Tony asked	"Any chance that McCoy is the Jock we keep hearing about?"
Shear said	"All Scots are suspect but there's too many of them to draw any conclusions."

Lewis said	"No Boss, whilst Bradley could still speak, he mentioned that he heard McCoy on the phone saying that he thought there was a leak at headquarters and that dealers were being tipped off by someone."
Shear said	"Any names?"
Lewis said	"No Boss."
Shear said	"We'll still need a lump on his car so we can stay close to McCoy."
Rohan asked	"I could never figure out why they call GPS a lump Sarge."
Shear said	"It's camouflaged, if anyone spots it, it looks like a lump of mud stuck to the underneath of the car, so it's called a lump."

The crew could see a number of youths at the river bank arguing and pushing and shoving one another, it was difficult to see who was on whose side. One lad fell to the floor when he was head butted by a Chinese looking guy. Shear told Ken and Tony to bring him over to the vehicle. These youths had little fear of the police, in the old days they would have run off at the sight of uniforms, but that was in the old days. The kid was dragged to the nearside of the van out of sight of anyone showing an interest.

Shear said	"Kong he fat choy."
The youth said	"What?"
Shear said	"Oh, you speak English, I thought you were a Triad."
He asked	"What's that?"
Shear said	"Chinese mafia."
He said	"What?"
Shear said	"That head butt was so well executed, so perfectly placed, so well balanced I thought you were some kind of King Fu master."
He replied	"Yeah, wasn't bad was it."
Shear said	"Trouble is, a judge would call it an act of gratuitous violence."
He said	"So what?"
Shear said	"Well, the blow lacked a certain Je ne sais quoi."
He said	"What's that?"
Shear said	"Are you familiar with the concept of pre-emptive reciprocity?"
He said	"What's that?"

Shear brought his forehead down on the kid's nose, he fell to the ground clutching his broken nose squealing and bleeding like the proverbial stuck pig. Lewis got out of the vehicle, put his hand in the kids' pocket and produced a plastic bag.

Lewis said	"What's in here son?"
He said	"Dunno, I've only got cannabis, that's all I use."
Lewis said	"You're nicked for possession of a class A drug with intent to supply and possession of cannabis."
Shear added	"And Section 5 of the Public Order Act."
The kid asked	"Why did you nut me?"
Shear asked	"Why did you nut the kid at the river?"
He replied	"'Cos he's a nasty little bastard who needed a lesson."
Shear said	"And a great many civilised people would say the same about you, my friend."
The kid said	"I don't believe this."
Lewis said	"The court will."

Back at the factory Lewis and Shear booked the kid into the system. Uncomfortable noises could be heard from the cells. A cell door slammed shut and Superintendent McCoy and Chief Inspector Bradley came out of the cell passage and made their way out of the custody suite.

Shear asked	"What are they doing in the cells unsupervised."
Custody Officer said	"Informal chat with a prisoner."
Shear said	"Somebody called Charlie?"
Custody Officer said	"How did you know."
Shear joked	"We ought to put posters up saying 'Help Your Local Police, If Your Name's Charlie Beat Yourself Up'."

Shear and Lewis rejoined the crew. Time for plain clothes for the second part of the shift. They drove the banger to the canal and parked up. Shear and Boots made their way along the bank on foot until they were in sight of the Narrow Escape. Time to sit and take stock. They kept the canal boat in view waiting for sight of Tuppence or her mum. Twenty minutes passed when they decided on an impromptu visit. They climbed onto the bow over the cockpit and opened the saloon door where they found both women asleep, a dozen or so cans lay in front of them. Shear placed a couple of grams of coke on the table. Tuppence would know they've been.

Shear checked his Eyespy Tap and Track and found the Right Honourable was at home. Time to check all was set up for their weekend beano, numbers, transport and the like, he rang his home landline. Ting confirmed that he'd let the staff go early and would be alone in half an hour, perfect.

The Right Honourable was in buoyant mood when he greeted Shear.

Ting said	"All well for the weekend beano Sergeant."
Shear said	"Yes, all well, just a question of how many and any special requirements really."
Ting said	"Well besides the Home Secretary and I, there'll be a Major General, some admiralty fellow, a dear friend of mine from banking and a name."
Shear enquired	"Name?"
Ting confided	"Yes, someone who cannot be named. Now tell me are the girls all set?"
Shear said	"Yes, they are indeed, I saw both earlier and they are looking forward to the weekend."
Ting said	"How splendid, now we'll need some extra white powder, and of course, you know…"
Shear said	"Know…?"
Ting said	"Yes, Jonnies dear man, you know condoms."
Shear said	"Only teasing."
Ting said	"Now we're in for a rollicking good weekend and as usual security is the watchword, your department dear boy so no hiccups eh."
Shear replied	"Hiccups do not happen."
Ting said	"A final word dear boy, he who cannot be named will be arriving by private car…"

Control room called Foxtrot 13 and directed 'go now to M5 junction 23 southbound exit and report arrival over'. Other units were sent to specified locations. Two dog handlers were heard to go 10–1 and make their way to motorway exit points. An incident was up and running. Shear's crew reported their arrival at the junction and waited. A motorway traffic unit came on air.

Tango 3 reported	"Suspect vehicle has moved into the nearside lane and is indicating exit at junction 23, is there a unit there to block over?"
Shear replied	"Foxtrot 13 in plain task force van at exit, say when to block over."
Tango 3 called	"Block now over."

Saaz pulled the van across both lanes at the bottom of the junction, the crew got out and made out that the vehicle had broken down as the suspect vehicle came off the motorway followed by Tango 3, game on. The suspect was seen to be stuffing stuff into his mouth, drew to a halt with the Tango unit close on his tail. The driver was wrestled from the vehicle, he was clearly drunk. Tango 3 reported one in custody and administered a breath test which was negative indicating no signs of alcohol. Shear arrested the driver on suspicion of drink-drugs and took him back to the nick. Superintendent McCoy and DCI Bradley were waiting.

McCoy said	"Get him booked in, Mr Bradley and I will interview him in half an hour."
Shear said	"Can't do that, sir, he's off his head, he can hardly speak."
McCoy said	"Half an hour."

Shear spoke to the Custody Officer and agreed that blood samples were needed and that the prisoner could not be interviewed as he was unfit. The Custody Officer called the police surgeon whilst Shear went to speak to McCoy and Bradley.

Shear said	"We're arranging blood to be taken, sir, but as far as interviews are concerned this guy is well psychoactive on something so we had…"
Bradley said	"PACE allows interviews of nutters in cases of emergency so that's the plan, we need…"
McCoy interrupted	"Do you know who this is Sarge?"
Shear said	"No but my guess is his first name is Charlie."
McCoy confirmed	"Yes, Charlie Lloyd, he's a player and a serious suspect for wholesale importation of Class A, so we'll be interviewing him whatever happens."

Again Shear spoke to the Custody Officer who was of the view that as soon as they had blood the prisoner would be locked up on the grounds that it was impossible to interview someone who was incapable of speech. Custody assured Shear that McCoy and Bradley would have to wait 'til morning. Shear agreed to speak to custody in the morning when he came back on duty.

Shear stirred when he heard ringing, he looked at his watch it was 5.40, he answered the phone. It was Dave Clarke the Custody Officer.

Clarke said	"Dave here Paul, I've got a problem, I need you to come in."
Shear enquired	"What's up Dave?"
Clarke said	"I'll tell you when you come in, use the prisoner's side entrance."

Shear opened the prisoner's entrance door and found himself in a secure cubicle, a bit like a lift. He pressed the bell and was let into the cell block by the Custody Officer who was purposeful but clearly rattled. Shear began to speak but was hushed by Clarke who pointed to his office. They went indoors and Clarke took the phone off the hook and beckoned Shear to close the door.

Shear said	"What've we got mate?"
Clarke said	"They've dropped a dead body on me."
Shear said	"What are the facts?"
Clarke said	"After Lloyd got banged up last night, I went off duty. I came back for earlies at about half five. It was busy, the cells were full and unusually the Night Inspector was here. The handover only took five minutes. We checked the prisoners but most were asleep. When we got to cell ten, the Inspector said the bulb's gone so the lights stayed off. Next thing is they've gone off duty and I went to change the bulb and...come on, I'll show you."

Clarke led the way, the place was like a submarine on red lights. No windows, still air and the stench of humanity. Cell ten door was yanked open by Clarke who shone his torch on Lloyd's bench. He lay on his right side facing the wall, his blanket up to his chest. Clarke put his finger to his mouth and whispered shh...They both looked and listened, nothing, there was no chest movement and the silence palpable. They approached the body and Clarke shone the light on the exposed left shoulder which showed dark patches like heavy bruising.

Shear said	"Hypostasis."
Clark said	"What's that?"
Shear said	"When someone dies, the heart stops pumping the blood so it's subject to the effects of gravity and it falls to the lower parts of the body where it lays before rigour set in, you know what that means."
Clarke said	"This guy's been found dead and then turned over."
Shear said	"Right."

They both returned to the office and began checking the custody record. Nothing, just routine visits about every hour.

Clarke said	"Death in police custody, this is not going to end well."
Shear said	"Yes, it is. We sit here and we think, check all the custody records and think again."

Time passed at the speed of a glacier. Shear found that the prisoner in cell number seven had been arrested by two traffic units following a high-speed chase. He had crashed his car and had run off. The dog handler found him and a bit of a battle ensued. He had been injured in the accident and added to his injuries by fighting two traffic officers and a police dog, he had been well battered. He would do nicely. Clarke called in the police surgeon while Shear informed the Coroner's Officer of the sudden death. They knew that blood would show that Lloyd died from an overdose of drugs. They had blood taken the night before and the blood they would take now to show that the stuff he put in his mouth at the time of arrest must have been drugs. The problem was, he had been found dead in the cells, why was he then turned over, it may have been that the Night Sergeant found him dead and panicked or was it something more sinister. They now put the operation revenge into action. Clarke rang the Night Sergeant who had left the dead body in cell 10. He knew he'd be waiting for the call.

Clarke said	"You'd better get your ass back here now mate we've got a big problem."
He replied	"What problem?"

Clarke said	"The guy in number 7 is dead."
He said	"What?"
Clarke repeated	"The guy in number 7 is dead."
He said	"Number 7."
Clarke said	"Yeah, he's dead."

The receiver went dead. Clarke and Shear grinned broadly.

Shear said	"Just think, he found a dead body in the cells and instead of just dealing with it the normal way he chose to be really naughty and leave it for you. How bad is that?"
Clarke said	"Yeah, but he didn't figure on hypostasis giving him up. What is it they say about revenge?"
Shear said	"A dish best served cold."
Clarke said	"And there's none colder than the dead."
Shear said	"Don't forget, he knows Lloyd in 10 is dead which we didn't mention, so he's coming in thinking he's the only one who knows there's two dead, if he couldn't cope with one what's this going to do to him?"

The Night Sergeant appeared in the cell passageway bewildered but trying to put a brave face on events, clearly, he was a troubled soul who was about to be unmasked. He followed Shear to the cells. Clarke was at the door to number 10 honing his look of dismay. The sergeant paused at cell 7.

Clarke said "In here, mate."

The Sergeant said "I thought you said number 7."

Clarke said "Why would I say 7, he's in 10."

All three entered the cell. Lloyd had been placed in his original pose with Hypostatis where it should be, at the bottom.

Clarke said "The custody record shows that he was OK at 05.11."

The Sergeant lied	"Yes, I checked them all about 5, he was OK then."
Clarke asked	"Did McCoy or Bradley come down the cells in the night?"
The Sergeant said	"No, no one did."
Shear said	"McCoy's visits are never recorded, if he did come down best to say so now."
He insisted	"No, he didn't."

As they left the cell passage the Sergeant opened the hatch of number 7, how could he not.

The Sergeant said "What now?"

Clarke said "No sweat, somebody died in a cell, it happens, just deal with it in the normal way, what else."

The Sergeant left the cell area unabashed, his brazen attempt at skulduggery teetering on a knife-edge. He guessed that if Clarke or Shear knew anything they would keep it to themselves, sergeants always stick together do they not. A close-run thing.

Clarke said   "Do you think he knows?"
Shear said   "He knows we know, yes."

The police surgeon arrived and looked at the body in situ. He opened his bag and went with Clarke to the surgeon's office to get the blood kit. In his absence, Shear removed the small digital thermometer from his bag. They returned to the cell and took blood samples, the doctor made notes and made marks on his small body map. He reached for his thermometer, and for a moment he was thrown, but passed it off when he returned his notes to the bag. Shear had ensured that the body temperature had not been taken. The doctor asked.

"When was he last checked?"

Clarke said "Eleven minutes past five, Doc."

The doctor noted the estimated time of death as between 4 and 6 am, body temperature 95.6 with the onset of lividity. The doctor took the safe option in the knowledge that the blood taken before and post mortem would show accidental overdose. Perfect.

Shear's crew were waiting for him in the canteen, they got tooled up and began their reconnaissance of the route proposed for the royal visit. The route was no problem, the problem arose from threats made against the visit by the lunatic left and the mentally challenged, the usual suspects really. Special branch were looking at creditable threats and likely locations of attack, standard stuff. Shear's job was to plot all locations from which immediate medical assistance could be summonsed and how best to get the royal patron to accident and emergency, or, as a remedy of last resort to the 32 Squadron helicopter for immediate evacuation. Not so much a wedding more a blueprint for a major disaster, but like all such visits the most likely thing to happen of note was that the Hoy Polloi would in some way disgrace themselves, it often happened.

As anticipated Shear was called by control room and directed to return to the police station and confer with Superintendent McCoy. Shear replied that his royal duties were incomplete and that McCoy would have to wait. Shear smiled at the deference everyone showed when the word royal was mentioned. It was never challenged except that McCoy had sent DCI Bradley to speak to Shear who joined Bradley in his car.

Bradley said	"Mr McCoy wants to speak to you urgently, how long will you be?"
Shear said	"What's the problem, sir?"
Bradley gushed	"You know what the problem is, there's a death in police custody."
Shear said	"Well, it was his turn to die, everyone manages it."
Bradley said	"But he died in the cells."
Shear said	"You've got to die somewhere, he was in the cells when it happened."
Bradley said	"You're not taking this seriously Sergeant."
Shear said	"No, I'm not, do you know that anyone who dies within 24 hours of leaving a police station is deemed to have died in police custody."
Bradley asked	"What's your point?"
Shear said	"Semantic somersaults and linguistic limbo dancing, Home Office speak for deaths in cells must somehow be sinister."
Bradley said	"Well, they are until we prove they're not."
Shear said	"No, what's sinister is finding someone in the cells dead and trying to cover it up."

Bradley had reached the end of his common sense approach to the problem. He knew that Shear suspected foul play but he didn't know how best to proceed. He knew that he had stalled to gain thinking time and that Shear knew it.

Shear continued "I know for an absolute fact that when they tried to wake him this morning he was dead, and in a state of panic they turned him over but forgot to turn him back, resulting in lividity showing where lividity shouldn't show."

Bradley was clearly thrown by the disclosure, all his university learning was of no help, what was needed now was actual knowledge only obtained from experience.

Shear went on	"Good thing is, Clarke and I got to him before the police surgeon, so all the little school boy errors were sorted. All anyone has to know is that he took a mouthful of drugs when he was stopped and as a result he died of an overdose. Blood taken before and after will show that to be the case and the coroner will record misadventure. No problem."
Bradley said	"I sincerely hope so."
Shear said	"I'll bet you do."

Bradley's silence told Shear that McCoy and Bradley had visited Charlie in the night for one of their little chats. Finding him dead didn't figure in their plans and panic took over. Their main suspect was dead, good or bad Shear wondered. Time now to dismiss Bradley.

Shear said "Well I'm busy with this royal visit, sir, perhaps you'd let Superintendent McCoy know I'll come and see him as soon as we finish here, that's if he still wants to see me."

An uncertain Bradley said nothing and gunned his motor. Shear joined his crew and continued his duties. Bradley drove off looking quite perplexed. Shear somehow knew that McCoy would now adopt a different approach when they next meet.

Shear said	"Let's make sure we get a lump on Bradley's car, he and McCoy are bang at it and McCoy's weakest link is his bagman Bradley."
Lewis said	"On it, Boss."
Shear said	"While you're at it, get the home addresses of Hanson, Bradley and McCoy, these three have much to tell us, all we have to do is expose their sordid little secrets."
Boots said	"Doesn't look like McCoy's involved Boss, Bradley said that McCoy thinks that someone's tipping the bad guys off."

Shear said "Never listen to what people say, watch what they do, words are the deception and action is the truth, remember Hitler's speech to the world 'we have no territorial demands'."

Foxtrot 13 pulled into the station yard and made their way to the canteen. McCoy, Bradley and Farthing were seated by the window and had their heads together. Shear caught Bradley's eye who pretended not to notice. Shear knew that now was the time to make his approach to McCoy.

Shear said "Control room said you want to see me, sir." McCoy said "No, we've sorted it, thanks."

Shear stood over the three until finally McCoy looked up. He gave McCoy a knowing look and asked,

"Will there be anything else, sir?"

McCoy said "Get about your business Sarge."

Shear sat with his crew. He looks them over and felt pleased in the knowledge that these were a worthy bunch who would unravel what was going on. Who was Jock and who was Bubbles would soon be known? Lewis had a lump on Hanson's car, and one was about to be put on Bradley's motor. Ken and Rohan were well good at playing the heavies, and Saaz and Rohan could go anywhere disguised in their Muslim kit. Boots was his number two and could be relied on for just about anything.

McCoy approached the table.

He said	"I've got an operation pencilled in for next week Sarge. I need two wee black men to infiltrate a gang of black dealers in Bristol, I'm thinking of using these two…"
Shear interrupted	"Sorry, sir, no chance, these two are not quite black enough to infiltrate a West Indian gang, and besides their cover would be blown when they perform Salat."
McCoy asked	"What's Salat?"
Saaz said	"Our holy prayers. We pray five times a day, you can't possibly ask us to mingle with infidels…"
Rohan called out	"I refuse to deal with the dahriya…"
Shear said	"Sir, you'll cause a riot here, Allah and infidels don't mix…"
McCoy withdrew	"Bloody hell, worse than Catholics and Protestants, I'll leave your two wee black men to their prayers."

McCoy took fright and returned to his table.

Shear said "Well done boys, works every time, introduce religion and you can get away with anything."

Saaz said "I didn't know you knew about dahriya, Rohan."

Rohan said "I don't."

Chief Inspector Brown came into the canteen and made a bee line for Shear.

He said "Sarge I have to attend the IPA dance at Headquarters on Saturday, I have to take a sergeant and constable, that's you and Boots."

Shear said "Yes but…"

Brown said "No buts, you and Boots."

Boots asked what that was all about. Shear explained there was a do at headquarters every three or four months to celebrate the International Police Association, free booze, free food and a chance to meet cops from France, Germany and Spain, could be worse. Boots nodded.

Shear received a text from Fink. He's found a runner for the Liverpool job and needed to speak to Shear. Things were panning out nicely, Royal visit tomorrow morning, Beano at the Narrow Escape in the evening and only three more weeks to the election. Oh, and the IPA do, could be worse.

Chapter 8

Shear's crew were in their best uniforms for the royal visit. Cerberus was polished and was looking its best. His crew needed to be in pole position in the event of attach as they were tasked with conveyance to accident and emergency or evacuation by helicopter which was on a makeshift helipad in Victoria Park half a mile away. They're parked in Hammer Street overlooking Mary Magdalene Church entrance porch. A police cordon was keeping the public from the entrance. Some twenty-five people were in the church grounds looking mysteriously like members of the public. They comprised personal protection officers, special branch and HQ CID officers, no likelihood of attach then.

Shear said	"As soon as Princess Margarine leaves, we're off, much to do today."
Ken asked	"Why do they call her Princess Margarine, Sarge?"
Shear said	"Her nickname Ken, tells you a lot about people."
Saaz asked	"What's the plan if there's an attack, Sarge?"
Shear said	"In that unlikely event, we take the royal to hospital or the helicopter depending."
Saaz said	"Yes, but we're hemmed in by the public, we won't be able to move."
Shear joked	"Tactical contact."
Saaz asked	"What's that?"
Shear smiled	"Run them over."
Saaz complained	"You're joking, we can't run them over."
Shear said	"If a shot is fired Saaz, this street will be empty in seconds, don't worry it won't happen, no one wants her head."

The wedding ended, bells rang, bishops in their mighty frocks and lesser clergy left the church and saw out the bride and groom. Princess Margarine was then swept off to a local country house for overnight celebrations, thank the gods, the cost of looking after a royal was ten times more than the cost of the wedding.

When Foxtrot 13 returned to the nick, Chief Inspector Cole was on the lookout for Shear and Boots, an IPA briefing no doubt, in avoiding Brown Shear managed to bump into Chief Inspector Farthing. Shear took the initiative.

He said	"How's the murder enquiry going, sir?"
Farthing said	"Looks like the culprit made his way to Porto and we've recovered the murder weapon, enquiries are continuing but leads are scarce, looks like we're going to have another look at witnesses and see what we can wring out of them."
Shear asked	"Are Interpol having a look at it?"
Farthing said	"Yes, they're overseeing the National Policia in Spain, should get a result there, they're usually quite good."
Shear joked	"I'm at the IPA bun fight on Saturday, I'll have a word."
Farthing lamented	"No buns, just booze and women, if you see that little toe rag Fink on your travels give him a tug, I want a word."

So Fink was still of interest to the murder squad, if only as a witness, Fink will have to be briefed as to what if anything he has to say. Shear thought Fink should be pulled sooner than later whilst Farthing's expectations were low, and probably best done by his crew so he could keep an eye on events. Shear text Fink and told him to be on the streets in an hour. The location was agreed.

Shear now sought out Chief Inspector Cole, best to get it over with he thought, Brown was in the bar clutching his can of Coke.

Shear said	"Hi Boss, can I get you a drink?"
Cole said	"No, thanks Sarge. I've got to keep a clear head, Farthing's still on the war path about the murder weapon, he's never going to forget that."
Shear enquired	"About the IPA bun fight, sir, you wanted to see me."
Cole said	"Nothing really, just be at the nick at 7 pm, transport leaves at 7.30, should get there for just after 8, Do you speak any foreign stuff, most of them are high ranking Europeans."

Shear said	"I'm still struggling with English, besides it's their job to speak English, it's the international language."
Cole said	"I failed O level French."
Shear said	"I failed O level English."

Foxtrot 13 drove towards the farm and found Fink making his way into town, Saaz pulled up and beckoned Fink to the nearside of the vehicle. The door opened and Fink was unceremoniously yanked in and onto the floor.

Fink said	"What's up, what's going on?"
Shear said	"Just making it look good Fink, you don't want people to think you're helping the police with their enquiries."
Fink said	"Oh, nice one, looks like I'm getting turned over, got it."
Shear said	"DCI Farthing wants a word with you, just a little chat about the murder, just tell him what you told them before, Jonah was off his head when he stabbed the commissioner's son, you tried to stop it and he stabbed you as well, same as before, don't add anything."
Fink said	"Why me?"
Shear said	"You're all they've got, he's just looking again at all the evidence, so when you see him, you're still in big pain from your injuries so hold your side and make out you're in pain."
Fink said	"Yeah, no problem, it won't take long, will it? I'm really busy making a fortune, I reckon Jonah made a lot more than he ever made out."
Shear to him right	"You're making a fortune for us, you get good pay for not doing much."
Fink complained	"Now that I'm a boss I should be getting a rise, I'm taking all the risks."
Shear asked	"What do we think boys, does Fink get a rise."

Everyone in the crew bus agreed, Fink deserved a pay rise, and it was voted that Fink's money would double. Shear reminded Fink that being a boss brought extra responsibilities whereupon Fink began to brag about how he'd opened a book and had at least a street name for his buyers and in some cases their actual names.

He said	"I've got a runner to go to Liverpool, well two actually."
Shear said	"We don't want two, we only need one."
Fink bragged	"I've got this girl who deals and never been caught, never even been turned over by the cops and she's out dealing every day."
Shear asked	"How does she manage that?"
Fink said	"She borrows her mate's kid, it's spastic…"
Shear said	"We don't use that word, Fink, he's got Cerebral Palsy…"
Fink asked	"What's that?"
Shear said	"Spastic is what it is and we don't say spastic in the same way that we don't use the 'n' word for black folk."
Fink said	"What's the 'n' word?"
Shear said	"Tell me about this girl."
Fink continued	"She's eighteen and borrows her mate's little girl, she's five, and she pushes her buggy about the streets dealing, bold as, no one ever looks at her like they're embarrassed 'cos she's a…you know."
Shear said	"She's got Cerebral Palsy, just call it CP Fink."
Fink said	"Yeah, that's it, that's what she's got."
Shear said	"Here's the deal. A week tomorrow Liverpool are playing Plymouth. All she has to do is get on a coach at Quanton and make her way to Liverpool. It's a direct journey to the 'Pool; overnight at the Pullman Hotel, which is nearby, and back the next day. Is she capable of that?"
Fink said	"No problem, cops don't stop coaches, how can it go wrong."
Shear said	"She'll have a small girlie Shaun the sheep backpack to take. A man will come to her room swap her pack for another Shaun the sheep backpack. She doesn't open either OK."
Fink said	"No problem, Boss, a good overnighter that pays, couldn't be better."

Fink was taken into the police station and reminded by Shear that he was still in big pain from his injuries, and to play on it and to inform Shear by text when he was released. He was left with a detective to be taken to McCoy.

Control room called Foxtrot 13 and asked them to look at what was described as a strange man who was playing with himself and causing a nuisance at the entrance to the local park. As they pulled up the young man began to walk away from the entrance. Shear lowered the window.

He said	"Just a minute, we need a word."
The lad said	"I don't speak to the filth."
Shear said	"If you don't stop, you'll become a casualty."

The lad drew to a slithering halt, turned to Shear and lowered his head in a stony faced 'so what' attitude. He was dressed in Doc Martin brown kicking boots, tight jeans, a long black overcoat. His red hair was crumpled beneath a black beret on which was a red star. Shear got out and pushed the lad onto the crewbus floor, Shear climbed in.

The lad said	"If I'm under arrest, you've got to read me my rights."
Shear enquired	"What's your name?"
The lad said	"I'm telling you nothing."
Shear said	"Well, we'll have to guess then. I reckon you're a dead ringer for Che Guevara, what do you reckon Ken?"
Ken said	"I'd have thought a young Leon Trotsky Sarge."

Boots searched the lad and found a bail notice returnable to Quanton police station for 3 pm that day, it was now 4 pm. Ken called Quanton custody unit who disclosed that the lad had been arrested for indecent exposure and that he claimed to be a revolutionary and was a card-carrying member of the Socialist Worker's Party. A further search found his membership card tucked behind his lapel.

Shear said	"People who don't tell the police who they are shouldn't carry bail notices and membership cards giving away their identity, all we need now son is occupation and address."
The lad said	"No chance."
Shear said	"Guessing time again boys, what's his occupation Saaz?"
Saaz said	"Court jester."
Lewis said	"Maybe he's a wandering minstrel Boss."
Shear added	"Or maybe the leader of the SWP."
The lad said	"You people know nothing of the SWP."

Boots said	"Ah the Socialist Wankers Party, were you holding a public meeting in Quanton when you were demonstrating the party's secret handshake and the audience mistook it for masturbation with you ending up in the cells, was that it?"
Shear said	"It's like this son, if you'd behaved yourself when we stopped you, you'd be well on your way by now, as it is you're now in custody, I'm sure you know your rights."
The lad said	"You won't get my address."
Shear said	"We have it, the cells, Quanton police station."

Having lodged the new age revolutionary in the cells, Foxtrot 13 responded to a call to reports of a sudden death in a known squat in the north end of town. The crew arrived to find a number of known addicts outside the premises who had nothing to say to the police. The informant had disappeared so forced entry was made. They made their way upstairs to find two young women on mattresses on the floor. Both had needles in their arms and were clearly dead, both were in their teens. Shear called for a forensic team and CID to attend. He had guessed what had happened. These two would have found a new dealer and instead of buying heroin at 30 percent strength, the new dealer supplied something much stronger, mixed with anything to hand. Death is no surprise. Shear briefed the teams as they arrived and was surprised to see Superintendent McCoy and his bagman turn up at the scene.

McCoy asked	"What have we got here Sarge?"
Shear said	"Two youngsters overdosed, sir, both still have needles in their arms so looks like they've seen a new dealer and bought a surprise."
McCoy said	"Yes, big surprise."
Shear said	"It won't take long to find who their supplier was, we're just about to speak to the squatters, most of them are outside."
McCoy disclosed	"We've had a run of these in the South West, two in Gloucester and two in Devon, see what you can find out."

Shear's crew spent time speaking to the squatters who were unusually cooperative. It was clear that their usual supplier had been hospitalised when he was attacked and robbed by a gang of Hells Angels who didn't like the deal he was offering. The Hells Angels had moved on after the attack. No one knew the new dealer's name but he was described as being a little guy, aged early twenties who wore a cream Panama hat and had a London accent. His description was circulated to all mobile units. The informant said there's no way he'd point the youth out, he only gave the description because two girls were dead, but he didn't see the youth's face, only his Panama hat.

Foxtrot 13 returned to the police station and changed into undercover gear and mounted up in the old battered van. Their briefing was standard patrol to support ground units, so it was general patrol and see what they could sniff out. They had a good look around the town centre for anyone wearing a Panama, no joy. Shear received a text from the Right Honourable asking for a meet. He tapped his Eyespy Tap and Track and sure enough Mr Ting was at home. Shear was dropped off at the estate with his crew tasked to stay in the area. As usual the Right Honourable met Shear at the door.

Ting said	"All the staff have gone home, Sergeant, I know that's always your first question."
Shear said	"Party time tonight then, sir."
Ting said	"It is indeed my friend, thought I'd get in touch, might need some more white stuff, that shouldn't be a problem, should it?"
Shear smiled	"Why don't I drop some off at the Narrow Escape, I can leave it in plastic bags in the watering can on the roof of the boat."
Ting said	"Good thought, and I'd ordinarily say yes, however we have a special guest here tonight and I don't really want any unnecessary visits as his presence must remain sacrosanct. You do understand?"
Shear said	"I absolutely do, sir, I'll drop it off here at about what time?"
Ting said	"Between 7 and 8 will be fine, we are meeting at the Narrow Escape at around 9.30."

Shear was picked up by his crew and they made their way back to town where they heard a mobile unit report that they had a young man with Panama hat in custody. They returned to the station yard to find the arresting unit unloading the prisoner. Saaz asked if there was anything they could do, the arresting officer asked that they search the prisoner's vehicle which was parked outside the library. Lewis was dropped off at the nick to gather intelligence. The crew made their way to the library. It didn't take long to find a large supply of drugs in the car. The surprise was that it was in NHS parcels and unopened. This stuff was pharmaceutical grade and kills if directly injected. How many had he sold they wondered and where did it come from. These questions needed answering and could be deflected at interview with 'no comment'. The crew knew a better way. Boots drove the car back to the nick. They stopped at the cottage and unloaded their find and then made their way to the station where Shear spoke to Lewis.

Shear said	"What do we know?"
Lewis replied	"Not much Sarge, he's done time for supplying and is well known in London but only for low grade coke and a bit of cannabis."
Lewis said	"Superintendent McCoy said to see him when you got back."

Shear found McCoy and Bradley in his office, they were clearly delighted with the arrest and expected big things following the search of his car.

McCoy asked	"What did you find Sarge?"
Shear said	"Nothing, sir, we turned the car upside down but it's clean."
McCoy insisted	"It can't be clean, bring it back to the Nick and have Traffic strip it down, this little bastard is well at it and we're going to find the evidence to get him well and truly banged up."
Shear said	"As we approached the car there were a couple of youths running off, it may be that they had cleaned it out before our arrival."
McCoy said	"They better not have done, get back to the library and find the little bastards, I want whatever was in the car back here."
Shear said	"We have the car back here now, it's in the rear yard."
McCoy asked	"What about the witnesses who gave us the description?"
Shear said	"No one saw his face, just a short guy in a Panama."
McCoy said	"ID parade a non-starter then."

Both McCoy and Bradley made off to the rear yard. Shear made his way to the cells and got the nod from the Custody Officer for an off the record chat with the prisoner. Shear spoke to the youth through the closed hatch.

Shear said	"Where do you keep your stash son, it's not in your car."
The youth said	"I'm not carrying anything, I don't even know why I've been arrested, something to do with my hat."

Shear left the cells and rejoined McCoy and Bradley in the rear yard. McCoy had two traffic officers and a dog handler searching the car. He knew that they would strip the car down nut by bolt until they found what they were looking for. It was going to be a long day.

Shear said "We'll get back to the library, sir, and see if we can find the youths that ran off."

McCoy said "See if anyone in the library saw them, passers-by, anyone, CCTV, just find them."

Shear said "If they're out there, sir, we'll find them."

The old battered van pulled out the back yard and made their way to the area of the library, Shear briefed the crew.

He said	"The youth in the cells is the guy we need to speak to. He knows that the only evidence against him is his description which isn't evidence and certainly not enough to hold him. He heard a voice through the cell hatch that the cops found nothing in his car so he knows that he'll be back on the streets before long, so we only have to wait."
Rohan asked	"How long do you think they'll keep him, Sarge?"
Shear said	"We have a couple of hours, it'll take forever to pull his car apart then he'll be interviewed, but the kid knows they've got nothing so he's only got to brazen it out and brazen he is."
Boots said	"They're all brave when the normal rules apply, the moment the rules disappear so do they."
Shear said	"You are so right, Boots."

It was beginning to get dark and there were three jobs to do, check on the uniformed officers at the country house looking after the Royal, see that the Right Honourable had enough coke for his Beano at the narrow boat and then when the youth was released from custody, introduce him to a no holds barred interview. Busy, busy.

The old battered van arrived at the country house as darkness fell. Shear left the vehicle and made his way to the rear of the house. It surprised him that no security was in sight, he could hear that a full-blown party was up and running so he thought it best just to talk to someone just to confirm his presence at the house. He knocked on the door in the certain knowledge that the music would drown any noise he could make, he then pushed open the door and saw the most of the on-duty cops, personal protection and HQ CID were throwing liquor back like it was their last day on earth. Margarine was the centre of attention. Shear closed the door and left having spoken to no one. Best to get away before any chance of an 'incident'. Shear rejoined his troops.

Lewis asked	"Everything OK, Boss?"
Shear replied	"Don't ask, what you don't know you can't give evidence about."
Tony enquired	"Bad as that?"
Shear said	"Bad as that."
Tony said	"What now Boss?"
Shear said	"Drop me at the Right Honourable's estate, I've got their coke for the Beano, then just wait to hear from Lewis about what's going on back at the nick."

Shear made the drop at the estate then parked up in town awaiting information from Lewis who was keeping his eye on events at the nick. An hour passed, nothing. Shear text Lewis 'What news?' Lewis replied 'No news'. Shear decided the crew could do with a break, the van was parked in the rear yard, the crew went for coffee and Shear made his way to the bar where he spotted Chief Inspector Cole.

Shear said "Hi Boss, fancy a drink?"

Cole replied "Yes, I think I might have a brandy."

Shear got a double brandy and learned from the barman that Cole had been there for over an hour. He moved to a table away from the bar where Cole followed with his Coke can. Shear could see that Cole's eyes were glazed and that he had had more than a drink or two. Easy meat.

Shear began	"So what's happening, sir?"
Cole said	"McCoy's got a youth in the cells he reckons is selling high grade stuff responsible for a few deaths in the last couple of weeks, so he's on the warpath."
Shear asked	"Is there any evidence?"
Cole said	"Well, we know it's him, the description is good, trouble is there's nothing else, they've pulled his car apart but nothing found and unless we can find something else to hold him, he'll walk."

Superintendent McCoy and Chief Inspector Bradley stormed into the bar. McCoy was bristling and clearly in a stinking mood. He approached Shear.

McCoy said "Did you find those little bastards who ran from the car Sarge?"

Shear said "Nothing yet, sir, we've searched everywhere and spoken to everyone in the vicinity but no trace, not a whisper, two CCTVs we've looked at told us nothing so we're left with speaking to local informants to see what we can come up with."

Shear asked "Anything in the car, sir?"

McCoy said "No, it's been picked clean, those thieving little bastards took everything, they didn't even leave a fingerprint, what is the world coming to."

Cole asked "Have you interviewed him yet?"

McCoy said	"Yes, but he's as smug as you like, making out that had been arrested because of his hat, he's a self-satisfied, righteous little git, ten years wouldn't be enough, a bloody good kicking is what he needs."
Bradley added	"During interview he just knew that we would find nothing in his car. I don't suppose his mates cleared it out after his arrest?"
Shear said	"We'll get back out on the ground and see what we can come up with."
Cole said	"I don't suppose we've got the wrong one?"
McCoy said	"Only you could think that Mr Cole…only you."

The Custody Officer came into the bar making a bee-line for the Superintendent, everyone knew that a battle royal was about to take place, the immovable object was facing an irresistible force. Shear was surprised by the Custody Officer's opening gambit.

He said	"Just to let you know, sir, I intend to release that little scroat shortly…"
McCoy interrupted	"You can't release him, we need to keep him in the cells overnight and we'll have another go at him in the morning when he might be more amenable."
The custody officer said	"Sir, I authorised his detention to secure and preserve evidence and to obtain evidence by questioning."
McCoy said	"Yes, yes, we know all that but I need him to sweat it out in the cells overnight."
Custody said	"Sir, you've searched everything and produced no evidence so there's no evidence to secure and your interview produced nothing so there's nothing to charge him with. All my reasons for detaining him have evaporated so I have to release him."
McCoy said	"There's no way he's leaving the police station tonight, he's staying in the cells."

An impasse had been reached, the Custody Officer was intent on refusing the charge and releasing him and a flustered McCoy was using bullying tactics, rank and sheer bravado to have his way. The Custody Officer still had an Ace to play, would he play it?

The Custody Officer said "Sir, I'm sure you know that where the custody officer is in dispute with a higher rank then the matter should be referred to the officer in charge of the police station for decision, now surely we can sort this matter between us."

McCoy said "If he stays in the cells, it's sorted."

Shear wondered if Superintendent McCoy or Chief Inspector Cole knew what was going to happen next. The Police and Criminal Evidence Act favoured the custody officer but in the case of dispute the officer in charge of the police station had to decide, that was Cole.

Custody said	"Well, I have to refer the matter to Chief Inspector Cole for decision."
McCoy blurted	"I'm the senior officer here, I decide who stays and who goes, me, I decide. I decide…"
DCI Bradley interrupted	"The Custody Officer is correct, sir, it's the territorial rank that decides, not the senior rank if it is not his

141

station. Your station is HQ drugs not Aqua Ponds commander. "

Shear decided to intervene, McCoy had lost the argument but wilfully refused to accept the loss. The chief inspector could only agree with the custody officer who had law on his side and even DCI Bradley had abandoned his boss in favour of the custody officer. Shear saved Cole from indecision and acute embarrassment.

Shear said "There is another way."

McCoy took the bait "Go on."

Shear said "We could bail him 'til Sunday, that way he's out of the police station, which is where he'd be going in any case, but the pressure's still on 'cos he'd have to report back in two days, and we might find something before then."

Superintendent McCoy stood up to show that he was now about to make a decision and finally resolve the matter, he announced,

McCoy	"OK then, here's what we do, Shear's unit can spend what time there is chasing up the kids who robbed the car. We'll keep his vehicle here so he thinks we might still find something incriminating. The custody officer can bail him on a short surrender to Sunday night, is everyone OK with that."
Cole said	"Good decision, sir."
Bradley said	"Here here."
Shear said	"Result."

The Custody Officer smiled at Shear and left the bar. Shear went to the canteen and met Lewis in the corridor.

Lewis said	"Nothing to report, Boss."
Shear said	"I know, he'll be bailed in about an hour, stay here and text when you see him leave the nick. Follow him out and give us his direction of travel, he'll be on foot."

Shear gathered his troops, they mounted up and made their way into town and awaited a text from Lewis.

Shear said	"OK, he'll be on the streets in about an hour, his car is still in bits and pieces at the nick so he's on foot. Lewis will text us his location and we'll pick them both up."
Boots asked	"What evidence have they got against him Sarge?"
Shear said	"They know it's him who supplied the girls but there's no actual evidence. The guy who gave the description doesn't want to come to the nick for an ID, nothing was found in the car and McCoy thinks it was plundered by some kids after his arrest. So they have nothing."
Boots asked	"What about the interview?"
Shear said	"He knew that nothing had been found in his car so it was a no reply interview. We'll soon see a different expression on his face when he learns that all his kit was in fact recovered and is in our possession."

Lewis finally text Shear to say that the prisoner was leaving the police station and was on his way to the taxi rank near the park gates. The crew picked Lewis up and watched the youth walking in the direction of the park. It was dark and wet, the streets empty. Time to offer help. The crew bus pulled up alongside the youth who was pulled into the van, his resistance was minimal as he was trying to work out whose hands he was in. The game was given away when the radio crackled with chat between the control room and a traffic unit. The youth was handcuffed and sat in the seat in front of Ken.

Shear said	"Where's your mobile phone?"
The youth said	"The cops kept it, I'm getting it back on Sunday."
Shear said	"Salt Marsh Saaz, no hurry."
Lewis asked	"Do you want tide times Sarge?"
Shear said	"Yes, please."
The youth said	"I've just been bailed from the police station, the boss is expecting me back Sunday night, I've got the bail form in my pocket."
Ken pulled the form	"Says here your name's Mr Horrid."

The youth was confused but showed no fear, he brazened it out.

He said	"They only arrested me 'cos of a Panama hat, nothing else, they didn't find any drugs 'cos I haven't got any."

Shear said	"A cream Panama, a little guy who's exactly your size whose name is Mr Horrid, that's you to a tee son, it says so on this form."
Lewis said	"Low tide half an hour ago Sarge."

The youth began to doubt himself, maybe he should do a deal with the crew…

He said	"I don't do drugs myself anymore, but I can give you the name of a major dealer in Gloucester. I mean I really want to help so long as it doesn't' come back on me."
Shear said	"We're not interested in Gloucester, we're interested in Wessex, what major dealers do you know here?"
He replied	"I've only been here a couple of days, I'll get you the names and pass them on to you, no problem."
Shear said	"You Mr Horrid supplied two young girls with pharmaceutical grade morphine which they injected, guess what happened then?"

The youth knew the game was up and that his position was looking bad.

He said	"Two little whores, they're both on the game, they sell themselves to everyone and anyone, they're well at it, what do they expect."
Shear said	"Your morphine killed both of them, they still had the needles in their arms."
He said	"Well how stupid are they, if I didn't sell it to them somebody else would, nothing to do with me is it. I can't help what people do, can I?"
Shear said	"You sold this stuff in Gloucester and Devon knowing that if they injected it straight from the packaging, it would kill them."
The youth said	"Not my problem, they're smack heads, morphine users die sooner or later, they're so bloody stupid they don't mix the stuff before they inject it, how daft are they?"
Shear said	"Looks like you're in total denial, nothing to do with you, everyone else's fault except yours, is that it?"

He replied	"If I didn't sell it to them somebody else would, they're lucky I sell quality kit, most stuff they buy is about twenty or thirty percent so they get ripped off at the time but they're only smack heads and nobody cares if they live or die."
Shear said	"So it sounds like you're doing them a favour."
He replied	"Listen mate, I know the guy in Gloucester who steals the stuff from the main NHS supply depot at the Express Park in Aqua Ponds. I can set him up for you no problem, he's the one who's sending it out at a hundred percent, not me, if anyone wants doing, it's him."
Shear enquired	"Name?"
The youth said	"Oh no, I'll give you the name when you drop me off in town, I'm not that stupid."

The van arrived at the salt marsh and pulled up in the car park by the channel. It had just gone midnight and begun to rain. Rohan and Tony began to pull the Sainsbury's bags over their boots when Ken pulled a bag over the youth's head. Shear climbed on the concrete base to check the directional arrow. Twenty minutes later the crew were on their way back to the cottage, two more hours before they were off duty, time to have a sit down.

At the cottage, Shear asked his boys to look again at the photographs they had taken at the Freemason's Lodge. They knew that McCoy and Cole figured in the pictures. Cole was in half a dozen or so but McCoy only showed in one, increasingly it looked as though McCoy belonged to another lodge and that he was on a visit to the lodge at Aqua Ponds for one of their ceremonials. Shear checked his high-tech kit. His Eyespy Tap and Track showed the Right Honourable at the Narrow Escape and the solicitor Hanson was somewhere between Bristol and Aqua Ponds, need to check him again in ten minutes to find his direction of travel.

Shear asked "Did we manage to get that lump on Bradley's car yet."

Lewis said "It's fitted Boss but not yet tried out."

Lewis gave Shear some stuff to input his phone. Meanwhile the boys turned on the TV and tuned into the Narrow Escape CCTV.

Shear said "Before you start on that, have a look at channel 7, Fink's CCTV should be up and running by now."

Sure enough the farm yard was in full view, poor lighting but enough to pick up number plates and faces. The boys went back to the Narrow Escape where things were in full flow. Both girls were present, the Home Secretary, the Right Honourable and four others, one with a mask.

Boots asked	"Who are the others, Boss?"
Shear said	"Don't know. Ting said something about a General, some high up naval guy, somebody else and he who could not be named."
Boots said	"If he took that mask off, we could probably name him."
Shear said	"If he took the mask off, you'd definitely know him, that's why he's wearing a mask."
Boots opined	"He must have something important to hide and it's not his willy, if that was mine, I'd hide it."
Shear said	"We need to see everything Boots, this is our insurance policy. A bit like the girl's menu, £10 hand relief £100 no holes barred. The full menu gives one hundred percent cover."

Shear checked Hanson's lump again, he was certainly moving south in the direction of Aqua Ponds. He texted Fink to see if he knew anything about Hanson's movements. Fink said that Hanson usually turned up without warning, but only on Saturdays, he wasn't expected until tomorrow. He told Fink to text if Hanson showed. Shear turned the TV off and said,

"OK boys, looks like things are on the move. Hanson is on his way down here, probably to see Fink, Fink never knows when he's going to arrive. He just turns up usually on Saturdays, I've told Fink to text if he shows up."

Lewis asked "What's the plan, Boss?"

Shear said	"If he turns up, I'll track his GPS lump, if he collects the cash then his next port of call is to deliver it, that's what we want to know, where's the money going."
Boots said	"Would be nice if Jock turned out to be McCoy."
Lewis said	"Doubt it, Bradley said he overheard McCoy tell someone that he thought someone was tipping off dealers remember."

Shear said   "No good speculating boys, just follow the evidence and see where it takes us. We have a lump on Bradley's car and we needn't get excited unless it gets too close to Hanson. Let's just wait and see. Just follow the evidence."

The boys turned on the Narrow Escape CCTV and were happy to speculate about the identity of he who cannot be named. Who on earth is so important that they cannot be named, they wondered?

Chapter 9

All operational personnel paraded in the briefing room for intelligence updates on current enquiries. Superintendent McCoy, DCIs Bradley and Farthing would lead matters on drugs and crime and Chief Inspector Cole would pick up what was left.

Farthing began,

"The murder enquiry is ongoing and is presently focused on Oporto and Spain, I'll be speaking to our Spanish counterpart at the IPA meeting in Bristol tonight who I hope will bring us up to date. Meanwhile the murder squad will continue speaking to informants and gathering evidence sufficient to indict Jay when we finally get him in custody. Are there any questions?"

An embarrassing silence followed. Everyone knew that things would peter out as the scope for gathering evidence became weaker by the day. Farthing was putting a brave face on things and looked to his squad of detectives for support.

DC Jenny Lee said	"With the evidence from Fink and the murder weapon showing a direct link to Jay, sir, looks like he'll be charged no matter what his defence is or how many alibis he can produce."
DCI Farthing said	"Yes Jenny, thanks for that, I'll see all the murder squad in my office after this briefing."

McCoy added to the embarrassment by telling Farthing that he could take his squad off now as the remainder of the briefing dealt with ongoing and immediate matters which his squad could not help with. Farthing left the briefing, his squad shuffled out behind him in silence.

McCoy said	"Now let's deal with some real stuff. Two young women overdosed yesterday using pharmaceutical grade morphine. We've had other deaths from the same morphine coming from an NHS distribution house somewhere in the South West, we'll know which house from Forensics sometime today. I know that DCI Farthing and his squad of lovelies want to get their hands on this but until it's declared a murder it's mine."
Cole asked	"Was anything found in his car yesterday?"
McCoy said	"Regrettably nothing, looks like after he was arrested his car was turned over by some local lads who had the evidence away, we'll know who they are if they turn up dead."
Cole said	"We ought to think about putting out a public announcement to warn people of the danger of..."
McCoy interrupted	"We'll do that when we know there's a danger, and until we hear from Forensics we know nothing except that the youth we nicked is surrendering to bail tomorrow evening..."
Cole said	"Carpenter."
McCoy said	"Carpenter?"
Cole repeated	"Yes, Carpenter, that's his name."
McCoy said	"When he surrenders to bail, he'll be interviewed by DCI Bradley and I when he'll tell us where he got the morphine or we'll shake it out of him and if he comes up no reply then a threat of a remand in custody for a week or two should do it."

Cole could see that any further conversation about Carpenter and the lethal drugs should be behind closed doors and asked that the troops should be released to continue enquiries in the hope of establishing who robbed Carpenter's car. McCoy ended the briefing and asked Cole and Bradley to join him in his office.

Shear's crew climbed into Cerberus, still gleaming from its wedding makeover. He texted Fink to ask about Hanson, Fink said he had heard nothing but expected him around midnight tonight. Shear then tapped into the GPS lump on Hanson's car to find that it showed up in the rear yard of Aqua Ponds police station. He checked again, yes, it was parked in the rear yard, Hanson had to be in the nick. On the way to the cell complex, he passed Hanson in the corridor as he was being shown out of the police station. The Custody Officer confirmed that he had attended an interview and that the prisoner had been bailed, charged with disqualified driving. He had been arrested by traffic as a known dealer but a search of his car revealed nothing in spite of their belief that he was carrying a couple of kilos of coke. Shear noted his name was Ian Curry with an address in Benmore, he then returned to Cerberus.

Cole and Bradley waited for McCoy to get off the phone. McCoy was clearly unhappy about what he was hearing and demanded a result sooner than later. All three sat down.

McCoy said	"That was the lab, they won't have a result until tomorrow."
Cole said	"We're going to have to announce that there's a particularly potent strain of morphine out there before anyone else is harmed."
McCoy said	"Rubbish, we don't know anything about the drug until we hear it from the lab."
Bradley said	"If anyone injects this stuff, we're going to have more bodies, we should…"
McCoy interrupted	"…We should do nothing until we know. If another body turns up, then we'll know who robbed Carpenter's car, won't we. We'll find out who did it one way or another then we can round his pals up and they can give evidence against Carpenter, that little bastard is going to jail."
Cole said	"If any more bodies turn up and it becomes known that we knew about the quality of the morphine, there will be hell to pay."
McCoy said	"The public know what we tell them to know, when these smack heads kill themselves don't think anyone cares a hoot, they don't."
Bradley said	"Sir, we've got to tell the public we just have to, I don't know if we'd survive any kind of enquiry if it goes wrong."
McCoy said	"I don't know how you two have survived this long, you're like a couple of frightened kids…"

The Control Room Sergeant opened the door clutching a log of papers. He said another body had been found in a flat next to where the two girls had been found and that packaging showed that the morphine had been cellophane wrapped in NHS livery, looked like one hundred percent proof like it just come out of the factory. McCoy invited him in.

McCoy said "Yes, we're just formulating the words for a press release about the deaths which we believe have been brought about by pharmaceutical grade morphine, you can take this back to the control room and get it out to the press, tell them I'll be holding a press conference at 2 pm today."

Traffic officers were at the scene of the latest death, another young woman in her late teens. The needle was still in her arm. Shear's crew arrived before Forensics, enough time for Shear to take a picture of the wrappings and codes, traffic needed no help so Shear returned to the police station for a word with Chief Inspector Cole who, by this time, was back in the briefing room with DCI Bradley. Both were engaged in whispered discussion which Shear interrupted. Cole walked outside with Shears.

Shear said	"I've just come from the scene, it's another young girl, if there's any more of that stuff out there, we're going to have more bodies. This needs a press release now…"
Cole said	"Yes, I know, McCoy just described me as frightened little kid when I suggested it but with this new death he's decided on a press conference, begins at 2 pm."
Shear said	"I've got a picture of the packaging from NHS with its codes, that'll give us the location of the main wholesalers in the UK and the local distributor."
Cole said	"The Superintendent reckons we won't get a result from Forensics until tomorrow."
Shear said	"That's because he doesn't know the codes on the packaging, but we do, seems to me that if you ring the Chief Security Officer at Express Park, he'll be able to give you a quicker result."
Cole said	"I suppose I should tell McCoy."
Shear said	"There's a press conference at two o'clock, sir, it would be a major coup for you if you could announce that the drug was locally sourced and that its distribution suspended pending enquiries."

Cole thought long and hard. He guessed that McCoy would have to have some information otherwise he'd know he'd been usurped by Cole, but at the same time Cole needed this, he had to find a way to be seen to have prevented more deaths and be at least on the same footing as McCoy who would seize every opportunity to be seen to be leading events.

Shear said	"Why don't you give McCoy the picture to think about, by the time he's been on to the lab you could have a result from the local distributors, that would keep McCoy off balance, he wouldn't guess you had inside information."
Cole asked	"What inside information?"
Shears said	"I have a strong feeling that the morphine came from the distribution centre at Express Park."
Cole asked	"How strong?"
Shear said	"Very, if I go to McCoy with the picture, he'll pass it to Forensics to be checked out, that means a nationwide search, and if you call the local distributor at Express Park, you'll get an immediate result. You'll just have to come up with a reason you called Express Park."
Cole said	"McCoy will smell a rat."
Shear said	"You make the call then when you're speaking at the press conference, I'll come in with a piece of paper which I pass to you. You then look delighted and pass the paper to McCoy, at the same time announcing that the source has been traced and distribution suspended."

Cole could see himself as an unsung hero here, he would be seen to be as astute as McCoy and maybe even a little ahead of him whilst leaving McCoy as the driving force in the enquiry, besides he wasn't about to jeopardise his almost assured promotion. This press conference would show him in the public eye again, yes, he'd go for it. So it was agreed Shear would take the picture to McCoy and Cole would make local enquiries with the NHS distribution centre.

Shear made a call to his friend at Express Park who headed security. A retired DS and an ex running partner of Shear who was able to say from his computer screen that the serial numbers and bar codes on the packaging came from Express Park. Shear asked him to wait for a call from Cole. His friend was also able to say that the consignment of drugs was overseen by a junior manager at the Park who had reported damaged packages having been destroyed.

The control room was awash with activity, calls were being fielded by an incident room manned by Special Constables. These deaths had created a stir which was ripe for the picking. Shear bypassed the queue waiting to see McCoy, knocked on the door and pushed his way in.

He said "You'll want to see this, sir, this is the packaging from the stuff they injected themselves with, Forensics should get you a result with the picture and serial numbers."

McCoy told his two sergeants to wait outside and beckoned Shear to sit.

McCoy said	"Who else knows about this?"
Shear said	"Only you at the moment, there's a traffic unit at the scene and Forensics just arriving but they take hours so it won't be common knowledge until later today."
McCoy said	"What about Chief Inspector Cole?"
Shear said	"He knows it's in NHS packaging that's all."
McCoy said	"OK, Sarge, tell no one what you found and delete the picture from your phone. I'll deal with this, now I'm sure you're busy."

The media were beginning to arrive at the police station, lots of them, so many they opened the rear yard to park their vehicles, some vehicles were large, incident rooms in themselves with large antenna and TV broadcasting discs. Shear detected some foreign broadcasters and guessed that three young bodies found dead in a squat were big news and the rumours that the needles were still in their arms made it seriously lurid and just what the public wanted to scorn, the more lurid the more scorn. People are so funny. An inverted schadenfreude. Shear decided to let a rumour spread and allowed himself to get too close to France 24 and was immediately engaged in conversation. He was able to deny that the numbers of deaths were five or more, he was able to deny that they were all found naked and subject to serious sexual assault and he was able to deny that they died as a result of a cult suicide pact. A good start. Tagensschau came next, seemed fair that the Germans should benefit from the same denials as the French. These two 'friendlies' would ensure that the news would be national headlines, at least in Europe, Reuters would do the rest.

Chief Inspector Cole was in the rear yard unable to find Shear amidst all the activity, it took a radio message to unite the two.

Cole said	"I haven't seen this much activity since the floods."
Shear said	"This is going to be big, sir, there's a dozen TV crews here now, I expect it'll double."

Cole said	"Get your crew and dig up all the Wessex Constabulary livery out and onto the stage, everything for the TV backdrop and find the force blankets to go over the tables, make it look good."
Shear enquired	"Have you spoken to security at Express Park?"
Cole said	"Just about to do that now."
Shear said	"I gave Superintendent McCoy the picture, he wanted to know who knew about it. I told him that you knew that it was NHS packaging and the officers at the scene but nothing would be reported until after the press conference."
Cole said	"Good, let's keep it that way, this will make the national news and my opportunity to be at the centre of things, high risk but that's how it is."
Shear said'	"Remember, you're the local Commander, sir, DCI Farthing is HQ Murder squad and Superintendent McCoy HQ Drugs supremo, you are the boss here, you are the main man, everyone looks to you for leadership."
Cole said	"God, I need a drink, I'll make that call now."

Shear's crew sorted out the briefing room which was already beginning to fill up with TV crews. The earlier denials to the French and German crews had taken root. BBC asked Boots if there was any truth of the deaths being the result of a suicide pact and BBC Radio London asked if it was true that the deceased were members of a cult. How well it all went and still an hour to go.

Shear responded to a radio call to see Superintendent McCoy, DCIs Bradley and Farthing in the bar. He knew things were heating up and these three would be at odds, the press conference was looming closer. He joined them at their usual table near the window. Cole was clutching his can of Coke.

McCoy said	"The Press conference is in half an hour, Sarge and we want to make sure we have all the facts to hand before we make a start…"
Shear interrupted	"Are all three of you taking the conference, sir?"
McCoy said	"No, just me and Chief Inspector Cole…"
DCI Farthing said	"Well, now that it's a murder enquiry…"

McCoy said	"It's not a bloody murder enquiry, we've got three dead kids who have overdosed that's all, and until there's more information that's all we've got, so forget about murder until the evidence tells us that it is. Besides, how many murders do you want? You're up to your armpits with the Jay murder."

Shear could see that DCI Farthing was making a case to be at the top table and that McCoy would ensure that he wasn't. McCoy was like a bull clawing at the ground and inviting all corners, he alone was taking charge of events and he was laying his marker down now. Farthing fell silent. Perhaps he needed some help.

Shear said "Nothing to do with me, sir. I know, but doesn't Section 23 Poisoning by Administering a Controlled Drug…"

McCoy said	"Correct Sergeant, nothing to do with you."
DCI Farthing said	"But he's right where the drug is administered then the dealer is guilty as a principal where it results in death."

Things were approaching boiling point, McCoy and Farthing's voices were raised and both had become animated, time now for a turn of the screw.

Shear asked "What are your thoughts Mr Cole?"

Cole took a long swig from his can of Coke…

McCoy said "Now, everyone, listen to me. Murder is not an issue here. I'll be taking the conference with Mr Cole, DCI Farthing will continue with his enquiries into the Jay murder, it's a simple case of an overdose involving three of them, perfectly simple, nothing else."

Farthing stood up and made off without a word.

McCoy continued	"I've forgotten why we asked you here Sarge, oh yes, is there anything else to tell us about these three deaths. I don't want to get ambushed by the press at the conference."

Shear said   "No chance of you being ambushed by the press, sir, that won't happen, they're not smart enough for the game if you ask me."

McCoy and Cole got up and made for the briefing room. DCI Bradley confided to Shear that he was right about procuring drugs and the dealer being guilty as a principal. Shear said that he was disappointed that he didn't say so when it mattered.

The briefing room was filling up. There was something in the order of 25 cameras with their attendant technicians and anchor men. Word had got out and unexpected observers were in attendance. The Right Honourable Khom Ting and the Police Commissioner sat quietly at the back of the room and remained incognito throughout. Finally, McCoy and Cole climbed onto the stage and sat at the top table. Lighting, sound and cameras had their final check. Cole began:

"Ladies and gentlemen good afternoon and welcome to Aqua Ponds police station, I am Chief Inspector Cole, local commander and this is Superintendent McCoy Wessex Constabulary Drug Czar. This briefing arises as a result of the three sudden deaths brought about by morphine overdoses recently detected in a local squat, where it is believed that pharmaceutical grade morphine was injected resulting in the tragic deaths of these three young people."

BBC asked "Is it true that the drug is of extraordinary high strength and being made available to other drug users who are in immediate danger if they inject themselves; what steps are being taken to alert users and avert the danger and do the police anticipate an early arrest in this matter?"

Cole and McCoy made the usual noises about how the drug was still being analysed by a dedicated Forensic team and lied about how a large number of officers had been drafted in to expedite enquiries in the drug community.

Shear left the room and remained listening at the door. He would let the conference continue until the time presented itself when he would make a dramatic entry and pass information to the Chief Inspector who would make his dramatic 'save the day' announcement leaving McCoy high and dry, if not speechless and all this on National news. He let the conference continue awhile.

France 24 "Can the police deny these awful reports that it is expected that the other casualties of this high-grade drug are in danger of dying in the immediate future?"

And so it continued...

Tagesshau asked "Can the police confirm that all bodies had been found naked and that it is part of your enquiry that this was a result of a cult suicide pact..."

Shear let the conference continue until the foreign press had enough to shock their viewers and establish conspiracy theories sufficient to feed offshoot programs viewed by the lower orders in the wee small hours. Time for action.

Shear swept into the room creating a silence as he purposefully mounted the stage. He appeared to whisper something to the Chief Inspector at the same time handing him a piece of paper. Shear withdrew behind the cameras.

Feeling at a disadvantage Superintendent McCoy took the paper from Cole with deceptive ease feigning that it was something he was expecting. Such deception was what kept McCoy at the top. Before McCoy could read the paper, Chief Inspector Cole announced,

"The news is good, I've just been handed a piece of paper which tells us that as a result of enquiries I made earlier, the source of this drug has been found and that its distribution has ceased..."

McCoy spoke "Yes, this was something I tasked Chief Inspector Cole with earlier today, information received from my informant has brought the distribution of this devastating drug to an end and I thank all of those who helped me with this matter in particular those whose identities must remain secret."

McCoy waved the piece of paper in the air, all cameras were upon him close ups from every angle were shot and crews waiting in line for individual interviews. McCoy was revelling in the applause and attention. He had established himself as uncontested Alpha Male and he knew it. Chief Inspector Cole left the stage amongst the tumult and joined Shear behind the cameras, they both left the room to McCoy who by now was basking in his own reflected glory. Top dog.

Cole said	"McCoy will love that, he thinks he's the cat's whiskers, bees' knees and the dog's bloody bollocks."
Shear corrected	"Testes. What are 'Bollocks'?"
Cole said	"Carpenter won't appear for bail now after all this publicity and McCoy will be there telling me I told you so, I could kill that bastard."
Shear said	"You're right, sir. Carpenter won't appear for bail and it'll be all your fault. Is McCoy attending the IPA meeting tonight?"

Cole said	"Attending, he's the UK organiser, there are twelve on the international committee, he's ours, he knows everyone who's anyone of importance in Europe, never underestimate him. Remember it's not what you know, it's who you know."

Shear replied "No Boss, it's not who you know or what you know, it's more what you know about who you know."

Both the Police Commissioner and the Right Honourable Khom Ting left the briefing room and made their way to the door to the rear yard. Shear left Cole and waved Ting aside. He asked,

	"Did all go well last evening, Mr Ting?"
Ting replied	"Indeed, it did, thank you Sergeant; so well that four of our number will be staying over until Sunday, he who cannot be named had to leave early this morning to attend to other engagements in London."
Shear said	"Not too early I hope."
Ting said	"5 am, I fear, 32 Squadron flew him back in time for breakfast."
Shear asked	"32 Squadron, I thought that was the Royal Flight."
Ting said	"Good try Sergeant, no 32 Squadron deals with all VIPs in and out of Northolt not just Royals."
Shear asked	"Is there anything you need for your second bash this evening, sir?"
Ting said	"The Home Secretary was intrigued by the wine you produced last evening, perhaps two or three more bottles I think."
Shear asked	"White or red?"
Ting said	"It was something biscuity with a sharp nose and showed a clean set of heels I recall."
Shear said	"That'll be white then."
Ting said	"We now have three more members who have been introduced to the brotherhood and very pleased they are too."
Shear asked	"The brotherhood, yes, High Priests, they have been introduced to the concept of ambush from behind, I must say it's greatly favoured by the girls, it makes them incredibly receptive, even he who cannot be named was quite overwhelmed by the response, I think that'll be his party piece to liven up the party."

Shear left Ting. He made a note to see to it that the Narrow Escape had another case of white delivered and then made his way to the cottage to dress for the IPA bun fight, he managed to escape from the police station without being ambushed by McCoy a narrow escape he chuckled.

Boots turned up at the cottage dressed as the country gentleman, hacking jacket, cavalry twirl trousers, brogue shoes and regimental tie, quite the gentleman farmer. Shear was more contemporary in an off the peg suit, not quite haute couture, but passable.

Shear said	"I didn't have you down as a fashionista Boots."
Boots said	"Just wearing this kit so as not to disappoint the foreigners at the bun fight."

They discussed what they knew about the prisoner Hanson had visited at the police station. It was known that when Hanson turns up Jock is behind it. Neither knew Curry or had read any intelligence on Benmore. Shear tapped on the lump on Hanson's car, it was on the motorway and clearly on the move. It was worth taking a punt and calling Curry. Boots made the call.

Boots said	"Hi Ian, Hanson had a word earlier and said Jock was sorting stuff at the police station, just to let you know that prosecution file will be going missing so a good result all round."
Curry said	"Great, how did he manage that?"
Boots said	"'Cos the prosecution file comes to me and I can put it in the Crown Prosecution tray or the bin, guess where your file's going."
Curry said	"Hanson said he'd speak to Jock and try and sort it, nice one."
Boots said	"Traffic were really surprised you weren't carrying."
Curry said	"They nearly had me but I spotted them so I pulled in to get petrol and dumped the stuff in the bin at the petrol station, they pulled me as I left, two minutes too late."
Boots said	"Don't forget to pick it up, will you?"
Curry said	"Just as soon as it gets dark."

Boots called the custody suite and found that Curry had been arrested in Quanton Road, only one petrol station in Quanton Road. Shear called Fink and told him that a stash had been placed in a bin at the garage and that he was to pick it up. He reminded Fink to use a nondescript car and do what it takes to ensure he didn't appear on the garage CCTV, when the job was done, Shear wanted to know.

On his arrival at the police station, Shear and Boots met Chief Inspector Cole in the bar. He was dressed in civvies strongly suggesting he was an off-duty chief inspector. Cole began to brief them on what lay ahead when a determined McCoy appeared at the door, he fingered Shear and pointed upstairs, Boots wished him luck. McCoy's office door was closed, Shear knocked and waited. Shear guessed that a psychological game had begun, he waited and waited. McCoy finally opened the door and sat down.

McCoy said "Well?"

Shear said "What are you asking me, sir?"

McCoy "What have you got to say for yourself?"

Shear began "Good result today, sir, bound to make the national news."

McCoy said nothing. He was leaving Shear to self-interrogate in the knowledge that it always resulted in worst possible scenarios. Shear didn't bite. He who spoke next would lose…Time passed in super slow motion. Shear was no stranger to interrogation techniques, he mused at the certainty that the rule of physics stated that every vacuum had to be filled and that when someone stopped speaking the other party was compelled to fill the vacuum. Shear decided to help McCoy by looking at his watch. McCoy spoke.

He said	"When you passed that piece of paper to Mr Cole, what had you two stitched up?"
Shear said	"I was passing the note to you, sir, but the Chief Inspector took it out of my hand as I reached over."
McCoy said	"Know this wee man, if I find that you're trying to have me over I'll see to it that you are well and truly fucked."
Shear said	"Before there can be a meeting of thighs, Superintendent, there has to be a meeting of minds and on that front, we are miles apart."
McCoy said	"Don't fuck with me, wee man, I don't fuck."

Shear left McCoy's office and found the Chief Inspector and Boots waiting for him at the back door. They drove off to the IPA bun fight at Police HQ Bristol being briefed by Cole on the dos and don'ts as expected at the bun fight. He said that if things went well, it was no problem to arrange reciprocal invites from the

Europeans. They could easily find themselves on away weekends in the likes of Dusseldorf, Paris and Barcelona all paid for by the IPA.

Boots enquired "I wonder what's the best language to learn?"

Shear said "English."

As they arrived at Headquarters, the cops directing cars to parking were dressed in pre-war uniforms, magnificent old-style helmets and white gloves, Cole drove through as if this was the norm, a number of coaches were off loading large groups of European senior officers who made their way into the main building and into the gymnasium where the vent was being hosted. Cole explained that the officers in uniform were either chief inspectors or above, the people in civvies were guests of the officers and were mostly sergeants or bare assed constables. The Oscar unit could be overheard bringing in the IPA president and entourage to the party. The force was really showing off, clearly the IPA was a very wealthy association that attracted only the best and the force helicopter was the best.

Shear asked "So who is the head of the International Police Association, sir?"

Cole replied "Haupt Kommissar Jurgen Weiss is the main man."

The gymnasium was decked out in Wessex finest. Even Boots opined that he didn't recognise the place and that he was quite chuffed that the Force could put on such a good show, they even had police cadets mingling with trays of drinks, the Force was showing itself off very well. There was something in the order of two hundred officers present and almost as many women. A quality band gently playing national anthems in an understated way, almost emotional. Food was laid out on tables on a help yourself basis. Shear received a text from Fink. He and Boots left the gymnasium and went outside. Shear rang Fink.

He said	"Hi, Fink, what news."
Fink said	"Hi, Boss, I picked up the gear, I used a mate's car and kept out of the CCTV. The bin was next to the car wash so no problems."
Shear asked	"How much?"
Fink said	"Six little packs, probably just over a kilo."
Shear said	"I saw that being dropped on CCTV, looked like more than that to me, weigh it when you get back and let me know."

Boots said Fink couldn't help himself, he wasn't smart enough to get away with a simple shop lifting, why he should try to steal stuff from us was a mystery.

He asked if Fink believed the stuff about the CCTV. Shear nodded. They could hear speeches being made in the gymnasium and decided to stay outside until festivities began. McCoy arrived and exchanged uncompromising nods with Shear and disappeared into the gym. Looked like a long night.

Shear and Boots joined the festivities, it was immediately obvious that the uniforms worn by European cops were of better quality than the Brits, their angular cut suggested a certain non-negotiable gravitas. The Germans sported the best uniforms and Shear found himself wondering if they might be improved by adding the occasional Iron Cross, maybe not, but it made him smile. The music changed from the softly orchestrated National Anthems to loud popular music. The mood changed, people were up dancing and alcohol was freely flowing. Shear and Boots remained on soft drinks, unlike Cole, who continued to hold his can of Coke while helping himself to doubles from the bar. When the wine is in, the wit is out. Rich pickings lay ahead.

Fink text Shear just after midnight saying he had weighed the find and sure enough Shear was right it was almost exactly two kilos in weight. Shear thanked him and sent him a smiley face. He told Boots that Fink had a rethink and decided stealing a kilo was best avoided, Boots agreed it was best avoided. Shear tapped into Hanson's lump, he was travelling south toward Aqua Ponds, Shear alerted Fink that Hanson might show, and in that event, he was to text if he arrived. Unusually Fink asked if he knew that he was going to arrive or was just guessing. Shear replied that it was a feeling in his water.

Shear and Boots sat at a table with a few other Brits watching activities. As the night progressed, people got louder and less inhibited. It was noticed that the main man Jurgen was making his way around the tables chatting to each in turn, Cole was quite drunk and would certainly make a fool of himself before close of play, the faux pas happened almost immediately.

Cole said   "They're queuing up to dance with that woman in the LBD."

Shear said   "Yes, she's very popular with our European guests."

Cole said   "Yes, I think it's the way she throws herself about on the dance floor, sooner or later her bra won't be able to cope and its contents will be up for grabs if you ask me."

Boots said   "No one's asking."

Cole said	"Well, she's been dancing with the German, the Frenchman and the Spaniard, I wonder who's going to get her knickers off tonight?"
A guy said	"I am."
Cole asked	"Who are you?"
The guy said	"Her husband."

Shear and Boots remained po-faced. Cole spluttered and tried to stand up but only managed to tip the table enough to cause the drinks to spill and one to fall over. Cole finally got to his feet and was immediately overtaken by the effects of gravity. The gallant Boots and Shear bundled him outside and left him dazed on a sofa in the foyer.

They returned to their table in time to meet Jurgen Weiss bedecked in a sort of Herman Goring outfit obviously created by a military outfitting fashion house. He was a tall, broad, blonde and blue eyed, the perfect hun, speaking perfect English. The conversation touched on the usual niceties of law and order and how the world could be made a better place. A high-ranking politician of the future. The chat lasted longer than Shear expected and Jurgen, as he insisted on being called, moved on to another table.

Boots asked "If his name's Jurgen, how come all his entourage call him Blashen."

Shear guessed "Nickname I suppose."

Shear received a text from Fink saying Hanson had arrived. Shear tapped onto his mobile and brought up the CCTV showing Hanson's car.

Shear said	"When Hanson leaves, we'll clock the lump, he'll be on his way back up here. This is our chance to watch and see where he goes."
Boots asked	"What about Cole?"
Shear said	"What about him, he's a big boy, probably asleep now."

Shear noticed that as drinking increased so did the number of people at McCoy's table. He recognised that most of them were Headquarter drug squad officers but there were others he didn't know. He and Boots made their way toward their table and pretended to take pictures of themselves but with the drug people in the background, this they could scrutinise later. They went in to the foyer and sure enough Cole was asleep. They sat and watched Hanson leave the farm with a briefcase, things seemed to have gone well. It would take him about forty minutes to get back to Bristol so monitoring the GPS was the answer. Fink text to say that Hanson had left with ten grand but had expected twenty. He said he'd collect the rest next week.

Boots noticed that Jurgen had been chatting at the HQ drug squad table for some time with no hint of movement.

He said	"Looks like Jurgen and the drug squad are big pals, he's been there a long time."
Shear said	"Yes, McCoy said he'd be speaking to him tonight. I expect they're in the same Lodge."
Boots said	"What Masonic Lodge?"
Shear said	"I'd bet that ninety percent of this lot are in Lodges throughout Europe, don't forget this is the police branch of the illuminati and the illuminata was founded in Germany so Jurgen is probably near the top of the tree, now that's power. If you want to get invited to a European IPA paid bun fight just speak to any of these guys."
Boots said	"I won't be speaking to any of the French cops."
Shear said	"Nobody wants to speak to the French, the old enemy, What's your reason?"
Boots said	"I've been to the Loo twice in the last three hours and on both occasions, I became aware of unsolicited admiring glances, both were French chief inspectors."
Shear said	"You ought to introduce them to each other."

McCoy stood up and walked towards the bar with Jurgen, they were alone and in ear-to-ear conversation. Something was going on, the laughing and jokes had been replaced by something more serious, there was an obvious deal being struck ending in a vigorous handshake.

A uniformed cadet approached Shear and asked if he could do something with Cole who had come to and was trying to find his way back into the function room. Shear picked up Cole's can of Coke and remaining brandy and joined him in the foyer.

Shear said	"Hi, Boss, I've just been to get you a drink."
Cole slurred	"Thanks, mate, I was just coming in to dance with the lady in the LBD."

Shear joked	"Too late, Boss, she left ten minutes ago with one of those Spanish chief inspectors."
Cole said	"Bloody hell, I've missed my chance."
Shear said	"Boots here can introduce you to a couple of Frenchmen looking to play some lacrosse."
Cole said	"That's a girl's game."
Shear said	"Not the way they play it it's not."

Jurgen and his party came out of the gym closely followed by McCoy and a number of HQ drug squad officers.

Jurgen waved	"Auf wiedersehen."
McCoy said	"Wiedersehen Blashen."

Jurgen's party left the building together with a number of drug squad officers. McCoy went back inside.

Boots said "McCoy's on nickname terms with Jurgen, Boss, he called him Blashen."

Shear said "Yes, it's a worry, isn't it?"

Shear and Boots returned to the dance. Cole had nodded off again. Half an hour elapsed and Shear tapped on Hanson's lump to discover he was in the vicinity of the Headquarters building, he was parked in a nearby street just outside the Headquarters perimeter. He and Boots made their way outside to find the GPS showing Hanson moving off in the direction of the city. Missed him by a whisker. Cole came staggering toward Shear, complaining he felt sick and wanted to go home. Boots and Shear took Cole back to the car and threw him in the back seat to sleep it off.

Shear said "Get back in there, Boots; we need a picture of the drug squad table, we need to know who's here and who's not, find out if McCoy is still here. Just find out whatever you can."

Boots returned within minutes saying that McCoy was still present but half the squad had gone. They both got in the car and started it up. Cole came to and said,

	"Are we here yet?"
Shear said	"No, Boss, we're just leaving, we'll have you home in just a wee while."

Cole said   "2 am Sunday morning, bloody hell it's the general election in a fortnight, just two more weeks, it's like waiting for Christmas."

Boots asked "What are you getting for Christmas, sir?"

Cole said   "A promotion."

Chapter 10

Chief Inspector Cole was disappointed to have missed the call from the Right Honourable Khom Ting, the answerphone message told him only that he had missed the call. How could he have slept through that. He told himself what he always told himself, drink less, drink moderately, don't get stupid drunk and try and remember what happened, he was too near his promotion to mess things up now. A couple of pints of water would sort him out before he returned the call. Too late, Ting rang.

He said "I've just watched you on the National news dear boy, excellent performance, the Home Secretary thought you acquitted yourself very well. Only two weeks to the election so things are very much going to plan, we must get together soon and iron out the nitty gritty, don't you think?"

Cole was confused and feeling anaesthetised, the events of yesterday slowly began to come into focus, he remembered some of the press conference stuff but little of the IPA bun fight, just as well Ting was talking about the press conference. Cole practised moving his lips.

He said   "Yes, it seems to have gone well, I'm glad you and the Home Secretary are pleased with the result."

Ting said   "The Home Secretary will be here for the hustling next weekend, final push before the election, feels that Wessex should be the home base as things were trialled here and it's from here that the final dash should be made, what say you to that, dear boy?"

Things began to dawn, Cole now remembered the conference ending with McCoy's hand in the air clutching a piece of paper suggesting 'peace in our time', the international press corps trying desperately to introduce a salacious slant on events, and the actual facts of ending the tragedy of young lives being lost as a result of chemical poisoning. Yes, a good result which should be celebrated.

Cole said "Yes, good idea, a final chat before the home run, I agree."

Arrangements were made to see the Right Honourable at his estate later that day. Cole decided to freshen up and get himself sufficiently sober to face what the day would bring, time now for a couple of pints of water…or maybe a Coke?

Superintendent McCoy was in the custody suite at 11 am to confirm that Carpenter's bail was returnable at noon, it was. He knew that all the publicity would have scared him off but there was a slim chance he might turn up, failing that a warrant would be issued for his arrest. Bradley was making enquiries with security at the Express Park attempting to establish how much morphine had been 'destroyed', how, where and who was responsible. It transpired that part of the shipment sent to Gloucester was reported as being received damaged, and against procedure was destroyed by the local manager. McCoy put in train arrangements for the local manager to be arrested, it being Sunday Gloucester police would arrest him at home and bring him to Aqua Ponds. How wonderful it would be if Carpenter and the manager were in the cells at the same time at Aqua Ponds.

Shear's crew were on a rest day and had agreed to meet at the cottage after lunch for an update. A Home Office Pathologist was pencilled in to perform Post Mortems late Sunday, no surprises were expected. DCI Farthing arranged to see the pathologist in an attempt to have the deaths linked to his murder enquiry which was losing momentum, a few more deaths would re-energise his enquiries and keep him in his post as Senior Investigating Officer. He had to make a link between the three young deaths and his murder, drugs was the obvious answer but McCoy wanted to keep the matter separate from the murder for reasons of his own. Another battle loomed between Farthing and McCoy, Farthing had better be prepared for the next exchange and McCoy was prepared for everything.

Shear was at the cottage mulling things over, trying to make sense of the evening's events. Hanson appeared at Police Headquarters with ten grand, half the drug squad had just left the gym at about the same time, McCoy was not with them and remained at his table throughout. The question was, who collected the money from Hanson? They were no closer to finding the identity of Jock or Bubbles, more needed to be done, more needed to be done soon.

Shear received a text from the Right Honourable who wanted to see him today at about 2 pm, it didn't sound negotiable, 2 pm was agreed. As Shear's thoughts became more focused a plan evolved in his head which he needed to thrash out with his crew later. Meanwhile he checked his Eyespy Tap and Track to find the Right Honourable at his Estate and the lump on Hanson's car was stationary in Bristol. No movement. Things seemed quiet. What had the Right Honourable in mind, he wondered. Cole called Shear.

Cole said	"What time did we get back last night, Sarge?"
Shear said	"Just after three this morning, sir."
Cole asked	"Didn't do anything silly, did we?"

Shear noticed the 'we' word and decided not to take advantage.

Shear said	"No, it went very well, you were on remarkable form, hardly stopped laughing all evening."
Cole said	"Oh good, I seem to remember I probably had a glass or two too many."
Shear said	"Nonsense, everyone was a bit drunk, it was a party, that's what people do at parties, get drunk, even Jurgen had a few, you had him laughing, you played a blinder there."
Cole said	"Oh yes, I remember, a good night, wasn't it?"
Shear said	"The news showed you on remarkable form this morning Boss, you're quite the local celebrity you will soon be a regular on morning and evening news."
Cole said	"I have to see Mr Ting later today, just wondered what your thoughts were on the recent deaths in relation to our new drugs initiative, it looks to me that these deaths will make a nonsense of our sixty percent reduction figures."
Shear said	"No change on that front, sir, the theft of the morphine and the sale took place in Gloucester, not Wessex, our figures are in relation to dealers in Wessex only, so the figures stand."
Cole said	"Oh yes, of course, I didn't think of it from that standpoint, thank you for that Sarge, just as well I spoke to you."

Shear knew that Cole was taking soundings on the activities of last evening and seems to have swallowed Shear's account of events hook, line and sinker, and he now has a story to put to the Right Honourable concerning the figures on the new drugs initiative. All was going well…so far.

McCoy watched the clock in the custody suite. Noon had come and gone with a 'no show' from Carpenter. He knew that Carpenter would have been frightened off by the press conference and made do with an application for a warrant to arrest following breach of bail, McCoy was furious. He turned to his bagman and said,

>"I told you Bradley, I told all of you, that little bastard should have remained in cells like I said, now he's done a runner there's no telling when we'll get our hands on him again."

Custody said   "We had no grounds for holding him, sir, even the criteria for bail was a bit iffy, ordinarily he would have been released without charge."

McCoy said   "No one's asking you sonny."

McCoy and Bradley left the cell complex. Bradley's usual objective view of events was becoming strained. He knew that he had a good job but didn't know how long he could continue to cope with the outrageous shortcuts taken by McCoy. He decided boundaries had to be set, he said:

>"Sir, if we're to continue together we need an understanding of what we can and cannot do. I don't fancy I'll get much thrift from the complaints department or the courts if I come up with the Nuremberg defence…"

McCoy said   "What's that?"

Bradley said   "Saying I was only obeying orders."

McCoy said   "Listen to me, we don't have to continue together unless the understanding is that I give the orders and you just obey them. We're not Nazis on trial for war crimes, we're the people trying to stop the villains ripping off the public and if your university training can't think of a way to do that then you had better submit your resignation to me now and get back to Research and Development where I found you, and remember this, Bradley, you're in it up to your neck son, you've been party to every move, every stroke, all unrecorded chats in the cells so time to grow up son and grow some balls."

The only boundaries that had been set favoured no boundaries set by McCoy.

Time to stand up and be counted or cow tow to his dictates. Moral fibre deserted Bradley who would now be guilty of passive acquiescence by doing no more than he was told. He lowered his head and was conscious of making no reply. McCoy was still the main man. A very dangerous main man.

Shear made his way to the Right Honourable's estate. He spotted Chief Inspector Cole travelling in the opposite direction and guessed that he'd briefed Ting on the drug initiative being sacrosanct and the three deaths could be put down to Gloucester Constabulary as the offences of theft and handling took place in Gloucester, not Wessex. As usual, Ting was waiting at the front porch for Shear whom he greeted warmly.

He said "Sergeant how lovely to see you, all well with you, I trust?"

Shear said "Never better, sir, I hope your Friday and Saturday was a success."

Ting said "Never better, a cracking weekend, come in, come in."

Ting busied himself making coffee whilst Shear sat himself on the Victorian sofa. He noticed an ashtray on the coffee table and an open packet of foreign cigarettes brand name HB. Shear tapped HB cigarettes into his mobile Wikipedia and sure enough it was a popular German smoke. What German of import could be in these marbled halls, he wondered. Ting appeared with coffee.

Ting's phone rang and was answered before it could repeat itself. Ting said, "Yes, you have Blashen shall I bring them up?" Ting excused himself and made his way upstairs with the packet of HB cigarettes. He returned shortly.

	"Weekend guest, now where were we?"
Shear said	"Slogan for the final push, or should I say putsch?"
Ting said	"What like a new drug-free Britain?"
Shear said	"My god, that's it, that's perfect, yes, rolls off the tongue with ease, easily understood, easily fitted on every front page, only five words which when heard is never forgotten, I see it now:

A NEW DRUG-FREE BRITAIN.

Every election is won on a slogan. 'A Land Fit for Heroes', 'Britain Deserves Better', top advertising sells most 'Melts in Your Mouth Not in your Hands', 'Because You're Worth It'. Yes, well done, sir, you have it and you coined it here at the heart of the trial in Wessex, well done."

Ting rose to his feet as though to receive an academy award, yes, he sees it now. If McDonalds can get away with "I'm Loving it" and sell millions worldwide, what can we in Wessex do for Great Britain with 'A Drug-Free Britain'?" Ting picked up the phone and rang the Home Secretary. No reply, he left an answerphone message. "Our new election slogan, sir: 'A New Drug-Free Britain'. I'd be grateful for your thoughts on the matter. Coca Cola do 'Open Happiness' so we can do this, surely?"

Shear decided to test whether Ting would disclose the name of his weekend guest. He spoke of the IPA gathering and said how impressed he was with his European colleagues, he mentioned that Superintendent McCoy was an organiser and that they were even graced by the presence of the IPA Chief himself. Ting showed no sign of acknowledgement, a silence that suggested he had been briefed to remain silent. Interesting times.

Shear said "So was there anything specific you wanted to chat about, sir?"

Ting said "No, no, just to let you know that the launch would be taking place here and we'll be kicking off with the usual press gathering, so just giving you the heads up and we'll be relying on your usual support, Sergeant."

Shear left the Estate wondering what Jurgen Weiss was doing there and more importantly why the Right Honourable chose to keep his presence quiet. The most important question was why Jurgen had briefed Ting to keep his presence a secret. Shear quickly checked on the location of Hanson. GPS showed he was mobile and was travelling south. He resolved to keep a close eye on Hanson who would, as always, be up to no good.

The Custody Officer rang Superintendent McCoy to tell him that an escort had just arrived from Gloucester with the prisoner Curry. Curry was in charge of the NHS sub unit who had received the morphine which subsequently killed the three young women. He had a great deal of explaining to do and had to explain it to McCoy.

DCI Bradley entered McCoy's office.

He said   "Sir, Curry's been nicked and is being booked in now."

McCoy said   "I know custody just told me, take a seat we need to talk."

Bradley closed the door and took a seat. He knew that this was the time he would be required to resign his position or enter the conspiratorial world of noble cause corruption. It was his call. McCoy made it easy.

McCoy said "Well Bradley, are you in or out?"

Bradley said "In, sir."

The matter was sorted.

McCoy and Bradley made their way to custody intending to start their interview of Curry but were told by the Custody Officer that they would have to wait until his solicitor arrived. His solicitor was Hanson who was on his way to the police station.

DCI Farthing entered the office and said,

"We need a word, sir."

All three gathered in the corridor outside the custody suite.

McCoy asked	"What's the problem?"
Farthing said	"I've been to the post mortem of the girls and according to the pathologist, if toxicology show that they overdosed as a result of morphine then the matter can properly be viewed as homicide and be investigated as murder, the reason…"
McCoy said	"You can't wait to get your hands on another murder can you Farthing, well it's not a matter for you or the pathologist to decide, it's a matter for the Chief to decide when he's got the toxicology report."

Farthing appealed to Bradley knowing that he had agreed that where a dealer sells drugs which result in an overdose then the dealer is aiding and abetting the transaction and is guilty as a principal. He was shocked by Bradley's answer.

He said "No, Mr McCoy is right, we only know that all three are dead and that it was self-inflicted. We don't know that it was a result of the morphine until toxicology are finished and tell us. We can't establish a link as to how they got the morphine, we may know where it came from but we don't know how they came by it, and we may think we know who supplied it but until we can prove it we've got nothing. So, we'll have to wait until we know and can prove it. Besides, the Chief is bound by Home Office guidance on when a murder is triggered for investigation. So you see, you are premature in declaring murder at this stage."

Farthing was outraged and stunned by Bradley's reversal, he could see that his opposition was overwhelming and that McCoy had somehow got Bradley on board. Farthing found it hard to believe that Bradley, usually known for his forensic analysis of events, could throw his hand in with McCoy who was a cunning low life who would get his desired results by any means and to hell with the consequences.

Farthing said "I'm not happy about this, when I get the toxicology report, I'll be reporting the facts to the Chief who can make a decision on the matter."

McCoy said "Good luck with that."

Farthing stormed off in a rage. He was beside himself and racked his brain on what his next move was to be. McCoy beat him at every turn and was determined to keep the deaths to himself, Farthing determined to outfox McCoy by fair means or foul and fair means have always failed to impress.

Shear was at the cottage and was monitoring Hanson's movements. When it was known he was at the police station, he rang Lewis and asked him to go to the police station and pick up what intelligence he could and bring what he had to the cottage. By now, his crew were beginning to arrive. Time to make sense of events. Shear knew that Ting had a weekend guest and that the weekend guest was Weiss, they knew that Hanson had appeared at the IPA gathering and was in possession of ten grand collected from Fink and he knew that Curry was to be arrested and brought to Aqua Ponds and would be interviewed by McCoy. At last, things were beginning to come together. He now had to wait for Lewis.

Lewis arrived at the police station just in time to see Superintendent McCoy and DCI Bradley take a man into the interview room with his solicitor. He positioned himself outside the entrance to the bar and briefing room hoping to spot the Custody Officer. He didn't have long to wait. As the Custody Officer approached the coffee machine Lewis engaged him in casual conversation.

He said	"Busy Sarge?"
Custody said	"The usual idiots, drunks, public order and shoplifters."
Lewis asked	"Who's that lot just gone into the interview room?"
Custody said	"He's just been nicked in Gloucester on suspicion of being involved in the death of those three girls, looks like he supplied the morphine, McCoy and Bradley are about to interview him."
Lewis said	"Who's his brief?"
Custody said	"Hanson from Bristol."
Lewis said	"Hanson seems to have opened a shop here, he's here a lot."

Custody said	"Yeah, he takes care of all our important little drug dealers, they all seem to know him."

Lewis texted the information to Shear who asked him to join the crew at the cottage. He noticed that the red light outside the interview room hadn't come on indicating that the interview hadn't started.

He said "Looks like the interview light is duff, Sarge, probably wants a new bulb."

The Sergeant knocked on the door and said,

"The interview light hasn't come on, sir, you'll probably be disturbed, no one can see that you're in here."

McCoy said "Just about to start, Sarge."

The red light came on showing that the recording equipment was now running. Lewis made a note that about 15 minutes had elapsed since they went into the studio and the light coming on. Lewis left the police station.

Twenty minutes later McCoy and Bradley went back into the Custody Suite without Curry. The Custody Officer asked,

	"Everything OK, sir?"
McCoy said	"It is."
Custody said	"Well, I need to know what's happening, I have to complete the custody record and if Curry's been left with his brief, I have to record it on his sheet."
McCoy said	"Listen Sarge…"
Bradley said	"OK Sarge, he stayed silent during the interview and his brief said he'd give us a written statement in reply to the questions."
Custody said	"Oh, full advanced disclosure then with time to talk over his answers with his brief, no wonder convictions of top dealers are so rare."
McCoy said	"Listen, son, it's our…"
Bradley said	"Time for a coffee, sir."

McCoy got the message and followed Bradley to the coffee machine, Bradley said,

"In the Custody Suite everything is written down, everything, so when we're in there we have to be seen to be squeaky clean. The Custody Officer calls the shots and he has the same powers as the Divisional Commander so we have to keep him sweet."

Lewis arrived at the cottage and briefed the crew as to the activities of McCoy and Bradley. Not much sense could be made of it except to say it was worth keeping an eye on. They mulled over the events at the bun fight and concluded that Hanson had handed ten grand to somebody, no doubt a member of the drug squad who had left earlier. They knew that Weiss the IPA boss was lodged with the Right Honourable and that the Right Honourable wanted to keep the matter quiet. DCI Farthing couldn't take his murder enquiries any further and there was a hate bubbling between him and the Superintendent, Room for mischief there. Bradley and McCoy seemed to have become best friends and Bradley would no doubt live to regret it. McCoy was poison, a toxic drip that could not be stopped.

The crew arrived for the pre-election briefing at 11 am. Chief Inspector Cole read the operation order and tasked each crew and individual officers with points to cover and polling booths to be visited, each was to do a dry run as the election was only ten days away. They were reminded that vehicles could be used without tax on the day of the election, a fact known only to policemen and party members tasked with taking those to vote who required transport, often used to call upon Homes for the Elderly who could be taken en masse to vote or whoever sent the vehicle.

Cerberus pulled out of the police station yard just before noon, time for a mobile patrol in favour of the good citizens of Aqua Ponds. As the crewbus approached the park gates, they were flagged down by a member of the public.

He said	"I've just come out of that loo and some guy passed a note and picture under the wall, it was a naked woman."
Shear said	"Have you got the picture?"
He said	"No, I didn't pick it up."
Shear said	"What about the note?"
He said	"No, I left it, I didn't touch anything."
Shear asked	"What did the note say?"
He said	"Well, you know, it was rude."
Shear insisted	"What did it say?"

The man was clearly embarrassed and leaned forward and whispered in Shear's ear,

"I like to be fucked."

With that the man indicated that the guy had just left the toilet and was making his way to the rear entrance to the park. Foxtrot 13 were parked at the exit as the guy appeared.

Shear called   "Just a minute my friend, a word."
The guy said   "What's up?"
Shear said   "Get in the van."
The guy asked "What for?"

The guy said nothing but clearly was behaving as though he had a great deal to hide, he said,

                  "I don't have to say anything."
Shear said   "Let me tell you what the complaint is and then you can decide if you want to talk to us or not. A man has just come out of the loo and said you passed a picture and a note under the wall."
He said   "I wasn't in the loo, I've just walked through the park."
Shear said   "We all saw you come out of the loo, so we'll forget niceties now turn your pockets out."
He said   "I haven't done anything you can't search me."
Shear said   "What's your name?"
He said   "Fred Forsyth."
Shear said   "I've heard that name before."

Lewis handed Shear a picture of the guy they found working at the mortuary four weeks earlier.

Lewis said "You live in Belvedere Road, that's right isn't it, Fred?"

Tony cuffed Fred and pulled the contents of his pocket onto the floor of the van. He handed a picture to Shear.

Shear said   "The note you sent to the guy said I like to be fucked, well we're the police, Fred, you're fucked."
Fred said   "No, I didn't, I didn't send any note to anyone."
Shear said   "Who's this in the picture?"
Fred said   "My girlfriend."
Shear said   "Does she always lay down naked with her eyes closed?"

Fred said	"Yes, sometimes."
Shear said	"Or is this a picture of a corpse that you took in the mortuary?"

Fred lowered his head, his body could hardly hold him, he began to cry and fell sobbing to the floor. Cerberus was fired up and Mr Forsyth was taken to the police station and booked in for public indecency. Shear informed Chief Inspector Cole of the arrest and attendant circumstances and suggested that Cole contact the Pathologist for a site meeting at the police station. Shear decided his crew should have an early lunch. Half an hour later Shear was asked to see Cole in his office.

Cole introduced the pathologist Mr Graham Carmichael and asked Shear to outline the events leading to the arrest of Forsyth, he began,

"Forsyth first came to notice when we spotted him on a Sunday morning outside the mortuary, his story was that he had a few things to clear up, we noticed he had no badge and he was up to his ears in deceit signals. He was nicked about an hour ago following an incident in a public toilet where he offered this picture as an inducement to a sexual encounter."

Shear handed over the picture to the pathologist. He looked at the picture and went noticeably grey, he said nothing and handed the picture back.

Carmichael asked	"What now?"
Cole said	"The question is, what damage will be done in the event of prosecution and the matter becoming public. It seems to be that this is a matter that does nothing to serve the public interest and is best dealt with in another way."
Carmichael said	"If it became public, I'd have to resign my post at the hospital."
Shear said	"Let me put this to you, if we can all agree then the matter ends here. I'll call in the force doctor and a social worker from mental health and give evidence that he's suicidal, he won't contest events as he'll see this as a way out. All things being equal he'll be sectioned for 28 days. We seize his mobile and computer and this picture will disappear. And all this under the heading of not in the public interest."
Cole said	"I agree."
Carmichael said	"I agree."
Shear said	"A meeting of minds, job done."

Shear received a text from Fink asking for a meeting. It was agreed that Fink would walk into town and would be turned over for a search in the van. Twenty minutes later Fink was found and pulled into the van for a chat.

Shear said	"What news. Fink?"
Fink said	"I managed to get rid of the two kilos of coke Boss so I can send the girls to Liverpool whenever you want."
Shear said	"How come you mistook two kilos for one kilo Fink, anybody would think you're trying to rob us."

Fink attempted to laugh the matter off but was unconvincing. He apologised for his stupid mistake and put it down to the heat of the moment and his inability to guess its weight which was put right when he weighed it. Shear let the matter go with a stark warning.

He said "Now that you're boss Fink you've got to get everything right first time every time. Another mistake like that and you'll find yourself replaced and you won't be looking for a new job. You understand that don't you?"

Fink said "Yes Boss, I'll make sure I weigh every one in future, I promise I will."

Shear asked "How much are we holding at the moment?"

Fink said "Sixty grand."

Shear said "OK, let the girls have twenty, that will bring us back forty fake, and when Hanson turns up on Saturday tell him you're short but you'll pay him forty on Tuesday, twenty for Saturday, ten for next Saturday and ten because he had to wait, have you got that?"

Shear made Fink repeat the deal three more times. Fink was sure he understood and Shear was sure he understood, this couldn't go wrong.

Fink said	"So when he turns up next week next Tuesday, Boss, what do I give him, real or fake?"
Shear said	"Let's get the money from Liverpool first, when that's done, I'll let you know."

Fink was dropped off near the farm dutifully repeating what had to happen on each day. He left the van with an uncertain smile on his face.

The Right Honourable rang Shear. He was agitated and demanded an urgent meeting. As usual the matter was urgent and, as usual, Shear guessed that Ting was in a tantrum about nothing. The crewbus dropped Shear off at the estate where a petulant Ting was waiting.

Ting said	"Come in, come in, I don't really know what's going on. I really don't, I don't understand it at all. Look at this and see if you can make sense of it. I certainly can't."
Shear said	"I'm sure this can best be done over a coffee."
Ting said	"Oh yes, of course, where are my social skills, take a seat old chap I'll be back in a moment."

Ting disappeared into the kitchen whilst Shear made his way to the top of the stairs, He could see no evidence of there being a guest present and decided to put the question to Ting. Coffee arrived.

Shear asked	"House guest gone, sir."
Ting said	"Oh yes, some time ago, now tell me what do you make of this?"

Ting played a recording of the National news. It was full of politicians telling bare faced lies about how there would be gravy today if only the people voted for them. Ting kept fast forwarding events until he handed Shear the monitor and asked him to do it.

Shear said	"What am I looking for?"
Ting said	"The Home Secretary's opening salvo on the election manifesto."

Finally, the Home Secretary was found and they both sat back to watch what the new Conservative Manifesto had to say. Ting sat forward on the edge of his seat, both hands on his cheeks and repeating,

"Now watch this, watch this."

The screen filled with the Union Jack being firmly slapped by the wind, solemn patriarchal music gave gravitas to the entrance of the Home Secretary appearing from the battlements of Windsor Castle, both arms outstretched to the heavens and calling out.

A New Drug-Free Britain

Archive footage heralded the muscular tones of Rule Britannia being sung by revellers from the Last Night of the Proms, eyes welled up and the need to stand to attention was overwhelming. Both Shear and Ting sensed the tide of emotion and sat basking in its reflected glory. As the Home Secretary began to speak to the strains of Land of Hope and Glory, Ting turned the TV off and said,

	"Well there!"
Shear said	"Well there indeed, sir, you have hit the jackpot, the new Conservative Party Manifesto spoken here by you and taken up by the party as its Flagship slogan. A New Drug-Free Britain! Five simple words that say it all, well done, sir. I'm so proud to have been here at its launch."
Ting said	"Oh, do you really think so?"
Shear said	"Of course, who could have possibly come up with as few as five words that would save the Nation, that every child would understand, that would strike the fear of god into the hearts of every dealer in the country and which make every thinking man look at every dealer as a traitor to the cause of a New Drug-Free Britain, again I applaud you."
Ting said	"But I left that slogan on his answerphone, there was no discussion, he didn't ring back…"

Ting said "You are so right, Sergeant, I must hold my nerve, of course the Home Secretary is a busy chap, and as you say, a Knighthood is in the offing."

Shear left the Right Honourable in higher spirits than he found him. His confusion gone and his subjective feelings of betrayal dismissed as a moment of temporary confusion. All was well.

Shear joined Cerberus which was called by control.

"Foxtrot 13, Foxtrot 13, 10–3 and confer with Foxtrot 1 over."

Cerberus returned to the Police Station and found Chief Inspector Cole who hurried him into his office.

Cole said "Sarge the Chief's coming down, he'll be here in less than an hour, I want your crew to get the rear yard cleared of vehicles and I want you and one of your boys in the yard to ensure that his arrival is incident free and more importantly, let me know when he arrives so that I can greet him. Happy with that?"

Shear said "Important matters of state then."

Cole said "Yes, when he appears things happen. He wants to see Superintendent McCoy and DCIs Bradley and Farthing, sounds like he's got an input on the murder and the overdose deaths."

Shear said "Good news is that he doesn't want to see you, sir."

Cole said "Oh, but he does, Sarge; he does."

Shear's men cleared the few traffic cars from the yard into the garages. No Waiting cones were strategically placed suggesting a semblance of order, Boots was asked to be near the entrance barrier and be ready with a premium grade salute. Shear pulled a reserved sign from the garage and placed it at the rear door. All was set. Shear radioed the Chief Inspector that all was set. They waited.

Shear met Superintendent McCoy and DCI Bradley at the barrier and told both that the car park was not to be used until after the Chief left. DCI Farthing was told the same. All three retreated without a murmur, reappearing on foot and silently making their way indoors. All combatants taking up their positions in preparation for what Cole guessed was to be a bloodbath. Shear knew better.

The Chief and his escort swept into the rear yard hardly noticing Boots' well practiced salute. His car took poll position at the reserved sign and his entourage parked to his left. Chief Inspector Cole opened the door with a "Welcome to Aqua Ponds police station, sir, everything is arranged as you ordered."

Cole climbed the stairs followed by the Chief, Assistant Chief (Crime), a secretary and Chief Superintendent (Complaints). All four took their positions in Cole's office and asked for coffee. Superintendent McCoy, DCI Bradley and Farthing sat tight lipped outside the office. Cole returned with coffee and joined McCoy, Bradley and Farthing. The office clock showed 4.05. Hushed murmurs could be heard from within with occasional polite laughter. 4.15, they waited in silence.

Five more minutes passed when the secretary opened the door and invited all four to be seated. McCoy took a central seat with his bagman on his right. Farthing took the outside seat distancing himself from McCoy, Cole was squashed between the main protagonists. Game on. The Chief opened,

"Thank you for attending this meeting gentlemen which arises as a result of the severe battering you chaps have undergone here at Aqua Ponds. First the murder followed by the tragic deaths of three young women…"

DCI Farthing looked as if he might speak but was silenced by a withering scowl from the Complaints boss, the secretary continued to record the events.

"I've come here today to thank you for your efforts in these matters. I know that you are fully stretched and you may occasionally feel unsupported from we chaps in the Ivory Tower…"

(Polite laughter…)

	"But let me assure you we are very conscious of what you do here and you have the full support of all my staff at Headquarters at all times. I've been thinking of how we might best help you and following discussions with the Crown Prosecution Service it seems to me that we could…"
McCoy said	"Join the enquiry."
The Chief said	"I'm sorry?"
McCoy said	"If we are bold enough to incorporate the three tragic deaths into the murder enquiry, in spite of Home Office advice on overdose prosecutions, which is not compelling, it seems to me that much time and money would be saved as enquiries unfold…"
The Chief said	"Exactly what we have in mind, Superintendent, the whole thing is time consuming and labour intensive and, as you say, if we call it a murder enquiry at this early stage, then much time, effort and taxpayers' money will be saved, will it not."
McCoy said	"Exactly what I think, yes, sir, I'm obliged to you for such forward thinking."
The Chief said	"Then it's agreed, OK chaps, onward."

The Chief rose to his feet and like the dutiful servants they were, everyone rose, keeping an eye on the Chief as he prepared to leave. Cole opened the door and as the Chief shook Cole's hand, he turned and said,

	"I'm sorry, Superintendent, I should remember your name…"
McCoy said	"McCoy, sir."
The Chief said	"Well done, McCoy, good man, that's the sort of blue sky thinking we need in the force, well done."

The office emptied, Bradley, Cole and Farthing stood in silence trying to make sense of what had transpired.

McCoy said "Like the Chief said, Bradley, onward."

With that, McCoy brushed through Cole and Farthing and swaggered from the office. Cole and Farthing were alone in the office, no one spoke, it was 4.35 pm.

Chapter 11

DCI Farthing was both confused and happy. Confused because McCoy, against all the odds, had given him the three murders he had been so anxious to secure in spite of McCoy's reluctance to let them go, and happy because his murder squad could not pursue enquiries where there was a real chance of charges being brought, thus justifying his position as Senior Investigating Officer. He would start with a conference in the morning with all dedicated officers in attendance. He needed only to brief himself on the prisoner arrested in Gloucester and establish his connection with the NHS morphine and the dealer who made the sales to the three deceased girls.

Farthing was astonished to find that Curry had been released under investigation, he hadn't even been released on bail with a surrender date, but released under investigation. He decided not to confront McCoy, better to speak instead to the Custody Officer and learn the reasons for his release.

Cerberus pulled out of the rear yard and made its way to West Street where Fink was to be met. Fink was a mess and clearly was confused as to what monies he had to give to Hanson and when.

Shear said	"Forget what you have to give Hanson, I'll tell you on the day so you won't forget. Now tell me about the Liverpool job."
Fink said	"Oh yeah easy Boss. They are both on a National Express coach to Liverpool tomorrow morning with twenty big ones, and back the next day with forty, that's right, isn't it?"
Shear said	"Yes, Fink, that's right. Just make sure it happens and keep me updated, I want to know that they're back and that they've got forty big, OK."
Fink said	"OK, Boss, I'll let you know when they're back with the dosh."

The radio squawked 'Foxtrot 13, Foxtrot 13, go now to the mortuary and confer with Doctor Carmichael re toxicology report over'. Shear and his crew arrived at the mortuary to discover that it had temporarily been taken out of use until the post mortems had finally been resolved. Now that the deaths were being dealt with as murders there was an increased chance of a second post-mortem and further more searching pathological searches to be made. Shear spoke to Carmichael in his office.

Carmichael	"I want to thank you Sergeant for your intervention in this most tragic case. I feel really bad about…"
Shear said	"No intervention, Doctor, Forsyth was sectioned as a result of his continual threats to kill himself, sectioned by a doctor and mental health officer, it happens all the time, almost routine. So forget interventions and remember, the public interest in a necrophilia would not only result in your resignation, your career would come to an end. The media wouldn't let it go, how many bodies, did full intercourse take place, did it include men, did it include children, what was the time frame, do we have DNA, do bodies have to be exhumed. No, Doctor Carmichael, it was just a troubled man who is now in the care of the hospital. So, forget it, it never happened."
Carmichael said	"Yes, I understand, thank you."
Shear said	"So how long is the mortuary going to remain closed do you think?"
Carmichael said	"About a week. I have the toxicological report here for your boss Superintendent McCoy."
Shear said	"I'll pass it to DCI Farthing, he's now in charge of the murder enquiry."

The crew mounted Cerberus and left the hospital grounds, Shear said,

| | "Good news, boys. We now have sole access to the mortuary. I seem to recall that Lewis had a brilliant idea in the furtherance of probationary training. Talk us through it, Lewis." |
| Lewis said | "Just a little game, Sarge, we find a new boy and tell him he has to attend the mortuary and go through the booking in procedure and continuity of evidence protocols…" |

Shear said	"Get on with it, Lewis, come to the point."
Lewis said	"Well, the bottom line is, when he pulls the drawer out, I sit up and give it 'Bugger off, this drawer's occupied'. He'll have a bloody fit."

The crew laughed heartily, Gallows humour is the stock in trade stuff of all emergency services, the more gallows, the more humour.

Shear said "I'll organise a new boy to sacrifice later today."

DCI Farthing studied Curry's custody record in disbelief. The Custody Officer sat with his coffee and asked, "Problem, sir?"

Farthing said "Curry was in custody in connection with three murders and four hours later he's back on the streets under investigation, what's going on?"

Custody said "No, he was nicked for theft of Morphine which during the course of interview he explained he thought that damaged packets were to be destroyed. His solicitor made representations for his release and in the absence of evidence he was released pending further enquiries."

Farthing said "But that morphine killed those three girls."

Custody said "Bring me evidence to that effect and I'll be happy to charge him. No evidence, no charge."

Shear entered the custody office and spoke to Farthing.

"Toxicology report from Pathology, sir."

Farthing opened the envelope and read the last paragraph. Cause of Death: Opiate Poisoning. The report continued with: Brought about by: 'Opioid overdose triad'. Just as he suspected, and yet the only link with the deaths had been released under investigation. Before Farthing could speak, Shear made sense of the situation.

He said "We know that Curry received the drugs and we know that the three girls died as a result of overdose. All we have to do now is link Curry with the kid who sold the drugs to the girls' deaths and we're home and dry, trouble is, the Doctrine of Remoteness rather gets in the way, and the argument that a butterfly spreading its wings in Borneo contributes to a storm in England doesn't cut it. We need evidence beyond reasonable doubt that that morphine killed those girls, an actual causal link and we're a million miles from that."

Custody said	"Two million."
Farthing said	"I'll listen to the taped interview."

Shear followed Farthing from the custody office and continued the conversation in the corridor.

	"I'll deny having this conversation but, what you need to know is that when Superintendent McCoy and DCI Bradley entered the room with Curry and his brief, the interview didn't start right away. You'll need to check what time he was booked out for interview and when the interview actually started, you'll find that there's about fifteen minutes not accounted for."
Farthing said	"Thanks, Sarge."
Shear said	"No, thanks, this conversation didn't take place."

Shear saw Chief Inspector Cole making his way to the bar, he followed him in.

Shear said	"Can I get you a drink, sir."
Cole said	"A brandy would be nice, thanks Sarge."

Shear took a large brandy to the table and invited himself to sit.

He said	"What news, sir?"
Cole said	"Where to start, election is a week away, we've got four murders on our hands, Superintendent McCoy and DCI Farthing are daggers drawn, add to that…"
Shear said	"What I meant was, I understand things are to be kicked-off here for the election."
Cole said	"Yes, I believe the Home Secretary is using Wessex as the lynchpin for his 'A New Drug-Free Britain' campaign, sounds catchy, easy to remember, popular with the public. A master stroke really, I expect his whiz kids at the Home Office came up with that one."

Shear decided to put the question to Cole about his knowledge of any relationship that exists between Weiss and the Right Honourable, he'd use his nickname and watch for any reaction.

He said	"I thought that Mr Ting might have attended our bunfight at Headquarters, he missed an opportunity to meet Blashen."
Cole said	"Who's Blashen?"
Shear said	"Sorry, forgot, you'd had a drink or two."
Cole said	"Or three."

It was clear that Cole knew nothing about Weiss being a guest of the Right Honourable. This matter seems to be a closely guarded secret.

Shear made his way to the control room where he found a probationary constable undergoing his one-week attachment to communications. He spoke to the Control Room Sergeant and arranged to borrow the constable for mortuary duties. His name was Jeff.

Shear found his crew and announced that he had found a sacrificial lamb for the mortuary spoof, a young constable just back from training school with four month's service. Perfect. The whole crew was quite excited about the prospect of the horror that would appear on the Constable's face and began to lay bets on the outcome – running for his life was favourite.

The crew made their way to the mortuary and parked up outside the near entrance where Shear wanted to go over what was about to happen, a sort of rehearsal.

Shear said	"OK, it's getting dark and I've arranged for Jeff to be brought here in about twenty minutes, the plan is, we go into the mortuary and open up the booking-in register, prepare the toe identification labels, identification forms and cameras, all ready to receive the deceased. When Jeff arrives, I'll explain all the stuff and ask him to pull out a bottom drawer in preparation for the body, any questions?"
Lewis said	"How old is the probationer?"
Shear said	"Jeff is in his early twenties, about 23."
Lewis said	"Great, this'll be a scream, he'll pull the drawer out and I'll sit up giving it 'Bugger off, this drawer's occupied'."
Shear said	"Yes, I'm sure the contents of his bowels will escape him."

The crew much excited and giggling with anticipation went inside and opened up the mortuary. The booking-in register was opened, toe labels laid out together with the camera.

Shear said "Get in the drawer, Lewis, and try to remain perfectly quiet."

Lewis pulled open the drawer and climbed in, lay down and covered himself with the white sheet. Shear pushed the drawer closed. The new boy Jeff was in the next drawer and said,

"Cold in here, innit?"

Lewis shruck and spontaneously tried to sit up crashing his head into the drawer above. Great peels of belly laughter escaped the crew and Jeff was helped out of the drawer and thanked for his participation. Lewis said,

"This isn't fucking funny."

Shear said "You're right, it's absolutely hilarious."

The crew rocked with laughter, some were holding their stomachs anticipating they might explode, the laughter increased and became a lather of self-congratulatory plaudits, would it ever end.

The next day the murder squad waited in anticipation of the arrival of DCI Farthing who entered the briefing room with a spring in his step. He climbed the stage and placed himself behind the lectern, he looked purposeful. A small round of applause spontaneously arose from the murder squad detectives, clearly what Farthing had to say had somehow leaked, his smile increased as did the applause.

Such excitement. Everyone knew they were on the brink of what would be a national favourite, three young women dead with much salacious intrigue, so much in fact that the national sense of curiosity had been excited sufficiently that the newspapers were hungry for more, true or false came a poor second to the need to answer the already asked questions, was this a cult, a suicide pact, a sexual triple murder, the press had their big guns out in force and the big guns did not recognise boundaries.

Farthing outlined the proposed schedule of enquiries. A team would re-interview the staff at the NHS site, a second team would investigate the antecedence on Curry and lay bare all intelligence on his activities and the third team would be tasked with making a link between Curry, the sale to the dealer and the dealer's sale to the girls. They had their work cut out, a small miracle would be useful. After the briefing, Farthing spoke privately to two of his detective sergeants. He alerted them to the fact that twelve minutes had elapsed from the time Superintendent McCoy and DCI Bradley entered the interview room with Curry and his brief. The tape was not turned on for a full twelve minutes and an explanation was needed. He invited possible explanations. A silence followed while they processed all possible eventualities. Both agreed that something sinister was afoot and the matter was best put directly to McCoy or Bradley.

With that Farthing got the heads-up that McCoy and Bradley had just entered the corridor and were heading their way. He decided on confrontation in a nonconfrontational way. As McCoy and Bradley drew near, he said,

"Ah there you are, sir, I've just listened to the interview tape on Curry, it seems that he was in the interview room for some time before the tape was turned on, was there a problem?"

Both McCoy and Bradley knew they were being confronted and spoke as one, as though from a well-rehearsed script,

They said	"Sick."
McCoy said	"He was so nervous he could hardly speak, said he felt ill."
Bradley added	"Yes, he had a couple of glasses of water before we could get started, I thought he was going to be sick in the interview room."

Farthing was thrown by the reply that seemed a perfect explanation that accounted for the delay. He was at a loss as to how to proceed so limply said,

"Ah that explains it, thanks for that."

Bradley had assumed the same level of arrogance displayed by McCoy and Farthing's urge to bring both the bastards from their high horses was reaching uncontrollable levels. His pot was near boiling.

McCoy said "I'll leave you to your wee murders, Farthing. You've got four now, I would have thought you'd have charged someone by now, you better get on with it, the Chief will be wanting results and as sure as hell so will the press. I'll be calling another press conference at the weekend. Have answers by then, won't you?"

Farthing's toes curled, he could feel his blood reaching boiling point, his two sergeants cajoled him back into the briefing room where all three stared at the floor clenched knuckles and steaming with a collective hate of both McCoy and Bradley. No words were needed, they just knew that somehow, they had to cause harm to them both...very serious harm.

Election fever was mounting, only six days to go before ballots were to be cast and a new government appointed to take control of the country. Shear's crew decided to have lunch in the bar and watch the national news. The second item showed the Prime Minister leaving Downing Street for PMQs. The usual political pundits shouted the usual questions and unusually the Prime Minister walked to the cameras and spoke,

"I ask the good people of this country to join me in our new bold and determined effort once again to take charge of the country under the watchword of…"

He leaned into the camera, paused and in as solemn a face as he could compose said:

"A New Drug-Free Britain."

The public clamour from the gates of Downing Street echoed the words 'A New Drug-Free Britain', the chorus was tumultuous, it was loud and it was virtuosic. There was honest unity in their cries whose intensity increased as the PM was driven through the crowd to the exhalations of the public. The cameras captured the emotion of the moment and the tear-filled faces of the crowd. Clearly the PM was on a winner.

Chief Inspector Cole smiled broadly as he played with the new title that must surely come his way; 'Superintendent Cole, QPM'. How well it sounded. Richly deserved and long overdue. Cole caught the eye of Shear and beckoned him to his table.

Cole said	"Well, Sarge, what a powerful speech from the PM."
Shear said	"Yes, wonderful, sir, this time next week he'll continue in office and his supporters will be generously rewarded I'm sure, there is a promotion in this for you I'm sure."
Cole said	"Do you really think so?"
Shear replied	"It's screamingly obvious, it was here that the new initiative was trialled, it was you who were here when it was born, it was you who saw it through all its challenges and setbacks and in spite of everything you have been instrumental in delivering what is now the Prime Minister's watchword, 'A New Drug-Free Britain'. My god if this doesn't deserve a Queen's Police Medal I don't know what does. Even Superintendent McCoy had better look out, there's a real danger that the new Drug Supremo could be you, by God there is."

Cole smiled the smile of the righteous, he could hardly contain himself, he could feel himself glow.

Shear gathered his crew together for a mobile patrol of Aqua Ponds, Cerberus took them to a quiet road near the town gardens for a spot of reflection. Shear looked at this crew. Saaz as always drove Cerberus, a quiet thinking man who was always reliable. Rohan and Saaz being Muslims were running mates but Rohan was the more assertive, he could always be relied upon when the chips were down. Boots sat in his usual seat behind Shear, the oldest of the crew, a dutiful servant always up for challenge. Tony was at the rear with Ken, Ken was a Force Majeure, a bruiser who could think. Being next to Ken was his conscience, Tony. Tony was a deep thinker who kept the crew noble in times of necessary corruption. That left Lewis, a tall gangly individual always full of bright ideas and up for any activity however challenging, although smarting from his humiliation of the Mortuary incident he now laughed about the matter, stoicism personified. A solid crew of worthy individuals, Shear felt privileged to command them.

Shear said	"Well, boys, are we any nearer Jock or Bubbles, your thoughts."
Boots said	"Those pictures we took at the IPA bunfight were quite useful Boss. When Hanson rolled up with the money, we know that half the drug squad had left the party and gone outside. If you look at the pics, you'll see who left and who stayed. There's a tall blond WDC who left as Hanson turned up…"
Shear said	"Yes, go on."
Boots said	"Look at her hair."

The phone was passed around the crew, each looked in turn at the picture wondering what it was that was about to be disclosed.

Boots said "Well?"

Shear said "Well, what?"

Boots explained that her hair was a mass of loose blonde curls and looked like she just lifted her face out of a bubble bath. If anyone was called bubbles, it would be her. They all had another look at the picture and agreed that had she been a member of their crew she would probably be called Bubbles.

Shear said	"What's her name?"
Boots said	"Belinda."
Shear said	"And her nick name?"
Boots said	"Bindy."
Shear said	"Not Bubbles then."

Boots felt a little silly and began to explain his thoughts. Shear said,

"Nice try, Boots, but she's not Bubbles."

Shear asked	"Were any of the others who left Scottish thugs?"
Boots said	"No, Boss, four English and one Welsh, no Scots."
Shear said	"We're no further forward, so it's time for us to take charge of events and flush them out. That's Jock the tipster and money man. His Boss Bubbles and while we're at it we'll see if we can bring Hanson down. In fact, we'll probably have to use Hanson to collar the other two."

Shear laid out his plan to the crew who were delighted with how brilliantly simple it was, they were especially tickled by the Catch-22 implant which would result in their exposure however they defended their position. A sort of double jeopardy finale. Not unlike the best laid plans of Lewis when attempting to put the frighteners on the new boy. It would blow up in their faces. Yes, the crew and Shear fell quiet and contemplated the action. They decided to call it the Nuclear Option. Ken pointed to the park and said,

"Look, isn't that Tuppence?"

Everyone looked and sure enough it was Tuppence making her way through the park in the direction of Cerberus. Shear left the vehicle and caught up with her at the wooden bridge. Tuppence knew Shear as a policeman but was unaware of his connection with the Narrow Escape.

He said	"Hi, Tuppence, how are you?"
She said	"Hi, I was just going to the shops for my mum, she's run out of food."
Shear said	"Oh, I thought you'd have taken care of your mum better than that."
She said	"Oh, you know what she's like, always a bit drunk and if I'm not there she doesn't look after herself."
Shear said	"Oh, have you been away?"

Shear could see she was dying to tell him. She lit a cigarette and in an effort to impress Shear, she said,

"I know one of your bosses."

Shear could see that she was fingering a packet of HB cigarettes, much enjoyed by smokers in Germany. Her next disclosure was staggering…

"Do you know Bubbles?"

Shear said	"Bubbles."
Tuppence said	"Yes, I'd thought you'd know him, he's a big boss."
Shear said	"Where did you meet him?"

Tuppence became hesitant and knew that had been sworn to secrecy but thought she'd give enough to Shear just to show him that she had some clout in the world.

	"I was away in the country for a couple of days and I met Bubbles, he's a proper gent."
Shear said	"Yes, I think I've heard of him now that you mention it, where in the country did you meet him?"
Tuppence said	"That's a secret, but a friend of mine has a big house in its own woods."

Shear asked to use Tuppence's phone while she popped into the corner shop. She reappeared a few minutes later and said,

	"You haven't wished me happy birthday."
Shear said	"Oh, happy birthday, how old are you now?"
She said	"15, but I'm big for my age."

They both laughed, Tuppence continued her journey and Shear returned to the crewbus checking his Eyespy Tap and Track which was now an app showing the location and movements of Tuppence.

Shear climbed into the crewbus and said,

"We know that the IPA boss is Jurgen Weiss, and we know that his pals use his nickname, remind me Boots, what's his nickname?"

Boots said   "Blashen Boss."

Shear said   "Lewis, type Blashen into Google and ask it what Blashen means in German."

Lewis set about the interrogation of his mobile phone and tapped on enquiry.

"Christ almighty!"

Shear said   "And?"

Lewis said   "Bubbles, Bubbles Boss."

A silence overtook Cerberus, the crew looked at one another as the revelation took hold, eventually Shear said,

"So, we now know who Bubbles is, the top Cop of the European Division of the International Police Association. We only need to identify Jock whoever he or she is. And guess what…?"

Boots croaked   "Bubbles will lead us to Jock."

Shear said   "Correct."

Tuppence unwittingly gave me Bubbles' name, I happen to know that he was a guest of the Right Honourable when I visited him at his estate. He had left his German cigarettes downstairs and rang down to speak to the Right Honourable who said he'd bring them up. He used his nickname Blashen. Oh, and guess what type of cigarettes I've just found Tuppence smoking, yes German cigarettes, the same brand as Blashen, oh sorry, the same brand as Bubbles. That tells us that Tuppence had been a guest of Bubbles who was a guest of the Right Honourable which explains why it was such a secret. There's no way that the top cop in Europe is going to engage in sexual activity with a 14-year-old in a gang bang scenario, no too many witnesses, he's too smart for that. The good news is that I've just put an Eyespy Tap and Track on Tuppence's phone.

Lewis said   "I thought she was 15 or 16."

Shear said   "We all did, she's a big girl."

Boots said   "So how many have we got GPS on now Boss?"

Shear went through their intelligence sources. We have CCTV at the farm covering Fink. We have CCTV at the Narrow Escape covering the players. We have a lump on Hanson's car and we have Eyespy Tap and Track on the phones of the Right Honourable's and Tuppence's, that's it.

If we keep an eye on Tuppence's location, the moment she gets out to the estate, we know Bubbles is there. If we keep an eye on the lump on Hanson's car then we'll know if he gets near Jock, best time to track him is after he picks up his money from Fink, this is the last weekend before the election and I have a strong feeling that's what's going to happen and will happen soon. Jock is the outstanding player, whatever happens, he's got to fall.

Boots said	"He's managed to keep his identity a secret so far, Boss, do you really think we can expose him?"
Shear said	"Hanson is the key. We know that every time one of his dealers is arrested, he sends Hanson as his brief. We know that Hanson picks the money up from Fink and then somehow gets it to Jock. We were unlucky not to get a result at the IPA bunfight but when Hanson collects the money this weekend we'll be as close to Jock as we're going to get, so it's all hands on deck and battle stations this weekend. A merciless surgical strike should do it."
Lewis said	"I can't wait, we've been at this long enough, we need a result and it needs to happen soon."
Shear said	"Fear not it will happen sooner or later, it may be later than sooner, but know this, it will happen."

Shear received a text from the Right Honourable, He wanted Shear to call around to reassure the Home Secretary of his facts and figures and brief him on the deaths of the three young women and how best they can be excluded from the Wessex figures relating to drugs. The meeting would be short and informal and needed to be in the next hour. Time was of the essence.

Shear arrived at the Estate within the hour and was taken directly to the Home Secretary who was sitting at the Bay window studying a mountain of papers.

Ting began	"You'll remember Sergeant Shear Home Secretary, you decorated him at Police Headquarters a month or so ago."

He replied	"Of course, the gallant Sergeant who unarmed a bank robber, or was it a post office. I suppose they're all of a muchness to you chaps on the front line. So brave, so bold, I expect you've been promoted by now, have you?"
Shear said	"Not yet, sir."
Kelvin said	"Good gracious me, our frontline troops should be rewarded for their acts of gallantry, speak to the Chief Constable Khom, get something moving on that front, there's a good chap."

The Home Secretary then outlined the strategy to his approach on his 'A New Drug-Free Britain'. He rattled through figures and scenarios with a pausing only to breathe, for occasionally looking up as though inviting approving nods from Shear.

Shear nodded approvingly.

Shear said "Everything you say is exactly so, sir, and may I say how well your 'A New Drug-Free Britain' has been so very well received by the voting public, how on earth could anyone not vote for such an ideal, it has everything to commend it…"

Kelvin said	"Yes, yes, well the public do what we tell them do they not, they just need to be told, then told again, and for those of them who find matters challenging we give them a slogan to rally around, they like that sort of thing, don't they, slogans?"
Shear said	"Yes, 'hands that do dishes can feel soft as your face' cannot be ignored."
Kelvin said	"Yes, that's the idea Shear, hear that Khom, if Shear is smiling then that tells us that the plebeian masses will smile too, and when they smile, they vote for us, do they not?"
Ting said	"Quite so, Home Secretary, quite so."
Kelvin said	"Now look here, I've asked you here to answer this question, so be honest man, can I exclude the tragic deaths of these two girls from Wessex drug figures, quite simple, yes or no?"
Ting said	"Three girls Home Secretary."
Kelvin said	"Two, three, whatever, can they be excluded."
Shear said	"Yes, they can, sir, those figures belong to Gloucester not Wessex."
Kelvin said	"Res ipsa loquitur, what?"

Ting laughed heartily and said,

	"It so is, Home Secretary, it so is."
Kelvin said	"Are you familiar with the term Res Ipsa Loquitur Sergeant?"
Shear said	"My colleagues and I at the police station speak of nothing else."

The matter was drawn to a close and Shear was shown to the front door by the Right Honourable who thanked him for his input. Shear rejoined his crew and reality.

Shear and his crew looked again at the facts as they knew them. Tomorrow the girls would be back from Liverpool with forty grand in counterfeit notes. Hanson would turn up at about midnight for his twenty grand as usual at which point, they would follow his GPS and establish where the money was to be taken, Ken and Tony would be in a plain car in the vicinity of Hanson's home address in Bristol and would attempt to follow as he returned with the money. With just a little luck they should be able to locate Jock and unmask him or her. The stakes were high, there was all to play for.

Lewis said	"What are we going to use the counterfeit for, Boss?"
Shear said	"We'll keep that in the event of an emergency, money talks, even fake money. We have GPS on Hanson, the Right Honourable, DCI Bradley and Tuppence, they will somehow gravitate together and when they do there will be a seismic occurrence, and when there's a seismic occurrence the walls come tumbling down."

The crew went off duty at midnight with a scheduled start at 10 am.

Chapter 12

Shear's crew paraded in the briefing room at 10 am. Half a dozen issues were dealt with in short order, election duties, murder squad support enquiries, press management and other low level domestic issues. A routine day at first sight, except to say it wasn't.

After the briefing, Shear's crew went into the yard to give Cerberus a much needed clean, while Shear sought out Chief Inspector Cole. Shear noticed that Superintendent McCoy and his bagman DCI Bradley had their heads together at the back door. What were they scheming, he wondered. He knew that there was to be a press conference that afternoon that McCoy had set up. No doubt another opportunity for McCoy to undermine DCI Farthing and the Murder team, not a difficult thing to do having regard to their unenviable job. McCoy would ensure that Farthing would be made to look inept at best.

Shear saw Cole in the canteen. He was alone nursing a can of coke. Shear began to speak and could see that Cole was in a world of his own, he seemed to be lost in thought and was startled when Shear spoke,

	"Good morning, sir, how are you?"
Cole replied	"Don't ask, the election is five days away, too much can go wrong between now and then."
Shear said	"Oh, high water or fire?"
Cole said	"It's no joke, we're starting with another press conference this afternoon, I don't know what that's about there's nothing new to tell them, Superintendent McCoy has set this up."
Shear said	"You don't have to attend do you?"

Cole said	"I do, yes, as the District Commander I have to sit between McCoy and Farthing and try and look intelligent not knowing what type of grenades McCoy is going to use to belittle Farthing, I just wish it was next week that's all."
Shear said	"Maybe something will turn up before the conference."

Cole said "I doubt it, I only hope that DCI Farthing gets back in time, I don't want to be alone with McCoy when the cameras roll. Farthing made an early start, something to do with the Gloucester end of the enquiry, he's gone to see Curry about something to do with his taped interview."

Shear excused himself and joined his crew in the back yard. It was time to have a quick word with Fink to determine how the Liverpool trip was progressing. He texted, 'How goes the business in the north.' Fink replied, 'Wot busnes.' No good trying to re-register his linguistic key to meet the limitations nature had imposed on Fink, Shear called,

	"What news, Fink?"
Fink said	"All done, Boss, they'll be back at 4.30."
Shear said	"Call me when you've got the stuff."
Fink said	"Will do, Boss."

Cerberus left the rear yard and took to the streets of Aqua Ponds. Yet another mobile patrol showing the flag and reassuring the good people of their continued safety and wellbeing. Ten minutes into the patrol the control room called Cerberus,

	"Foxtrot 13, Foxtrot 13 go now to the railway station and confer with BTP at Quentin."
Saaz said	"Roger that. ETA ten minutes."
Shear said	"British Transport Police, sounds like another suicide. Three hundred a year and in front of trains, you think they'd find a better way."

Cerberus pulled up at the station and called BTP by landline. The BTP controller said,

"We've had a woman hit by a train at Bishop St Mary, we've got some of her here but there's a few bits and pieces missing. The train will stop about half a mile short of Aqua Ponds, can your people have a look at the locomotive and see what there is of her at your end?"

Shear said   "What parts are you missing?"

BTP said   "Head and an arm. If you find anything, we'll have the loco grounded at your end and send a Forensics team up to deal with the crime scene."

Shear said   "Not a suicide then?"

BTP said "Until we know that it is, we'll treat it as a crime scene."

The crew began the long walk to the Train which was standing idle on the track, the driver was out of the Loco and was sitting on the bank towards the rear of the train. Shear left his crew to examine the Loco. He walked to the driver and engaged him in conversation. He was an elderly man, maybe 60, 65. He was clearly shocked and tearful. Shear asked,

"What happened, my friend?"

He said "This is the third time this has happened to me, if they want to kill themselves why do they have to involve me, I can't do this, I was off sick last year for three months with the last one, a young girl, pregnant, in care and only 14. I can't do this."

Shear spent time with the driver. He sat with him awhile and just listened, occasionally nodding and making supportive noises. This was the worst part of the job, just being there to support traumatised people who were temporarily broken, most could be mended, some not. Shear guessed that the driver would not be driving again. Shear asked again,

"Tell me what happened."

He said   "There were two of them, just standing there looking at the train. As we drew closer, she said something to him and pushed him away and that was it, I can't do this anymore."

Shear said   "What happened to the man?"

He said   "Don't know, I closed my eyes and that was it. I stopped the train and called BTP, they told me to stop here and wait for you, they're sending another driver."

Shear arranged for an ambulance land rover to attend the scene and pick up the driver. He then returned to the locomotive.

He said	"What have we got, boys?"
Ken said	"Just the arm, Boss, lots of blood, skin fragments and an arm, that's it."
Shear said	"OK, take a picture of the arm in situ then bag and evidence it, Forensics will take it when they arrive."

Shear noticed a guy walking towards the Loco from the direction of Aqua Ponds, he recognised he was a reporter from The Mercury, time now to take the heat out of the impending press conference with just a little mischief. Shear walked to meet the reporter.

Shear said	"What brings you here?"
He said	"Report of a suicide, do you know who it is, man or a woman, what happened?"
Shear said	"Well, I can give you nothing, or some strictly nonattributable."
He said	"OK, non-attributable."
Shear said	"There's a press conference in a few hours, you might want to ask if the police have found the man who ran from the scene when the woman was hit by the train."
He said	"Bloody hell, did he push her?"
Shear said	"You're the reporter, work on it, your best enquiries will be made at the press conference."

Foxtrot 13 returned to the police station and went about their reports and exhibit recording. Enough paperwork to see them busy for an hour or two. Chief Inspector Cole found Shear and asked for an update on the rail incident.

Shear said "I won't be five minutes, sir, I'll come up to your office."

Cole said "No, the bars open now, we can go down there."

They made their way to the bar, Cole took a seat by the window. Shear didn't ask if he wanted a drink, he knew he needed one. Shear returned to the table with a large brandy and a glass of water. Cole placed his brandy next to his Coke can and said,

"So what's in the rail incident?"

203

Shear briefed Cole as to the facts, the standard stuff that would appear on the incident report, another troubled soul unable to cope with the world who topped herself. No one would give it a second thought, but "I know you have concerns about the press conference this afternoon, sir, so here's the heads up on facts unearthed by The Mercury's reporter that only you will be privy to. He alone will be asking questions about the incident at the conference, this will keep the cameras on you, and everyone else at the top table will be able to do nothing except listen and agree with whatever you say."

Cole said "Bloody hell, Shear. Brilliant, I think, so what do I say?"

Shear continued with what only the driver knew. He explained that the driver was sedated in hospital and it very much looked like the reporter had got his information either from the driver or another source but more probably the driver. Cole began to smile and became quite animated, he said,

"Excellent, thank you, on the strength of that I think I'll have a drink."

With that, Cole finished his Coke, and then his brandy.

Shear asked "Shall I get you another drink Boss?"

Cole said "Well maybe a wee one, just to celebrate."

Shear got Cole another double and took his leave.

DCI Farthing drove into the rear yard, he and his two detective sergeants got out of the car and made their way upstairs. They were determined and purposeful, clearly they were on a mission, their tails were up and a confrontation in the offing.

Farthing tapped McCoy's door and pushed it open. McCoy and Bradley looked up. Farthing stepped forward. McCoy stood up and said to the two detectives,

	"You and you get out, and you Mr Farthing can close the door, sit yourself down and take that silly superiority look off your face…"
Farthing said	"I've just…"
McCoy said	"I've not finished, you're now gonna tell me some nonsense about how Curry told you that Bradley here offered him a deal if he came up with the truth about how the three wee girls got hold of the morphine and that took 10 or 15 minutes which was not recorded at interview, right?"
Farthing said	"Exactly right, how did…"

McCoy said	"How did I know, how did I know. I'm a detective Superintendent, sonny, that's how I know. Curry's solicitor rang me and said you spoke to him earlier today and offered him a deal if he'd say what really happened in the interview room. Well, know this, wee Man. What happened in the interview room is what we say happened in the interview room, not what you think you know what happened but what we say happened. So you see, Farthing, this isn't even a good try, it's typical of you and that bunch of ladies you lead who between you couldn't detect a fart in a spacesuit. And Hanson wants to complain about your unprofessional behaviour, but I put him right, it's not unprofessional, it's bloody criminal..."
Farthing said	"You can't..."
McCoy said	"Shut up, sonny, or I'll encourage Hanson to complain of your conspiracy to pervert the course of justice. Now, if you don't' know the first rule of holes, it's this; when in one, stop digging. Now get out of here and see if you can behave yourself, go on bugger off."

Farthing made his way downstairs followed by his detective sergeants, all three went into the briefing room where the murder squad waited to be updated. Farthing sat on an empty seat in the third row and lowered his face into his hands, he was tearful and it showed. The room was silent, no one stirred.

Chief Inspector Cole found Shear in the report writing room, he asked him to prepare the rear yard for the press and lay out the briefing room as per a National TV briefing, much the same as before. He took Shear aside and asked,

"What questions will The Mercury reporter be asking?"

Shear said	
	"Usual nonsense, was the woman pushed, is the man a suspect, do we suspect murder? Just stay with the fact, a man was seen to run from the scene and we're waiting to interview the driver who is traumatised and is expected to be in hospital overnight. The thing is, only you know that so you can play it anyway you like for as long as you like. That keeps you on camera and the Superintendent and DCI Farthing at a loss."
Cole said	"Thanks, Sarge. The press conference is in an hour."

Shear and his crew finished up in the interview room and went to sort out the rear yard where the press were already gathering.

Boots asked "Do you think the Chief Inspector's been drinking, Boss?"

Shear said "He's always drinking, he may have had a little extra today, he's under a lot of pressure."

As usual, the press were making every effort to get new information. Anything that would give them the edge on their competitors. Suggesting things that could be denied was always a good idea. Shear only confirmed earlier denials and kept the railway job strictly to himself. He did manage to deny that a team of officers had gone to Gloucester earlier that day to interview a suspect and was able also to deny that an early arrest was expected concerning the three deaths. He left the press interrogating each other as to the best approach during the press conference. Clearly, they anticipated something new, otherwise why had a conference been called?

Shear and his crew gathered in the briefing room to give it a makeover for national news, this was by now becoming routine. He noticed that DCI Farthing was seated at the back of the room. He looked quite unwell, Shear caught the eye of a DS and beckoned him over. He asked,

"How's the DCI, he looks poorly."

The DS said	"He's fine, we're about to take him for a coffee."
Shear said	"Is he at the top table for the conference?"
The DS said	"Yes, that's what's worrying him, there's nothing new to give the press."

McCoy and Bradley came into the briefing room, climbed the stairs and had a conversation about the top table, McCoy pointed to the far seat on the left and Bradley took the seat with McCoy on his right near the middle of the table. They had a shielded conversation then left the room.

The press had been allowed into the police station and slowly began to fill the room. The Control Room Sergeant came to the door and asked Shear if he had seen Superintendent McCoy. He has a confidential document for McCoy. Shear took it from him as McCoy was due back shortly. Shear put the envelope in his pocket and went to the toilet, locked himself in a cubicle and as it had just been sealed, he unsealed with relative ease. The paper read:

From: Interpol, Lyon France Subject: Jay Allan Wall

No trace has been found of your suspect in Portugal or Spain. There is no evidence that he landed in Porto. His fingerprints have been connected with the murders of two women in April last year.

Maria Gonzales Fernandes, 19 years, and Emilia Gabriella Martinez, 18 years, students domiciled in Barcelona. An international warrant has been issued for his arrest.

Shear resealed the envelope and returned to the briefing room. McCoy's bagman came in looking for Shear. Shear held up the envelope and gave it to Bradley who smiled and quickly disappeared. Shear now knew why the press conference had been called, McCoy had known about this for days and said nothing. He's now arranged this message to be received a few minutes before the conference and too late to pass the matter to the Senior Investigating Officer, DCI Farthing. Cunning beyond belief. Shear text Cole and asked him to bring DCI Farthing to his office for a very quick briefing before the conference.

The Press Conference started on time. Chief Inspector Cole introduced the top table and revisited the deaths of the three girls and confirmed that their deaths were now being treated as murder and that Detective Chief Inspector Farthing was the Senior Investigating Officer. The crowded press corps jostled for best position in the pecking order and as convention would have it, they deferred to the BBC who asked,

"Is it true that a man from Gloucester has been arrested in connection with murder of these three girls?"

In response, McCoy picked up a wad of papers as if to read a prepared statement. The cameras focused on him. He tapped the papers into position on the table and sprung his ambush on Farthing.

He said "As you have heard, these deaths are now the subject of a murder enquiry and the Senior Investigating Officer, DCI Farthing, is here to answer your questions…"

McCoy continued "DCI Farthing…"

Farthing was still smarting from his recent confrontation with McCoy and had resolved on a do or die continuum. Farthing gave a masterclass performance when he outlined the three tragic deaths and the subsequent enquiries resulting in an arrest of a suspect, who, at this stage had not yet been charged, he continued with new information concerning Jay who was the subject of the first murder and the latest information from Interpol confirming Jay's involvement in a number of other murders in Europe, Farthing ended with a coup d'état with the words that the police were now on the trail of a highly dangerous European serial killer. As an afterthought his coup de grace was his asking the community for their help in building 'A New Drug-Free Britain'. Turmoil engulfed the press corps. Farthing answered questions from the French and German media and in particular the Spanish who were astonished at the news of a serial killer of Spanish citizens was for the first time being named in England. Somehow the local reporter from The Mercury managed to blurt out his question to the top table.

He said "Is it true that the woman killed at Bishops St Mary earlier today was pushed into the path of the London Plymouth train, can you tell us about the man who was seen to run from the tracks, is an early arrest anticipated?"

Farthing saw his chance for a counter ambush of McCoy. He said,

"Perhaps Superintendent McCoy can help…"

McCoy moved uncertainly in his seat, he picked up his papers and began limply to say…Chief Inspector Cole, awash with perhaps one brandy too many, but still perfectly articulate intervened,

"This matter is being treated as a suicide pact at this stage, enquiries reveal that one of their number lost courage at the last moment and fled the scene, you may be aware that that makes him the subject of a separate charge of complicity and a separate statement will be made in the fullness of time."

Cole unexpectedly stood up bringing the conference to an early end. The whole of the media flocked around DCI Farthing who continued his masterful performance even managing to answer the Spanish questions in Spanish.

Bradley and McCoy, silent and deflated, shuffled from the room, McCoy was convulsed and furious harbouring murderous thoughts.

Shear got his crew together and mounted up in the old battered van. Time to get out of uniform, into mufti and take their afternoon break at the cottage in preparation for their strategic objective. Now was the time to unfurl the nuclear option. Exciting times.

As they arrived at the cottage, Fink texted to say he had the package from Liverpool.

Shear rang him; he said,

"I'll send someone for the stuff from Liverpool, Fink. All you have to do tonight is let Hanson have his usual ten grand plus the ten he's owed, so that's twenty grand. Give it to him in a Sainsbury's bag, got it?"

Fink said   "Yeah, got it, Boss."

Shear said   "Repeat what I've just told you."

Fink said   "Give Hanson twenty grand."

Shear said   "And what will the twenty grand be in?"

Fink said   "A Sainsbury's bag Boss."

Shear asked Lewis to pick up the forty counterfeit and bring it back to the cottage. Shear checked his GPS intelligence. The CCTV was alive and well at the farm covering Fink. The CCTV at the Narrow Escape was in order showing Tuppence's mother drinking from a can. No sign of Tuppence. He interrogated the App which showed Tuppence was back at the Right Honourable's estate and so too was the Right Honourable. Interesting times. They now had to wait for the return of Lewis by which time they'd be off duty and free to play.

Lewis returned just before 6. Shear looked at the notes, all new and each bearing the same serial number, this could only be described as Kryptonite, or the nuclear option. All was set except for one last phone call. The call was made, the game was afoot. Boots and Ken were tasked to go to the Right Honourable's estate and recover the coke previously secreted by Boots, two packets of two kilos, four kilos in all.

The bar opened at 7 and was usually beginning to get busy at about 8. Tonight was unusual, the bar was crowded. Most of the murder squad were still cock a hoop with their boss' performance at the press conference and many of the media had been invited by the squad to celebrate the events of the day. The media were there hoping for more off the record vignettes that flow with the beer. They were not disappointed as the senses dulled with alcohol so the stories became louder, brasher and somehow took on a life of their own. The two murdered Spanish students soon became, well we're sure there must be more, those two were killed on one evening and we know he was there for a month, so it follows that two was just a starting point, he is after all a serial killer. There was no time for taking notes, the media would make it up in any case, so long as their stories gelled, they could substantially print whatever they liked under the heading of, a source close to the Senior Investigating Officer. The squad awaited their boss who was just about to leave his office.

McCoy and his bagman happened upon both Farthing and Cole as they made their way to the bar. The encounter was short. McCoy said,

"Know this, wee man, I'm going to break you."

No one answered, Farthing and Cole continued to the bar where they were met with rapturous applause from the Murder squad who already had drunk too much and were intent on partying hard. McCoy and Bradley opened the back door and walked into the night in silence.

At the cottage, Shear went through the plan for the night. The only thing that was certain was that Hanson would turn up at the Farm about midnight and collect his ten grand retainer plus the ten previously promised, twenty grand in all. Simple enough then. Hanson would leave the farm with the money and return to the North where Ken and Tony were waiting. He would be followed at a distance by Saaz, Lewis and Rohan so that on his arrival with the money they would have manpower sufficient to deal with whatever went down. Shear and Boots would monitor events by GPS. No more could be done. Time for Shear to make a confirmatory phone call.

The crew watched the evening news. The usual stuff except there was more of it. 'A New Drug-Free Britain', it was on everyone's lips, Union flags, the strains of Land of Hope and Glory, the Prime Minister and the Home Secretary hand in hand on a castle's battlements. If this could be believed then a landslide victory was in prospect for the Conservative party, and sure enough opinion polls came up with the goods favouring the Tory party. The little time afforded the Socialists was drowned out by choruses from bystanders of 'A New Drug-Free Britain'. It was almost embarrassing. They turned the TV off and monitored the lump on Hanson's car. No movement yet. The Eyespy Tap and Track showed the Right Honourable to be at his estate and so too was Tuppence. There was no activity at the Narrow Escape and the farm CCTV showed no movement. They just had to wait.

Shortly after eleven Hanson's car appeared on the GPS, he was on the move South towards Aqua Ponds. Ken and Tony were despatched to the North to take up their positions for Hanson's return. Saaz, Lewis and Rohan made their way into town and sat up awaiting instructions from Shear. Shear and Boots made their way to the farm and parked their vehicle just outside the main gate. It was dark and it rained, it rained hard.

Hanson appeared as expected, parked up and went into the farm. Shear and Boots approached Hanson's car and did their business returning to their car well before Hanson appeared with his twenty grand in a Sainsbury's bag. Hanson began his return journey being monitored by Shear who gave Saaz, Lewis and Rohan the heads up.

Instead of taking the main A38 back to town, Hanson drove into the country in the direction of the Right Honourable's estate. Shear waited and kept his eye on the GPS. Sure enough Hanson arrived at the estate and almost immediately left.

Shear could see that the Eyespy Tap and Track showed that Tuppence was in Hanson's car and five minutes later the car passed Shear and Boots who could see that two men and a woman were on board. They followed the vehicle into town and stopped for an RV with Saaz, Lewis and Rohan. Again Hanson had left the A38 and entered the town centre. Shear followed them on GPS. The car went to the Narrow Escape where the GPS showed that Tuppence had become stationary. Hanson's car moved on, back onto the A38 and drove North passing Shear's crew. Two men were on board Hanson's car.

Ken and Tony were alerted and anticipated Hanson's arrival in about forty minutes. The rest of the crew followed Hanson keeping half a mile behind him and monitoring his movements on GPS. Thirty minutes later Shear asked Ken and Tony to start moving slowly south. Finally GPS showed Hanson's car turn left off the A38 just before Redhill. GPS showed it stop two hundred yards along The Pound where it remained stationary. Shear drove along The Pound and saw two men leave Hanson's car and enter an up-market house with a large drive.

It was time for Shear to make his last telephone call and press the nuclear button.

Less than three minutes later four large black 4x4s pulled into the drive disgorging about a dozen NCS officers. The front door was battered down and armed police entered the house.

Boots asked   "Who are they, Boss?"

Shear said   "National Crime Squad, they deal with serious and organised crime nationwide. They've been monitoring the Liverpool gang responsible for counterfeit notes for the last eighteen months and guess what, someone gave them the heads up that they could nick a major player tonight."

From a distance of 200 yards Shear and Boots watched the large drive. Three officers were searching Hanson's car and placing stuff in exhibit bags, A few minutes later four men were brought out into the driving rain in handcuffs. The head of the IPA Herr Jurgen Weiss was first, followed by Hanson. Then came DCI Bradley and Superintendent McCoy. All were struggling and protesting their treatment. A camera caught all the activity and speech. Each prisoner was placed in separate vehicles and driven away in convoy.

Shear's crew parked up in the forecourt of the Darlington Arms. The rain had stopped and they gathered for a chat.

Ken said	"So what have we got, Boss?"
Shear said	"The National Crime Squad have been looking at the counterfeiting business in Liverpool for quite some time. I tipped them off the day the election was called and have kept open communication through a private Crime Stoppers channel. They've had an eye on Herr Weiss for a long time concerning child transportation and drug importation but the other three are extra…"
Lewis said	"These four bastards will be able to talk their way out of anything, Boss, they'll probably say the twenty grand came from donations during the IPA bunfight, they're always making donations."
Shear said	"Trouble is, the NCS found two Sainsbury's bags, one with twenty grand and the other with forty counterfeits. All new notes with the same serial numbers. Add to that there were two packages in Hanson's car. Two kilos of coke beneath the driver's seat and another two beneath the passenger's seat, they seem to be in a spot of bother, don't you think?"
Tony said	"It couldn't get any worse for them, could it?"
Shear said	"It could, the NCS have been bugging Hanson and McCoy's houses for the last three weeks, every conversation has been recorded, they're done, I think they're all looking at something in the order of 25 years."
Lewis said	"It's a corrupt world we live in."
Shear said	"Some of it's noble, Lewis; some of it's noble."